A Mother's Loss

Caroline Rebisz

CAROLINE REBISZ

DEDICATION

For my family Alan, Danuta and Beth who inspire and support me.

CONTENTS

PROLOGUE

His fist connected with her jaw.

He grunted with the effort. Her legs crumpled and she fell back, hitting the ground with brutal force. Her head jarred whiplashing with the force of her fall.

Blackness surrounded her as she slipped from consciousness. Fog enveloped her mind. Where was she? What was happening?

All too soon the mist in her brain started to clear and she became aware of the sounds and smells around her.

Darkness surrounded her. The cold crept into her bones chilling to her core. She lay on long grass which was sodden and clung to her hair, wrapping her in its all-encompassing fetid smell. Her fingers reached up to her face and felt wetness. Blood seeped from her mouth and she tasted its metallic flavour. Her head was pulsing with pain as she struggled to understand what was happening. Shaking her head from side to side she tried to free herself from the fog in her brain.

Looking up to the sky, she could see the stars shining down as if to guide her away from this place. "Get up and run" they implored. Despite her overwhelming fear, she could not move. Frozen. She felt rooted to the ground and dug her fingers into the soft soil. Panic enveloped her. Her heartbeat sounded like a drum in her head; a cruel reminder of her need to fly and her inability to move.

Suddenly he threw himself down onto her, grabbing her arms and forcing them back over her head. A sharp pain streamed up her arms as her fingers went numb. She was pinned down, unable to move. Her head was forced back, arching her neck. He closed in, driving his face into hers.

The smell of him hit the back of her throat. Putrid breath with an animal scent of the unwashed. Sweat dripped onto her face, stinging like acid. His breathing was ragged as his excitement of what was to come took over. He slobbered like a rabid dog dripping his rancid saliva into her hair.

He ripped her blouse open and groaned. Hard callous fingers grabbed at her soft skin. He snatched at her breast gripping hard. His nails scratched at her nubile skin. She recoiled, trying to creep backwards up the grass and his twisted foot clamped down on her thigh pinning her to the ground. His teeth bit into her nipple and she screamed. His hand clamped over her lips stifling her cries. She could smell the dirt on his fingers as they crushed into her lips. His grotesque face pushed against her cheek, his foul-smelling breath panting with his repulsive desire.

"Slut" he whispered in her ear. "You keep your mouth shut, you whore".

Her skirt was riding up as he dragged his knee up between her thighs. He used his legs to push her thighs open beneath him. His hand grabbed at her underwear and she felt the rip of fabric as he pulled them away from her. Her head was screaming "stop please stop" but she could not get the words out. His fingers continued to clamp down on her mouth, making it difficult for her to breathe.

Time stopped as she waited. The blood beating through her body was the only sound she was aware of.

Then a ripping pain as he entered her. He thrust into her cruelly, without a care for her pain.

Grinding his body against her, oblivious to the distress he was causing.

In her mind she left that place of pain and humiliation and drifted away trying to ignore the grunting and burning as he took her. She stopped the struggle and lay there passive and unresponsive.

"Please let it end" her heart screamed out.

As quickly as he took her, it ended.

He pulled himself away and wiped himself on her tattered dress.

"Whore."

Her head cracked back as his fist drove into her jaw. Blood seeped from an open wound at the back of her head.

Then came blackness.

She was gone.

CHAPTER ONE

Two cars swung into the gravel driveway with a satisfying crunch. Giles pushed open the door of his racing green Jaguar and stretched as he unfolded from the driver's seat. It had been a long journey in the heat and he was definitely looking forward to moving about again. His 6ft build stretched skywards as he uncoiled his frame. A handsome man, lean with a well-defined muscular body, he carried himself with confidence not arrogance. He tipped his sunglasses up his forehead to rest on his well-groomed chestnut hair. Giles was sporting chinos and a designer shirt; his standard dress when not at work.

His 14-year-old son, Harry, was out of the door the minute the car pulled up and could not contain his excitement at seeing their new home. With eyes darting around, he took in the impressive looking house and gardens which were so different to their mid terrace home in North London. He nodded silently in approval of his parents' choice. Harry and his elder sister Jo had not visited the country house chosen by their parents and were keen to explore.

"Mum come on. Get a move on" sighed Jo as their mum took her time getting out of the other car, a red BMW. Jo grabbed her younger brother and rubbed his head affectionately. "What do you think kiddio?" she smiled. "Looks good to me."

Brother and sister were like two peas in a pod except that Jo had her father's chestnut hair and Harry took after his mother. Jo at 16 was developing into a woman. She was tall, nearly reaching her father's height; slim with long athletic legs. She had a face which lit up as she spoke, a testament to the beauty she was growing into. Harry was a typical 14-year-old lad. He was short for his age and without exercise would have a tendency to run to fat. His hair looked like it hadn't seen a brush in weeks and his track suit had a lived-in look. Harry hadn't reached that awkward age when the inclination to obsess about his personal style would kick in.

Liz smiled at the kids' enthusiasm and pulled her mobile phone from her bag. The estate agent had text the number of the lock box where the keys would be found during their journey. Having located the box, she called out to her husband.

"Giles, darling, will you do the honours and open the key box. You know I can't do it with my nails" Liz laughed. She was very particular about her acrylic nails. They were a constant fashion accessory she couldn't do without. Packing up the old house had been achieved without any breakages and that success was not going to be wasted now. Who knew how long it would take to find a new nail bar out in the sticks.

Liz was in her early forties but could easily be mistaken for younger. Her excellent skin tone and her fitness regime had helped to keep her youthful looks. Her blond hair was pulled back from her face in a ponytail; when released it would fall down her back like a silk curtain. Golden hoops jingled in her ears as she gazed around the impressive drive lined with apple trees, heavy with early fruit. She let out a huge sigh of contentment. This was a new beginning for the family. Seeing the house again after all these months was all the confirmation she needed that her heart had made the right decision. This move meant big adjustments for all of them but they needed this change of scene to recover as a family and find a way through their pain together.

The house was an impressive brick and flint cottage which had been added to over the years and was surrounded by an extensive garden ready to be explored. It had stood out from all the other houses they had viewed as it was such an attractive looking cottage. The search had been intensive and at one stage Liz despaired that she would find somewhere suitable for them all. Crown House soon became the only viable option. It had grabbed hold of Liz's heart the moment she walked through the door. She had felt a calming peace as the home enfolded her in its arms. She smiled as she remembered Giles exasperation at her reaction. He always made decisions with his head and was already compiling the list of items to bring up with the agent as part of the negotiation process. He would be keen to get a good deal on the asking price. Liz's enthusiasm during their initial visit was never going to help him achieve his plan. It was obvious to Giles and, more importantly, the estate agent that Liz had decided this was the house she wanted, at any cost.

Giles fiddled with the key in the porch door and grumbled to himself "that lock needs changing" as he struggled to connect the teeth in the old-fashioned lock. Giles pushed his floppy fringe back and put his weight behind the door as it creaked open.

Giles was the practical one of the couple. His role, as a Director in Corporate Banking for a large city bank, meant he spent most of his working life negotiating financial deals and dealing with complex customer issues. At home he was the one who loved to tinker with DIY. His job was stressful and working with his hands was his way of kicking back and relaxing. It wasn't always possible for him to do the home improvements he had planned due to the demands of his role. Even so he was fanatical in project managing any workers they brought into their house, alongside his passion for detail. Liz loved to point out to him that the word "detail" should be replaced with the term "OCD". Giles reluctantly accepted that description. Fortunately it had not harmed his career having that depth of enquiry.

The Stamford family crossed the threshold into their new home to explore. Shoes were discarded in a pile in the porch and their toes contracted on the cold flagstone floor. They started with the newer part of the house, an extension, which included a games room and office along with the guest bedroom and bathroom. The games room was large and could easily fit the gym equipment which Giles had been keen to invest in once they got settled. Space was going to be something the family would need to get used to. They had lived all their married life in a terraced house in London which was compact in the extreme. All the available space had been used for bringing up their teenagers.

The guest room would comfortably house a king size bed which would be in frequent use as their many London friends had threatened to descend on their country home over the coming months. A number of their neighbours had expressed concern that Giles and Liz were moving away from their close circle of friends who had been their support mechanism after they lost Rebecca. Whilst they understood the need to leave the house which held so many dreadful memories from the last year, the thought of the Stamford family being so far away was a concern to those who loved them.

The office was going to be Giles's domain. It would give him the option to work from home on the days he didn't need to travel around the country or make the long journey into London. Having the space to work in private was important to him and his clients. He spent whole days in audio meetings which he could easily manage from home rather than waste time on a train. He realised this fresh start was an opportunity for him to get control over his work life balance. He worked hard and was rewarded well for it, but current circumstances had made him rethink his priorities. Recent events had shown him that he needed to be at home more to support Liz and the children. Unfortunately burying himself in piles of paperwork didn't make the pain go away.

The older part of the house was originally a country pub but had been totally renovated by the previous owners into an impressive country house. Wooden beams and bare floorboards, so quintessentially country cottage, were a feature of the ground floor rooms. A large wood burner set within a granite hearth was the focal point of the lounge. Liz imagined the family settling down around the fire on cold winter nights. The dining room looked out over the fields and would be a great place for entertaining or for family meals together. Liz always made a big deal of Christmas. It was a special time of year for the family. The thought of hosting the festivities in these surrounding excited her.

With the absence of furniture the teenagers' voices echoed as they exclaimed at each room they surveyed. "Mum, do we seriously have 2 kitchens?" asked Jo as she twirled around the cooking space. She touched each cupboard and workshop as if subconsciously she was familiarising herself with her surroundings. "And what the hell is this thing?" as she grabbed hold of the ancient green Aga.

"Well darling, that's the cooker and also a boiler" explained Liz. "I reckon it's going to take some getting used to but should be fun trying it out." Liz didn't want to share her nervousness about the ancient stove just yet. "We have a separate cooker in the summer kitchen as another option if I can't get on with it. So don't worry, you won't starve."

Liz was apprehensive about attempting the first meal on the Aga. It's not something she had considered when she had listed out her key requirements for the house hunt but at the same time she was intrigued as to the impact it would have on family dinners. Liz was an imaginative cook and loved to entertain; or at least she had before it had happened.

In the centre of the house there was a wide steep set of stairs which the family ascended to take a look at the bedrooms. The staircase was a feature in itself. Wooden slats almost wide enough for the family to walk side by side. Hanging from the ceiling was an ornate chandelier which would be a bugger to dust, thought Liz.

As Giles expected, there was a mad rush from Jo and Harry to decide on which bedroom they would claim. He could hear Jo and Harry bickering over their choices. Harry was clearly throwing a strop as he tried to get his own way. As usual, Jo gave in to her baby brother far too easily, decided Giles. His son had taken first dibs on the room at the end of the corridor which looked out over the garden. Harry wanted to be as far as possible from his parent's room. Giles's snoring was legendary and extremely frustrating for the rest of the family trying to sleep. Harry had always been a light sleeper and couldn't cope with the ear plugs which Liz had spent most of her married life using.

Jo was, in fact, delighted with the other double bedroom as it had the most fantastic view over the fields across the road from the house. She may have given into Harry in the interests of family peace but in her mind she felt she had ended up with the better option. Her feet dug into the deep pile carpet as she gazed out of the window. Sheep were grazing in the field and gazed up at the newcomers with little interest.

Giles and Liz walked into the master bedroom. It was a beautiful room with floor to ceiling windows looking out over the fields. It was huge compared to their previous bedroom which had always looked cluttered and disorganised. This room felt welcoming. The light streamed through the windows and bounced off the clean white walls, enveloping them with warmth. This was a room to help the healing process, thought Giles. He wrapped his arms around Liz as he could see the tears start to flow.

"Rebecca would have loved this house." Liz's voice was cracked with emotion. She snuggled close into his chest for comfort.

"She certainly would" he agreed, kissing her gently on the top of her head. "She will be with us here in spirit. That's what we have to hold onto." He sighed. "It will get better darling."

Giles and Liz took a private moment of reflection whilst they listened to Jo and Harry excitedly extol the virtues of their new rooms. The previous arguments seemed to soon been forgotten. They took comfort from the early enthusiasm of the children to the change they had foisted on them.

Attached to the master bedroom was the en-suite bathroom which was set off to one side. The walk-in shower covered the entire wall of the bathroom and would no doubt be used by the whole family. There was a family bathroom off the main corridor but the power shower in the ensuite could be too good to resist.

Liz's attention was suddenly drawn to an intriguing door on the other side of the room. She couldn't remember seeing this when they viewed the property. If she recalled correctly there had been a huge wardrobe covering that wall. It had been an ugly dark wooden structure which Liz had been determined was not going to stay when negotiating the fixtures and fittings schedule. It just would not go with the design she was looking for in her bedroom.

Giles cracked the door and peered in. After fumbling around in the dark, he couldn't seem to find a light switch so pulled out his mobile phone and tapped on the torch function. The light revealed a huge space which seemed to stretch out across the vast staircase. Cobwebs hung down from the ceiling adding to the unused and mysterious look of this unexpected room. The space had a sad look of neglect. Obviously this hadn't been included in the renovations and, if Giles recalled correctly, wasn't included in the estate agents floor plan details. Out of the gloom in the corner of the room, Giles made out the shape of some furniture underneath a piece of old sacking. The pile was covered in dust and cobwebs and looked like it hadn't been touched for years.

"Well this is interesting, Liz" Giles remarked. "It looks like this was some form of old storage space. It's going to need a lot of work to clear it out and make it useable. It's one to add to the list for now. I bet you won't fancy rooting around in there with all those spiders."

Liz smiled "Oh my god, spiders. I hate them. They serve no purpose." Liz shivered exaggeratingly. "It feels a strange space. I don't like the feel of it. Creepy. I wonder what it was used it for. Maybe we could use it for storage or something."

Their investigations were cut short by their noisy son.

"Mum, Dad, can we check out the gardens now" shouted Harry from the landing.

"Ok, darling. Let's go together shall we as I haven't figured out all the keys yet." Liz and Giles followed the children downstairs. "We need to look in that pile and find out which opens the back door" said Liz. There was a huge pile of keys left on the floor in the dining room and it took some minutes to figure out which one fitted the door out of the summer kitchen into the back garden.

"That's another job for me!" joked Giles. "There are enough keys here to secure Fort Knox. How can any house need so many keys?" Giles shrugged as he fiddled through the pile trying to sort into some kind of order. "You would have thought they would have labelled things up to make it a bit easier for us." The pile of keys was varied, some looking modern and new along with a good selection of rusty old-fashioned implements.

"Darling, not everyone is as efficient as you" laughed Liz.

Immediately outside the house was a stone patio edged with mature flower beds to define the boundary. Fruit trees lined the area nearest the conservatory and they were heavy with unripen plums and cherries. Behind that stretched the lawn; almost the size of a football pitch. The lawn was surrounded by various shrubs and trees which added colour and fragrance to the garden. Someone had taken a great deal of time and trouble designing this garden. It was clearly a labour of love.

At the end of the lawn, a laurel hedge defined a break in the garden. The children headed for it to see what surprises lay beyond. A large single-story building sat alongside a huge barn. The barn would be Giles's man-cave. He had already decided that his space would be out of bounds to the rest of the family. Everyone needs a space to chill out, he thought.

"Ok, let's open this building then" chuckled Giles as he winked at Liz. "I wonder what we have in here eh?" As he pushed open the door and flicked on the light switch the screams of delight from Harry and Jo were ear splitting.

"O-M-G, Dad. A swimming pool. Seriously? Why didn't you tell us?" squealed Jo. "If I'd known I would have popped my swimsuit in my overnight bag."

Both Harry and Jo were keen swimmers and had been members of a team in London. Weekends were often spent transporting the family to various meets. When Giles and Liz had first viewed the house, they had been overwhelmed by the pool house. It just seemed perfect for the family. They were all very sporty and would benefit from the facility.

"We wanted you guys to be surprised when you saw it" replied Liz. "I know it was a big decision to uproot us to a new home, darlings. You have been so understanding about it." Liz pulled both children in for a hug. "When we found out we had a pool we just knew it was the place for us. A place for you to practise and a fun place when we have friends over," smiled Liz.

"Trying it out will have to wait until tomorrow I'm afraid. I need to have a chance to check out the instructions." Giles put a dampener on the excitement. Ever the sensible one of the couple he added "I guess we need to figure out the chemicals and filtration system before we give it a go." It seemed a feature of the house that there was a lack of instructions for any equipment left by their predecessors. It was going to be fun finding out how everything worked.

Harry pouted with the rejection of instant fun in the pool. Both parents waited for the inevitable strop. It was a fleeting moment as both he and his sister recognised the longer-term benefit of this new toy. They could wait. There was so much to look at in their new home. Their excitement level was palpable.

"It will be such fun being able to invite your new friends around for a pool party, won't it" conceded Liz as she saw the play of emotions across Harry's face. "Ok who's for a cup of tea then?" she cried as they backed out of the pool room and strolled down the garden.

The family would have to rough it somewhat for the first evening as their furniture would not arrive until the following day.

"And how about checking out the local pub for dinner? Are we all up for that?" Liz suggested.

CHAPTER TWO

Later that evening the four of them wandered down to the village pub. Their new home was situated about a mile from Little Yaxley, a small village in the heart of South Norfolk. The village comprised of a single road populated on either side with chocolate box cottages. At the far end of the lane a terrace of workers cottages stood and bore testament to the farming nature of the area. A Norman church sat proudly at the centre of the village with a small and well-kept churchyard wrapped around. A shield of red roses grew across the fence surrounding the churchyard, adding to the beauty of the view. The Stamford's were fairly regular church goers and looked forward to joining that community over the coming weeks.

The Greyhound pub sat proudly at the edge of the village. Its white walls and slate roof made it stand out from the rest of the community. It was much more modern than the surrounding buildings. Two porches jutted out from the front of the pub welcoming the Stamford family in. A large rounded bar stood to the left of the entrance with a huge fireplace surrounded by big comfy sofas on the right. Ahead was the restaurant area with quirky tables and chairs with a passing resemblance to church pews.

"Welcome, come on in" a gruff voice from the bar greeted them.

"Hi there" replied Giles. "We have just moved into the village, so our first time with you. Are you serving food this evening?" Giles ushered his family into the bar area. The fire burning in the grate was a welcome addition as the heat of the early summer day had departed.

"Of course, yes. We have a full menu on tonight so grab yourself a seat and I will pop over and take your order. My name's Derek by the way. My wife Sally and I run this place."

Derek was sporting a huge stomach which was busting out from his tightly fitting shirt. His face was rotund with a bald head and a beaming smile. He puffed as he waddled around the bar to direct the family towards a table.

"Great to meet you, Derek. I'm Giles and this is my wife Liz and our kids Harry and Joanne. We have moved into Crown House today but our

furniture hasn't. Hence we thought we would treat ourselves to dinner out."
The family settled into a table with benches facing each other as Derek
rearranged cutlery and handed out clean placemats.

"Hey, welcome to the village. Nice to meet you all. Everyone was looking
forward to finding out who was moving in. The curtains have been
twitching all week" smiled Derek. "I do hope you will be happy here in
Little Yaxley. It's a great community. Me and the missus like to think the
pub is the centre of it. Of course, your place used to be an inn. Did you
know? It's got to be a couple of hundred years old at least." Derek revelled
in his story as he continued. "Our place is much more recent. When your
place became a house the village worked hard to replace it, about ten years
ago. You just can't have a proper village without a pub," grinned Derek.
Their host chattered none stop as he worked.

"The estate agent did tell us a bit about it being a pub in the past" chipped
in Liz. "I'm keen to learn more about its history once we get settled. It's
such a beautiful place and it's interesting to think of all the people who have
lived there over the years."

Derek expelled a deep booming roar of laughter. "Well don't worry, there
are plenty of old codgers in the village who will tell you loads of stories
about the goings on at your new place. Some of them will be true and a
great deal will be old wives tales" joked Derek. "You know, if you want to
find out the truth you should talk to Christine. She's the vicar. Got a
fascination in local history. I know she's done some research on the village.
She's definitely the font of all wisdom on Little Yaxley." Derek handed out
the leather-bound menus as he continued. "We have a specials board over
there on that blackboard. Let me leave you in peace to have a look and
decide what you fancy."

The Stamfords took their time reviewing the menus before making their
choices. Giles picked the ribeye steak, always a firm favourite with him. Liz
and Jo both wanted the seafood risotto. "Are you picking the burger by any
chance Harry?" said Jo with a cheeky grin. Harry looked across the table at
her, being sure to dramatically roll his eyes at the enduring family joke.

After taking their order, Derek handed out their drinks and asked where
they had moved from. He was keen to be the first in the community to find

out about the newbies. No doubt the news would be circulated far and wide by the morning.

Giles answered for the family explaining that they came from North London. "Lived there all our married life so this is our first experience of the countryside" continued Giles.

"Wow that's quite a move and you couldn't have chosen more country than 'round here. They call East Anglia the breadbasket of England because of all the crops we grow. Your new place is surrounded by fields." Derek exclaimed. "So what made you move to this neck of the woods? You have family 'round here?"

"Not exactly" Giles wanted to avoid too much probing. "We wanted to move out of the old smoke. I work in the city so will be doing the commute although I do have the luxury of working from home part of the week. Jo and Harry are transferring school to St Mary's college in the next couple of weeks so it's all change for us."

"St Mary's! Great reputation, if a bit pricey." Derek was already making a stereotypical assessment of the new villagers but wasn't going to share his thoughts out loud. St Mary's was an elite private school and you needed to earn big time to afford two kids there. Made their money in the city and now want a slice of the "Escape to the Country" life, he mused. "Right let me go and get your food sorted. It's my wife Sally who does the cooking so she may pop out a bit later and say hi."

Giles smiled at Liz as Derek disappeared out the back of the bar. Harry and Jo were chatting away quietly; comparing something they had picked up on Instagram. They were both enjoying the chance to log into the free wifi at the pub as they had been without it all day. For teenagers with busy social lives the free access to the internet was a lifeline. Tonight they could share photos with their London friends detailing the excitement of the move and no doubt friendly banter about the existence of a pool. Both parents knew that they were asking a lot of Joanne, who was 16, and of Harry in pulling up their roots in London and taking them away from their school and friends. The move was a chance to make new memories in a completely different house in a new county. Hopefully these new memories would help to heal the family. Liz could not have stayed in London after the attack and

Joanne and Harry understood the sacrifice they needed to make to help their mother who was struggling with her all-consuming grief.

Before they left the pub, they got to meet Sally who popped out between courses. Sally was a bubbly rotund character, just like her husband, who seemed to laugh at everything. She was dressed in chef's whites with her curly hair straining to be released from her hairnet. She welcomed the newcomers and offered her help over the coming days as they settled in. It did feel weird to be the centre of attention of the pub clientele but the family hoped that would only be temporary.

Dinner had been excellent and they all appreciated the asset they had within walking distance to the house. The family agreed that this was going to be a regular feature of their week, enjoying a night out together with good food and wine. In London, they often spent family time at their local bistro. It wasn't often that Giles and Liz spent a romantic night just the two of them. They had always been very family focused and from the day Rebecca was born they ensured that the children were very much part of their spare time. The children learnt early on that dinner was family time and an opportunity to discuss their days and plan opportunities. This approach had meant that Giles and Liz had brought up confident young adults who were at ease in conversations and interested in other people's views. They were particularly proud of this characteristic in their children.

As the night drew in Liz and Giles settled down on the blow-up bed they had set up in their new bedroom. Liz nestled into Giles's chest and wrapped her arms around him. She sighed deeply as she reflected on the day. All things considered, the first stage of the move had gone without a hitch. Leaving the house in London had been extremely difficult especially having to leave Rebecca's bedroom with all those memories both beautiful and grief stricken. So much of Rebecca's furniture had been given away prior to the move with only those most precious and personal belongings making the journey.

The decision to move had been strongly influenced by Liz's family doctor, who was also a close friend. She felt that the family needed to make new memories in a new environment. Liz clinging on to all of Rebecca's belongings was stopping her from accepting she was gone. She had taken to spending her nights sitting on Becky's bed and talking to her about what had happened that day as if she was still there. It was not helping either Liz or her family to see their mum almost obsessed with Rebecca's room.

Giles had become increasingly distressed with the amount of time she had spent lying on the small single bed and sobbing all night. It had been over a year since they lost Becky and whilst every day hurt, Giles knew that they had to carry on for the sake of Joanne and Harry. They were struggling so much with the loss of their big sister and they needed Mum and Dad to be there for them and make life seem normal again.

Giles kissed Liz's hair and squeezed her close to him as sleep started to take him into its gentle embrace. He had the amazing capacity to drop into a deep sleep within minutes of relaxing in bed. It was a skill that Liz was extremely jealous of. She had never been a great sleeper but the events of the last year had made it more difficult than ever for her to relax and fall to sleep naturally. She had tried sleeping tablets from her doctor but really didn't like the sluggish feelings she got the following day. She had tried herbal remedies but with little success. Liz found it hard to switch off her brain at the best of times and spent many a night chewing over the events of the day and worrying about what was ahead.

Liz knew that tonight was going to be another of those nights where she watched the clock and mulled over the move and its implications. She was conscious that Giles was exhausted so waited until he was firmly asleep before she got up. They had a long day ahead with the furniture arriving and Giles would be at the centre of sorting out where everything needed to go. Liz was used to functioning on little sleep so knew that she would get through the day ahead somehow.

Quietly Liz let herself out into the garden and found her way to the garden bench. She had grabbed another large glass of Chardonnay on her way out of the kitchen and took a gulp. The first thing that struck her was how dark it was in the garden. Other than the security lights near the house the rest of the lawn was pitch black. This darkness was so unusual, as life in the city was populated by streetlights and the glow from neighbours' homes. Their new home was remote from the village and only lit by the stars. Above her head was the most amazing night sky she had ever seen. The night was so dark that it looked like you could see every star in the universe.

Slowly Liz scanned the sky watching the twinkling lights. She fixed her eye on the brightest star which gleamed out of the darkness. Her Rebecca was that bright celestial body, shining down on the world. A star taken too early, leaving her family lost and confused.

As she held her watch on the twinkling light a tear started to fall gently down her cheek.

CHAPTER THREE

The alarm penetrated Giles' sleep heavy brain. Rolling over he grabbed the offending phone and pressed snooze. Through the fog of his mind he squinted at the screen and groaned. 6am on a Saturday morning shouldn't be allowed he thought to himself. Giles gradually remembered the reason he set his alarm the previous night; the removal van was coming early with all their furniture.

As he became more aware of his surroundings Giles noticed that Liz wasn't beside him. Was she up before the alarm? That's was unusual as Liz really wasn't a morning person. This had been made worse over the last year as she struggled to drop off at night and would often sleep through Giles's daily pre-work ablutions.

"She must be excited about the events of today" mused Giles as he struggled to get upright from the blow-up bed. "Oh god you cannot get off these things elegantly" he sighed as he levered himself onto his elbows and pushed up to a kneeling position. The bed expelled him from its rubbery structure with a loud belching groan.

Giles staggered into the ensuite and still half sleep allowed his bladder to empty before jumping into the shower. The lukewarm water hit him with its refreshing stream and he grabbed at the shower gel to wash away the last evidence of sleep. Stretching out the knots in his back he turned and took in the view of the bathroom as he let the water flow over him. His eye for detail examined the decoration and he made a mental note of the various jobs required to get the room up to his high standards. The house was generally in good repair and most of the improvements they need to do were superficial embellishment.

As Giles dried his body, he wandered back into the bedroom and pulled back the floor to ceiling drapes. The early morning sunshine streamed into the room warming his naked torso. It felt really liberating to expose his body to the world only to be observed by the lambs, who did not seem impressed in the least. Giles grabbed a clean pair of boxers from his overnight bag and selected shorts and tee-shirt to complete his look.

As he walked down the corridor, he popped his head around Joanne's door and saw his beautiful daughter curled up in a foetal position, cuddling up to Monkey. She might be a young woman but that didn't stop Monkey from sleeping with her every night; except of course when she had a friend to stay. Then poor Monkey was hidden away in an attempt to save Jo's cool image. Giles smiled as he gazed at his darling girl and decided to leave her to sleep for a while longer.

"My sleeping beauty" whispered Giles as he watched.

Joanne shared his colouring with her long chestnut hair and deep brown eyes. Whilst she was growing up so quickly, she still loved to cuddle her dad. She was tactile and full of affection for her parents.

He could hear Harry stirring so walked down the corridor to his room. "Morning son. You're awake early Harry" he said.

Harry groaned and rolled over onto his back. "What time is it, Dad?" Harry was entwined in his duvet with a leg sticking out from the tangled mess. His blond hair was sticking up in its usual morning haystack as he yawned and stretched.

"It's early mate. You can doze for a while if you want. I'll give you a nudge in half hour or so if you want" replied Giles. "Don't wake your sister up will you, as she is out for the count".

"Ok daddio" Harry mumbled as he gently slipped back into a light sleep.

Giles made a quick sweep of the house and was unable to find Liz. He realised the garden door was unlocked and wondered out into the fresh morning air. He wasn't entirely surprised to find Liz on her yoga mat stretched out on the lawn. Liz had taken up this form of exercise in the last year and tried to complete a warmup exercise every morning to prepare for the day ahead. Yoga exercised her body and the mindfulness was proving vital in supporting her mental wellbeing.

Giles was careful not to disturb Liz so that he could enjoy watching his wife stretch out her body. He felt aroused as she pushed herself up into Down Dog. Long supple limbs peddled out her hamstrings. Her long blond hair was tied up in a scrunchy and the ponytail slapped against her cheek. Her lycra exercise pants revealed her curves and the tight bra top enhanced her amble breasts. "She is one sexy woman" Giles thought as he silently observed his wife complete her exercises.

Liz became aware of Giles watching her and athletically stretched herself up to standing position. "Morning darling" she gazed across at him and smiled. "I was up early so wanted to try out a bit of outdoor yoga. It is a truly beautiful experience listening to the dawn chorus and feeling the early morning dew under my fingers. She grinned. "I know, soppy cow! Isn't it so peaceful here?"

Liz had watched the sun rise across the fields an hour ago and listened to the neighbour's cock crow his morning greeting. Outdoor yoga would be yet another benefit of moving up country. You just couldn't imagine trying to obtain peace in their previous garden where the noise of traffic and planes overhead would have disturbed anyone's karma.

Giles pulled her in for a hug and took a deep breath in, enjoying the scent of her exercise. He loved this woman with all his heart and would do anything for her. Even moving out to the countryside, despite his desire to stay in London with the life they had there. It was going to be more inconvenient for Giles but he was embracing the change with his usual stoicism and enthusiasm.

"Come on then love. Let's get some breakfast going and get ready for Ted and Roy to arrive." Giles pointed out the time. "The kids are still asleep so we may need to give them a nudge shortly".

Giles took Liz by the hand and led her back into the house. They were a tactile couple who didn't feel embarrassed showing the depth of their feelings in front of their children. The family all enjoyed a good cuddle and both Joanne and Harry were keen to snuggle down on the sofa with either parent whenever the opportunity arose. Giles was proud of the affection and love surrounding his family. He always aspired for that level of emotion in his adult life. He had not had the happiest of childhoods and was passionate at not making the same mistakes that his parents had employed in their child rearing. His childhood had been cold. His parents were very formal and old school, thinking children should be seen but not heard.

The kitchen appeared fairly bare other than the travel necessities they brought with them. The space looked huge when empty. Give it a day, thought Giles, and it will be filled with the various appliances Liz had acquired over the last 25 years of their marriage. As Giles filled the kettle for tea, his eyes followed Liz as she left the room. He wished he had the time to follow her into the shower, whilst the children were still asleep, but thought better off it as time was moving on a pace. It can wait, he sighed to himself with pent up sexual frustration.

Giles was apprehensive about the day ahead. Packing up the old house was hard enough but they had been under a time restriction which meant that they had employed help to pack everything and organise the move. Once the removal men had finished the job today, it would be down to the family to organise everything into its new home. Giles had taken a week off work to try and get as settled as possible. For Giles, a week off work didn't actually mean a break from work. His role meant that it was difficult for him to completely switch off and whilst his PA would field most of his calls, there would always be something urgent kicking off to keep him in touch with the office.

The house move had been Liz's project as she was no longer working. She had given up her role as an office manager for a large accountancy firm a month ago, ahead of the move. Giles knew Liz had a plan and would organise them all. Sometimes she was too organised for her own good and would work like a whirling dervish to accomplish a task. That was great as the job got finished in good time but often led to family arguments as not everyone was as obsessed as Liz with the task in hand.

The toast exploded out of the toaster with more force than was probably required. Giles grabbed hold of it and popped another couple of pieces in for warming. With the tea made and toast underway, Giles called the family down for breakfast. He smiled as he heard Jo and Harry moaning and groaning about the early start. They were still in their nightwear, with hair all over the place. A sight for sore eyes. Giles pulled them both in for a big dad hug; a speciality of his. Jo wriggled away first as early morning hunger took priority over affection.

The family grabbed their breakfast and strolled outside to eat. Pulling up a couple of garden benches, they ate and chatted as they prepared for the day ahead. Giles surveyed his family and reminded himself how blessed he was, despite their recent loss. He had two beautiful children who were confident in their skin. He was incredibly proud of the young people they were growing into. The hard work of parenthood was paying off including the cost of their education, he mused.

A loud bleeping noise broke into the silence.

Giles set off around the side of the extension to see the enormous removal van slowly edge its way onto the drive. The single-track road was a challenge to the size of the lorry and Ted, the driver, took a number of attempts to make the turning circle to avoid any damage to the wooden gates. As the van pulled up onto the drive, Ted and Roy climbed down from the cab to greet Giles.

Ted was probably in his mid-forties, a small man with little skinny legs which stuck out like pipe cleaners from his khaki shorts. He just didn't look the right build for his job. He grabbed a weightlifter's belt from the cab and pulled it round his middle. Giles had watched him load the lorry in London and was staggered by his strength. His ability to lift large pieces of furniture and boxes was astonishing. First impressions can be so deceptive.

Ted pulled a flat cap over his balding head and nudged Roy into action. Roy was the younger of the two. He was in his twenties; tall and slim but with incredibly broad shoulders. He was a quiet lad who was very much in the shadow of his partner but was a grafter who just got on with the job. Joanne had taken a fancy to Roy whilst the packing was taking place. She had been all giggly around him. To give Roy his due, he had carried on as if he was used to all the attention. With his slim build and striking good looks, he had a passing nod to Leonardo DiCaprio. With those looks, I guess he gets used to the attention, thought Giles.

The back doors of the removal lorry creaked opened and Giles noticed how the furniture seemed to strain outwards to escape its confinement. Ted and Roy jumped into action and made short work of emptying the contents and transporting them into the relevant rooms. Liz's organisation skills came to the fore. Not only had she labelled up all furniture and boxes with the correct end location but she had cross referenced this into a spreadsheet which she used to cross off as each item was unloaded and to direct Ted and Roy to the quickest route. Joanne and Harry were employed in holding open doors, making cups of tea and generally keeping out of the guys' way. Around mid-morning Ted and Roy were finished and were on their way back to London. The house heaved an imaginary sigh of relief as peace resumed after the frantic morning.

The family took a break and Liz cracked open a box of biscuits as they all enjoyed a cup of tea. It had been a manic couple of hours but the weather had been kind to them. The rain which had been predicted had stayed away. The main furniture was at least in the right room and boxes had been positioned to ensure Giles and Liz could work through the unpacking in an organised way.

"Now comes the hard work of unpacking it all" sighed Giles who had been heavily involved in helping Ted and Roy and was, once again, feeling the knots which had formed in his back. Harry, without prompting, started to rub at his Dad's back. Harry liked to think of himself as his Dad's wingman. They were inseparable most of their free time and were the best of friends. Giles relaxed and enjoyed his son ministrations. He could feel his muscles calling out as Harry's fingers pressed and released the built-up tensions of the morning.

"Ok" started Liz, "would it make sense if we prioritise the main things we want to get settled tonight. So kitchen, bedrooms and lounge? If I crack on with unloading the kitchen equipment and if Jo can give me a hand, then you chaps could finish putting the beds together and setting up the TV." Liz was mentally ticking off her list of things to do. "We can see how far we get in the next few hours and then decide what next." As a carrot to the rest of the family she suggested, "wouldn't it be nice to grab a dip in the pool later on so it's not work work work all day?"

Giles and the kids shared a secret smile at their mother's drill sergeant impression. It was a family tradition that Liz ruled the roost and the rest of them just better do as they were told.

"Sounds like a plan" responded Giles as he picked up his toolbox. "Come on then, Harry. Let's get these beds sorted and leave the ladies in the kitchen."

"Oh such gender stereotypes" laughed Jo as she offered out her hand to help pull her Mum up off the grass. "Women in the kitchen and the boys with their toys!"

CHAPTER FOUR

The sun had risen high above the gardens casting arboreal shadows across the lawn. The temperature was becoming uncomfortable within the house and Giles had already changed from one tee-shirt which had been starting to hum with his perspiration. He and Harry had worked hard until lunchtime to construct each of the beds, drilling on the headboards and sorting out all the bedding. The family would sleep well tonight with their familiar possessions around them. The TV and music system were all in place and working. The heartfelt strains of Adele were providing background tunes as they worked. Giles was into his music and not a great watcher of TV but he knew the rest of the family would be keen to settle down with a film tonight after a day of physical exertion.

He stuck his head into the kitchen to see a maze of removal boxes covering the wooden floor. Wrapping paper was neatly stacked to one side and across the work tops spilled piles of their crockery, awaiting its new home. Joanne was at the kitchen sink washing items as they came out of the wrapping paper and Liz was sat cross legged on the floor working her way through the latest box. Her hair was tided back and as she concentrated she bit on her plump lip. Giles smiled at his view of the two most important women in his life; obviously not including his PA in that description. She always maintained that her role was the dominant one in his life.

"Ok ladies. How about a tea break? I popped down the road to the village shop and have some snacks to go with it" said Giles as he contemplated his stomach growling with hunger.

"Perfect" laughed Liz. "I could eat a horse. It seems so long since breakfast."

As Liz pulled herself to her feet, Jo made a start on the tea. Giles grabbed a couple of plates to lay out the local delights he had picked up earlier. There was a homemade quiche, some mini pork pies and speciality crisps. He juggled his way through the chaos on the floor and found his way into the garden. The garden furniture was in place on the patio so created a readymade dining area for the family to relax and take stock of the morning's endeavours.

No-one spoke for a few minutes as they each enjoyed their picnic and slurped on strong builders' tea. Liz pulled the sunglasses off the top of her head and stretched back in the seat enjoying the sunshine. The sun warmed her face dancing shadows across her cheeks. Around her the sounds of birds warbling seemed to be the only interruption to the silence of their new surroundings. Off in the distance was the faint hum of machinery from the nearby farm but other than that the world was quiet and at peace.

"Choo, Choo" cried a shrill voice from the side of the house. Around the corner of the extension appeared a couple carrying a large cake tin. "Hi there. Sorry to disturb. We saw the removal lorry had left and just wanted to pop in and welcome you to the village" smiled the owner of the voice.

"I'm Joyce and this is my husband Malcolm. Welcome welcome." Joyce beamed with a grin from ear to ear as she approached the patio. Joyce was a bit older than Liz and was definitely carrying a bit more weight, although she carried it with a style of her own. She had a quirky dress sense with her bright purple leggings and white gypsy top pulled down over her shoulders. The ensemble was topped off with a huge floppy straw hat.

Malcolm looked much older than his wife. His grey hair was shoulder length and he gazed over the top of his glasses with a look of resignation. He seemed used to his wife taking the lead and happily followed behind her.

"Hi there. Come and join us." said Giles. "Lovely to meet you, Joyce; Malcolm. I'm Giles and this is my wife Liz and our children Joanne and Harry." As the introductions took place, the new neighbours exchanged welcome kisses and handshakes. Giles pulled over a couple of extra chairs for their guests.

"Would you like a cup of tea?" asked Jo as she spontaneously jumped up from her seat. Both teenagers were confident with newly met adults and could adjust easily to changing situations and new acquaintances.

"Oh we don't want to put you to any trouble my lovely" responded Joyce. "But if it's ok then, I would kill for one. White with no sugar for both of us. And Joanne, bring some plates and I will serve up some of my famous lemon drizzle cake."

The cake was truly delicious and clearly lived up to its top billing. While the group ate, they introduced themselves more fully. Malcolm and Joyce lived in the next house down the lane and were technically their neighbours even though that was about half a mile away. Malcolm had retired recently from his role with the NHS as a psychologist. He explained that he was still keeping his hand in with some private counselling work and doing some volunteering work.

Giles nodded with interest and took a mental note to pick up with Malcolm once they got to know each other better. His expertise may be a welcome support to his family and especially Liz.

Joyce was Professor of History at UAE specialising in medieval agricultural history. Giles apologised as he interrupted at that point of the conversation. "Joyce, that's so interesting to know. Joanne is obsessed with history and is already planning to study that for her degree. Jo, you will have to pick Joyce's brain over the best university for you as you start the application process."

"That's great to hear" replied Joyce. "I'm more than happy to help if I can. Joanne, what period of history are you most interested in?" Joyce looked encouragingly at Jo showing her desire to know more.

Jo squirmed with embarrassment at her dad trying to influence the neighbours before they had even got to know each other. But that was his way. Accepting her initial awkwardness she entered into the conversation even so.

"Most of the history we have done recently has been 20th Century. Mainly 1st and 2nd World War. I do have an interest in Roman history and I'm taking that as one of my specialist subjects for A level." Jo's love of the subject shone across her face as she made eye contact with Joyce. "I'm also taking Latin and English Literature at A levels. Starting after the summer."

Jo and Joyce carried on discussing the joys of history for a few minutes until Malcolm changed the direction of the conversation to get to know more about the Stamford family.

"So what brings you to Norfolk, Giles?" Malcolm was softly spoken and struggled to make himself heard over the buzz of conversation.

"We really were looking for a more peaceful way of life" explained Giles. "London is such a manic place to live and it felt like the right time to step off the hamster wheel." Giles thought the analogy worked in terms of their previous existence. They seemed to constantly run from one activity to the next and everything seemed to be organised by car; spending wasted hours in traffic jams. Everywhere had got so much busier too over recent years which added to the stress levels.

"I travel all over the country with my job and probably only need to be in London once a week so we had the luxury of choosing where we live. I spent many years as a child holidaying in Norfolk so it seemed a no-brainer to choose this part of the country." Giles explained his role as he and Malcolm discussed the ins and outs of their professional life.

"And Liz, do you work?" Joyce enquired as she sliced up some more lemon drizzle and passed it around.

"I did work as an office manager but gave it up when we decided to move" outlined Liz. "I'm not sure whether I will find another job at the moment. We've had a difficult year and I think I need to take some time out and concentrate on the family." Liz didn't feel ready to share Rebecca with the Peterson's, so quickly moved the conversation on to discuss Jo and Harry's introduction to St Mary's College and to get Joyce's view on the quality of the school.

Malcolm and Joyce had two children who had fled the nest. Ben was based in Liverpool and was a junior doctor whilst Vanessa had recently been taken on by a practise in Wiltshire where she could complete her training as a vet. Both of their children had attended the prestigious private school. The Petersons were delighted to recommend the establishment and extol its virtues.

Joyce stretched her legs out in front of her and rotated her ankles to get the blood moving again. "It's going to be lovely getting to know you guys" she smiled. "The Smith's who lived here before didn't really mix and kept themselves to themselves. Once you get settled you must come over for dinner or lunch and we can tell you all the gossip in the village" she giggled. "It's a quiet village but there's always something happening. And it would be good having fresh blood to liven up the social scene."

"That sounds brilliant," smiled Liz. "I'd love to get to know our new village better."

Joyce was on a roll. "We do try and get some regular events going at the church and at the pub. We often have a fish and chip supper at the village hall which goes down well. And there is a youth club which takes place Thursday evening which Jo and Harry may enjoy."

Joyce nodded to the teenagers as she considered the positive additions to the dwindling teenage population within the village.

"Oh that's so kind of you" smiled Liz. "We definitely want to throw ourselves into country life and a good social occasion helps to get to know our neighbours. Once we are settled, I may throw a bit of a housewarming drinks party so we can get to know people. It would be lovely to pick your brains on who to invite."

"Definitely, sounds like a plan" agreed Joyce. "Anyway we must let you good folks crack on with your unpacking. If you need anything at all over the next few days give us a call. Here's our phone number and my mobile. Malcolm, come on old fella. Let's leave these guys in peace."

As fast as they arrived the couple breezed out of the garden leaving silence behind them. The house breathed a sigh of relief once tranquillity had returned to the garden.

The sun was casting long shadows across the patio as Giles called it a day. They had made good progress with most of the kitchen equipment. Liz was confident that she could work her magic for dinner that evening. Jo and Harry had unpacked all their clothes and belongings and had started to make their bedrooms feel like home. Giles was finally sat on the patio with a beer in hand whilst he worked his way through the paperwork for the swimming pool. He was confident that he understood the pumps and chemicals needed to keep the pool filtrated and a note from the Smiths explained that they had it cleaned the week before they moved out. Usefully they also left a recommendation for the pool cleaner who Giles would contact and introduce himself next week.

Giles gazed across the gardens and sighed with contentment. Liz was right. This house had a good feeling. There was a quietness which gave one time to reflect and take stock. The pace of life in the country would give them all time to slow down and enjoy the important things in their world. The family will do well here, he thought.

Harry crept up behind Giles already in his swimming gear. "Hey Dad, can I have a swim now before dinner. Think Jo wants to swim also. She's just getting changed."

"Of course, son. If you don't mind I'm not going to swim. I've decided to have a beer and to be honest I'm blooming knackered" Giles laughed. "But I will come with you guys and watch, if you are ok with that?"

The heat of the sun had penetrated the glass roof of the pool building making it sultry and welcoming. The roof of the building was made with a reflective glass which took away the glare of the sun but allowed the building to retain its warmth. The pool was full size; around 50 metres in length which was ideal as the family would use the pool for exercise rather than for fun. They were all good swimmers. The main wall of the building was glass with full length cream blinds. Once opened these would bathe the pool with a golden bright atmosphere. Around the pool were tasteful large blue tiles creating an area which could be used for sun loungers. The bottom of the pool had a mosaic of a dolphin cresting the waves. Rebecca's favourite creature was the dolphin. The choice of this decoration met with Giles's approval. The building was completed with a small changing room and shower which Giles was inspecting when the kids came running into the building full of anticipation.

Jo and Harry dived in while Giles pulled up a bench to observe his athletic kids. Unlike most teenagers, they didn't spend their time bombing each other and diving in an out of the water. They were both competitive swimmers and spent the next half hour racing each other, doing lengths of the pool.

Giles smiled to himself and congratulated himself on their choice. This house already felt ideal to heal his family. It was going to be a long slog but he was sure that the change in pace and the peace and quiet of this environment would give them all time to accept what had happened and find some form of closure. Time heals and here they would have the time as a family to do that.

CHPTER FIVE

The house was still.

Everyone was asleep.

Darkness crept with stealth along the corridors wrapping each room in its blackness. No streetlights penetrated the darkness, adding to the deep shadows. Stars twinkled creating a display of their glory across the night sky. As the house settled into repose there was the occasional sound of a creak or a groan. Shadows of trees swayed across the white walls making shapes in the gentle breeze. Curtains fluttered at the open windows offering a welcome relief to the night heat.

Liz rolled over onto her side pulling the duvet cover with her. Her bladder prodded her into wakefulness. There is a moment between sleep and waking where the body fights to stay in slumber but the physical needs of the body will not let that happen. Liz had reached that place and reluctantly pulled herself up to sit on the edge of the bed. She glanced over at Giles who had his back to her and was snoring rhythmically as he clutched hold of the edge of the duvet. Liz and Giles spent many a night fighting over the duvet as they were both light sleepers. Giles hated it when Liz created a tunnel with the covers sweeping cold air down his back. His normal response was to roll himself in the covers creating a papoose around him. Liz preferred to sleep with arms out and her leg flung out of the edge so between them the duvet took a good battering each night.

Rather than disturb Giles, Liz decided not to use their toilet but head down the passageway to the family bathroom. She quietly pulled open the bedroom door and looked out into the corridor. She was really only half awake and her body was functioning on autopilot. Shadows danced down the corridor which ran along the backside of the bedrooms. The window facing the back gardens cast further shapes across the walls.

Giles had joked earlier that the corridor reminded him of the scene from the film The Shining. He could imagine Danny Torrance riding his tricycle down the passageway of the Overlook Hotel. Fortunately neither Joanne nor Harry had seen that film or there would have been no chance of sleep that night. Liz grimaced as she thought of that scene and mentally gave herself a bit of a talking to. She didn't fancy running into Jack Nicholson in the middle of the night, she decided. It's just a dark passageway, she thought as she made her way along it, trying to avoid the noisy creaking floorboards. The blink of the alarm sensor broke the darkness, beckoning Liz towards her destination.

Liz was at the door of the bathroom when she felt it. An icy cold chill wafted across the back of her neck. It felt like someone had just breathed out deeply behind her. The temperature in the corridor dropped rapidly as Liz slowly turned to glance behind her. Her eyes told her there was no-one there but her gut told her something different. She strained to adjust her eyes and stare deeply into the shadows. There was nothing there but that didn't convince Liz. She continued to stare down the passageway dissecting the shadows for a clue to what she had felt.

"Don't be stupid," she whispered. "There is nothing there. You are just imagining it". As she turned her head back around and put her hand on the door handle she heard it. A low groan vibrated in her ear. A strong aroma of flowers filled the corridor. It was a sickly and overpowering smell, out of place in the still night air.

Liz gasped.

She pulled the door open, pushed herself through and quickly closed it behind her. Flicking on the light switch, she wrapped her arms around her breasts and breathed out deeply.

"Oh god," she gasped. "That wasn't my imagination surely."

She was shaking with fear as she stared at the door which was the only protection from whatever was out there. She could not face the return trip alone. Liz seriously considered calling out to Giles to come and help her. If she did that the commotion would surely wake the children up. She really didn't want to scare the kids.

She was petrified.

For a long moment Liz just stood there staring into space and shaking with fear.

Trouble was she couldn't really understand what she had just felt. It just seemed crazy to think it was something supernatural. Liz didn't believe in ghosts. She had desperately wanted to believe in some form of afterlife when they lost Rebecca but that comfort was never offered her.

It was probably just one of the idiosyncrasies of an old house. Cold spots or unexpected breezes from the badly fitted windows. The floors creaked as you walked on them so who knows what other noises were trapped in this old house. Her overwhelming feeling in this house was peace so Liz refused to believe something nasty could be happening. Liz continued to rationalise her fears as she went to the toilet.

Gradually her mind assimilated the situation and convinced her she had imagined the whole thing. She mentally pulled herself together and shaking her head vigorously she cleared the panic which had been building and threatened to take over.

"Ok silly cow, that's it. Get back to bed and stop letting your imagination run riot." Liz pulled open the bathroom door and sped back to their room. She felt foolish charging down the corridor like someone possessed. She wasn't brave enough to hang around in the gloom. Arriving back safely she sighed and convinced herself that she had made up the last few minutes.

Gently she pulled back the covers and slid under. She shuffled over and entwined her body along Giles's back for comfort. Giles moved in his sleep but didn't wake so she stayed put and tried to let sleep take her back into its embrace.

Breathing deeply through her nose, she started to relax and allow her mind to slow down its frantic thoughts. As she started to fall into a light sleep her eyes moved slowly across her eyelids and her muscles started to relax. Her breathing slowed as she moved towards REM. It was then that she saw her.

The girl.

Away in the distance.

It was like she was in half light, all fuzzy around the edges.

She was walking through a wheat field, swinging a wicker basket in her hand. The girl was on the cusp of womanhood, tall with developing breasts and hips. Her long dark hair cascaded down her back.

She was beautiful.

She looked familiar but not. Her clothes looked strange and out of place. She wore a long blue dress nipped in at the waist with a white pinafore covering her front and tied loosely at her back.

Liz dreamt on.

CHAPTER SIX – SUMMER 1860

The girl was daydreaming.

In her mind she was flying with the cranes who swept across the clear blue sky. She could feel the rush of the wind in her hair and her breath being sucked from her lungs as they climbed higher and higher. The ground rushed away as she flew over the wheat fields towards the horizon and freedom. As she looked to her left, the mother crane flew alongside her, flapping her huge wings slowly. Her grey plumage was magnificent with a group of 5 feathers reaching out at the end of her wings like bird fingers. Her neck stretched forwards with a steely determination to reach her destination. Behind, her mate followed in her slipstream. The majestic crane stared at her with its hooded eyes, urging her onwards.

Escape.

Her mind craved the freedom of those beautiful birds. She wanted the ability to take flight and find another home across the fields. A place where she could grow and be herself. A place where she didn't need to watch her words and, more importantly, keep away from him.

Suddenly she hit the ground with a thump.

The dream was over.

She lay at the edge of the field with the tall stalks of wheat swaying above her head. She must have fallen asleep for a moment. Sarah pulled herself up and noticed the wicker basket at her feet. She suddenly remembered what she should have been doing. She had been sent to collect the eggs from the henhouse in the yard and here she was wasting time, dreaming in the wheat field. If mother found her there she would be in even more trouble. Trouble was Sarah's best friend unfortunately. She never seemed to be able to do anything to please her mother anymore or to keep that dreadful man off her back.

She ran at full pelt back to the yard and skidded to a halt. Her toes hit the front of her wooden clogs chaffing her skin. The hen house was a basic wooden lean to, triangular in shape with a small wooden door. Sarah had to get on her hands and knees to access the booty. On all fours she stretched her arm into the straw to find the precious eggs. Ignoring the frantic pecks to her fingers she managed to retrieve a good dozen eggs which would please mother. She said a prayer to her beloved hens who had outdone themselves today and would perhaps ensure mother would not give her a beating for taking her time.

Easing her lithe body out of the henhouse, she stretched out her previous sleepiness. Her long hair was peppered with wheat chaff. Pulling her fingers through her hair she wound the brown tendrils into a bun which she secured in place with a tatty ribbon. Brushing down her dress, she straightened her white apron. There was no way any evidence of her slacking would earn her mother's displeasure today.

Sarah turned and took in the view of the house. Her home was primarily used as the local public house. The front of the building was given over as the tap room, where the local farm labourers would stop to drink themselves stupid after work. Most of them would then return home to take it out on their wife and kids.

The family had the use of a large kitchen and a couple of big rooms in the roof space. Mother and Jack shared one room with baby Emma. Sarah shared the other room with her brother and sister, Tom and Hannah along with stepbrother Arthur and stepsister Anne. Between the rooms was a large confined space which mother used to store belongings. Sarah knew that her father's belongings were lovingly kept there without Jack's knowledge. Her mother still missed her first husband. He had been a caring and loving father; the complete opposite of that monster her mother was now married to.

Sarah pulled open the kitchen door and maneuvered her way into the room balancing the egg basket carefully in the other arm. Her mother was kneading bread at the large wooden kitchen table and looked up at Sarah with a painful smile.

Mary Whiting had a gaunt face and wasted frame evidence of the toils of childbearing. She bore a passing trace of her youthful stunning looks which were fading with time. Her thick dark hair was dotted with grey. Her face was lined from worry and it seemed so long since her smile had lit up her countenance. She wore her normal working clothes of a grey check cotton day dress, fastened at the waist with matching cotton belt. The dress buttoned modestly up to the neck and her hair was covered with a white bonnet. She encapsulated the look of a downtrodden matron, with her weary expression and slow movements.

Without being told, Sarah placed the eggs into the kitchen basket and took over the bread making from her mother. She understood that her mother needed to get dinner ready for Jack who would be home from work shortly. It was never a good idea to keep him waiting. Jack seemed to enjoy her mother cowering from his fists. It seemed to make him feel like the big man. Sarah hated Jack with a passion. He was an evil man and she hated the changed he had inflicted on her mother. He had changed their family home from a warm loving environment to one of fear and anger.

As Sarah knocked back the dough and placed it on the stove top to prove, she watched her mother preparing the potatoes, carrots and turnips which were to be added to the weak broth warming on the top of the cast iron range. There would be a small piece of lamb in the broth, a left over from Sunday, and this would help to flavour the stew and be given to Jack as the breadwinner. Sarah found yesterday's loaf of bread which would be divided out around the family of eight to mop up the tasty liquid. Mary Whiting was a good cook and could make the dullest meal full of goodness for her growing family.

Dinner was almost ready when Anne and Hannah return from morning lessons at the village school. Hannah, at ten years old, was a bright child who was keen to learn as much as she could before her time in the classroom would be over. She would finish school this Christmas and would follow Sarah behind the bar and into the family business. Anne was Jack's favourite and his firstborn. At six years old she was developing into a sweet child with rosy cheeks and a rosy temperament. She was oblivious to the fact that her father treated her differently to her half siblings. Her beautiful nature ensured that the rest of the family could not hate her for his favouritism. To them Anne was an angel who had fallen from heaven to live in a child's body and was somehow protected from the evils of this world. She would wander through life with a fairy smile on her face bringing joy to all she touched. Her habitual white smock dress with matching white ribbon in her hair added to the angelic look.

As the kitchen clock struck twelve, Jack Whiting flung back the kitchen door and strode into the room. He kicked his work boots off and dropped them on the floor then threw himself into the chair beside the range. Jack was a thick set man with a jowly face and close-cropped hair. Tufts of hair grew from his ears and nose. Sweat dripped from his face, evidence of a mornings punishing effort. His was not a face you could love. It held no softness or joy but a countenance of anger and dissatisfaction with life. Despite his manual work on his farm, he carried some weight around his gut which was mainly due to the beer he consumed each night. His gluttony was renowned with his fellow farmers. As was his loose talk.

Before Jack had married Mary he had owned and managed Wood Farm which ran alongside the Crown and Hare pub. Mary's husband, John Cozen, had been the innkeeper. When John died unexpectedly it had seemed inevitable that Mary would agree to combine the two businesses for the future security of her children. Custom dictated that Mary could not manage the inn on her own. She needed a husband. Jack had been relentless in his determination to make Mary his wife, or if he was honest with himself, his pursuit of the inn. That partnership had helped to make Jack the most important man in the village, a fact he like to lord over his fellow labourers as they supped their beer in his taproom.

Behind him followed Tom, who spent the day working the farm with his stepfather. Tom was only twelve years old but was already becoming a young man, used to hard labouring. He was filling out and even starting to grow tufts of facial hair. Tom was a younger version of John Cozen. Tall, lanky with long slim limbs, ruddy cheeks and a smile to break hearts. He knew his worth as a worker which ensured that he took precedence over his mother and siblings when it came to the midday dinner.

The family took their places at the table where they were joined by the youngest children, Arthur who was four and the baby Emma at just over a year. Sarah strapped Emma into the baby rocking chair. The chair had a tray top for feeding and was on rockers which often cradled Emma to sleep after eating.

Meanwhile, Mary placed the heavy stew pot onto the table and served the meat and bulk of the potatoes to Jack. Tom was then given a decent helping in recognition of the work he would be doing that afternoon. The remainder was shared out between Mary, Sarah and the younger children with a large helping of bread.

The family ate in silence. They all knew it was best not to start a conversation. Sarah remembered how the family would laugh and joke over the midday meal when her father was alive. He loved to hear about everyone's day as they shared nourishment. Mealtimes had been a family occasion and the noise around the table had been comforting. Watching her mother and stepfather ignore each other, heads down in their bowls, saddened Sarah. Even though she hated Jack, she wished her mother happiness. Sadly that seemed for ever out of reach.

When Jack had finished eating he kicked back in his chair and pulled his clay pipe from his trousers. His face was set firm in concentration as he filled it and shaped the tobacco into the optimum position. Once happy he struck a match on the table and sucked in the musty fog deep into his lungs. He breathed out and filled the room with his rich smoke. Anne squirmed out of her seat and pulled herself up onto Jack's lap. His hand naturally came to rest on her hair stroking her like a kitten. She almost purred with contentment as she enjoyed her father's affection.

"Sarah, I want that bar spotless for this evening" he growled at the eldest of his adopted children. "Squire Cole has called a meeting of local farmers for this evening and I don't want him seeing a speck of dirt. Do you hear me?" The glare he shot at Sarah was in complete contrast to the affectionate embrace he was giving his own daughter.

"Of course, Father," Sarah replied. The word father almost stuck in her throat. He hadn't got a fatherly bone in his body when dealing with his stepchildren. Their mother had been insistent that they call Jack father. Sarah and Hannah both found this uncomfortable and did so under sufferance. Tom, on the other hand, looked up to Jack with much more respect. Working together daily had given the two males a relationship which didn't exist with his stepdaughters.

Sarah recalled the state of the bar area after last night's lock in and knew that she would be spending the rest of the day on her hands and knees trying to wash out the spilled beer and tobacco. Normally Jack was not concerned about how clean the pub was but the presence of the main landowner demanded that an image be upheld. Sarah was responsible for both the upkeep of the pub and spent her evenings serving the locals and trying to avoid their grabbing hands.

The atmosphere in the pub was another thing that had changed since her father had died. John Cozen had been much admired by the village and was renowned for running a respectable establishment. The men of the village spent time after their day had finished, sharing their concerns. Produce could be bartered over a pint of ale and many a neighbourhood dispute would be resolved in the cheery atmosphere.

Since her stepfather had taken over the running of the Crown and Hare the standards had slipped. Jack enjoyed the power over his fellow labourers and lorded it over the bar every night. He did not think it was his job to serve the ale and had left that task to first Mary and then when Sarah had grown older, to her. He was unconcerned that his stepdaughter was subjected to drunken fumbling from some of the more boisterous villagers and if she tried to object would often feel the back of his hand across her face. The fact that he was often the person responsible for that drunken fumbling was a secret he kept from his wife.

He lusted over Sarah as a younger and more nubile version of his Mary and, in his arrogance, had no concern at all that his grotesque affection was not replicated. He told himself that his touching was harmless. Mary would understand that he had needs and more often than not, his wife was asleep by the time he made it to their bedroom. A man cannot wait for ever for his needs to be satisfied and if things didn't improve soon then he was inclined to take things further to get what he wanted.

It was late afternoon and the sun continued to blaze across the summer sky, glinting through the open door of the taproom. Sarah was exhausted from her toils. She had cleaned the floor meticulously and she was certain you could see your face in the bar. She gazed longingly out the door, wishing she was a child again. She could hear the voices of Anne and Arthur as they played boisterously in the yard. Life was so simple for the younger ones. They were content in the love of their parents and the freedom of childhood. They were yet to learn of the troubles of growing up in this household.

Her work was all but finished. Sarah struggled to lift the bucket of dirty water, sloshing it out of the door and into the ditch which ran alongside the field surrounding the pub. As she stretched her back muscles, Sarah saw Hannah making her way round the side of the building carrying a ceramic flagon and wicker basket. She waved to her sister.

"Sarah, mother has told me to take some refreshment to the workers over yonder field. Do you want to come with me?" Hannah's face lit up with excitement at the thought of spending time with her big sister.

The last thing Sarah wanted right now was to hike across the fields to see her stepfather and his team of workers. She was tired from her hard work but she could not turn down her beloved sister. Spending time together was a precious gift and not one she could ignore.

"Come on then, Hannah. Let me take the basket off you. That looks heavy." With a sigh, Sarah heaved the basket onto her arm, noting the fresh bread chunks wrapped in linen. She could smell the freshness. A wave of jealousy washed over her as she contemplated the lack of fresh bread for the mid-day meal which was being saved for the men's afternoon break. Life was just not fair at times.

Sarah walked fast with a determination met by her younger sibling. Hannah was a strong child who was fast approaching womanhood. Her dusty blond hair hung neatly in a plait which touched the top of her buttocks. Her skirts were being gradually lowered by Mary as her daughter grew in age; a nod to the respectability required as a girl reached puberty. Her feet were covered by woollen stockings which were itchy and uncomfortable at this time of year and her toes were wedged into wooden clogs similar to Sarah's.

This summer had been hot and dusty and it had seemed weeks since the cooling rains had sent their sustenance to feed the parched ground. It was perfect growing weather for the wheat which stood tall as far as the eye could see. It wouldn't be long before the hard work of harvesting would occupy the whole Whiting family for days. Even the youngest children would be allocated tasks as the family worked together to bring in the wheat. For many communities the toil of harvest time would lead to the excitement and celebration of festivals. Not so for the Whiting children. Jack and Tom would celebrate their efforts with the other male workers with copious amounts of ale leaving the womenfolk to make do. Mary and her older daughters would spend their time cooking and providing for the men rather than joining in themselves.

As the two girls walked, Hannah linked her little finger with her sister's. The girls shared a bed each night and were devoted to each other. Hannah clung to her older sister in bed which Sarah found wonderful during those bitter winter nights. The recent clammy nights made sleep difficult especially when you had a sweat dripping body clinging to your torso. Sarah would not deny her sister the comfort. Since their father had died, she had taken the role of carer to her younger sibling. Hannah suffered with nightmares and having her sister to reach out for in her distress was a calming influence. Their mother's love was in short supply so they had learnt to lean on each other.

Hannah broke the comfortable silence as the sisters strolled arm in arm. "Why is Jack so horrible to you, Sarah?" When they were alone, the sisters called their stepfather by his given name. "He seems to find fault in all you do."

"I don't know, my lovely. He is just an angry man. He bullies mother. He shouts at Tom. And he hates me. Perhaps it's because I'm not frightened of him. He wants me to cower under his fists but for some stupid reason I really don't understand, I just want to laugh in his face." Sarah knew that her own behaviour didn't help the situation but she refused to bend to his will. There was stubbornness in her which she could not deny. "It's probably my own fault for standing up to him. I should maybe keep my head down and put up with his anger."

"I miss father so much." Hannah's sweet innocent face smiled up at Sarah's thoughtful visage. "Why did mother marry Jack? She surely doesn't love him. It is so sad. I don't think I will marry a man when I'm a big girl."

"Oh my lovely girl, you will marry a kind man. He will care for you and treat you fairly. Not all men are like Jack. Father was a gentle man and he loved mother so much. One day we will both find young men just like our father and live happily until we are old and grey."

Sarah wasn't sure if she believed her own words. Could she be that lucky? Most of the boys in the village irritated her with their loud cursing and dreadful behaviours. Most girls would marry from the village. There didn't seem a great deal of choice open to her.

"I don't know if I would like to marry, Sarah. If I did I wouldn't be able to live with you. I don't think I would like that." Hannah said with real concern in her trembling voice.

"Well I know what we shall do; we will marry brothers then. And live together for ever." Sarah smiled reassuring Hannah squeezing her fingers gently.

"Oh yes that would be the best idea. Let's make a pact now that we will only marry if two lovely brothers come along. Promise me Sarah."

"I promise darling."

Sarah could see the men ahead. They were working in two groups on parts of the stone wall which divided the two vast pastures belonging to Wood Farm. A number of stones had come away during the winter storms. Repairs needed to be done whilst the labour was available.

Being sensible Sarah and Hannah headed towards the team of men under Jack's guidance. The men were all casual labourers who travelled around the countryside picking up jobs for a few days at a time. Jack was a hard task master but paid well which led to him being popular with the wandering workforce. Sarah handed out the chunks of bread and poured ale from the heavy flagon avoiding Jack's eye.

As soon as they could the girls headed further down the field to find Tom. He was working on his own, wielding a stone axe which he smashed into the bigger pieces of flint. Once he caught sight of his sisters he dropped the tool and wiped the sweat from his face on his jerkin.

"What a sight you are," he shouted across at them; his ears not yet accustomed to the silence after the noise of the axe. "I am right thirsty. Pour me a drink Sarah."

The three siblings sat leaning against the wall while Tom ate the fresh bread. He pulled out the soft middle which was still warm and handed over to Hannah who grabbed at the dough and quickly stuffed into her mouth before he changed his mind. Tom reached across and ruffled Hannah's hair with affection.

"How are my favourite girls today?" he asked.

"Who is your favourite girl?" responded Hannah with a cheeky grin on her face.

"Oh you are my favourite, Hannah," he laughed as he winked at his oldest sister.

Tom was growing up fast but the bond between him and Sarah remained strong. In fact the bond between all three of John Cozen's children was formidable. Losing their father at such a young age had created a triumvirate which would not be easily broken. Tom held out his hand to Sarah as he took his baby sisters fingers.

"You are both my favourite sisters and I promise I will defend you to the end," he said.

Tom appeared to be looking across the field towards his stepfather as he said the words. He could sense the growing friction between Sarah and Jack. It worried him. He knew Jack was a nasty man. He had a dangerous temper. Tom had learnt to deal with Jack and most of the time they got on. He couldn't recall the last time he got a swipe from Jack's fist. On the other hand his big sister had a way of winding up Jack. She had a level of defiance about her character which just wouldn't buckle to her stepfather. It was dangerous and Tom worried what the future would hold and what part he would have to play in it.

CHAPTER SEVEN

Liz reached the end of the pool and forward rolled as she changed ends. She raised her face out of the water and took a breath deep into her lungs. Replicating the mosaic on the floor of the pool she swam with the grace of a dolphin. She moved through the water with a confident rhythm.

As she swam, she mulled over the dream. She could remember the dream so vividly. It felt like she was there with the family from the past. The house looked so familiar as if it was her new home but older and sparser. She visualised the girl from the dream. She looked so familiar but so different at the same time.

The girl shared many of Becky's features. In her mind the two faces blended into one to add to Liz's confusion. Was this some form of message from the past? Some form of shared pain? Was Becky trying to reach out to her mum and tell her something? Was she using this girl to reach out to Liz?

Liz reached the end of the pool and pulled herself out onto the side. Her black swimsuit dripped as she wiped the excess water from her torso. She raised her arms and stretched out as she continued to reflect on the message of last night. Normally Liz was sceptical of the supernatural. Her grief when Rebecca had died drove her to places she could not expect or control. She had been desperate to contact Becky after she had gone and that had thrown her core Christian beliefs into turmoil.

Giles had been angry and concerned when she told him she wanted to contact a psychic to reach out to Rebecca. He threw scorn on her plan and they had the most enormous row when she tried to book in a session. She had reluctantly backed down out of respect for his pain but hadn't squared it off in her conscience. Somehow she felt she had let Becky down by not trying to reach her and reassure her darling girl. Becky had been scared of the dark and would need her mummy to hold her hand through the journey ahead.

Perhaps this dream was a reminder that she had let her own daughter down. She was racked with guilt all over again. Why had she not picked Becky up that evening rather than let her take a taxi? She had allowed her daughter to be exposed to the evil side of London and had paid the ultimate cost. Why wasn't it her that was taken rather than her beautiful girl who had the world at her feet and had her whole future ahead of her? She would have had a successful life; a career; a husband and children of her own. All that was lost because she got in the wrong taxi with a pervert who robbed her of her beautiful life.

Liz grabbed a towel and wrapped it around her body as she sighed at her reflections. The pain was so intense. People shared platitudes that things get easier to bare but Liz could not imagine a time when she would be able to greet the day with a light heart. Things don't get easier; you just learn to live with the pain a little better every day.

She mentally needed to get herself together for the day ahead. Jo and Harry are due to start school next week and she and Giles had arranged to go into Norwich today to fit out their uniforms and ensure they had everything they needed. As a mother she had to keep functioning for her remaining precious children, despite the pain. They had promised the children a trip to the cinema and Giles had booked at table at Jamie's Italian for them to kick back and relax from the strain of unpacking whilst the kids enjoyed the film.

A fine rain was clinging to their hair as Liz and Giles ran into the Arcade after dropping off the children. They laughed at each other as they both pushed the hair out of their faces and shook off the excess water like a pair of dogs. The weather was still warm and steamy but a short and heavy shower had descended on the centre of Norwich driving the shoppers undercover. The couple pushed their way through the crowd of shoppers to find their way to the restaurant. They were both looking forward to some Italian food and maybe a large glass of red.

As they were shown to their table, Liz glanced around the busy restaurant which was mainly occupied by couples catching a break from shopping. Their table was next to the main windows looking out over the Arcade. The shopping mall was crammed with quirky boutique shops which Liz took a mental note to go and visit after lunch. Their prime location next to the window was ideal for their favourite sport. If people watching were an Olympic sport then Liz would be confident of a gold medal. She loved observing others and imagining what was happening in their lives. Her and Giles would often make up bizarre stories about the people they had watched and these narratives often had them in stitches as they belly laughed.

Having chosen their lunch, they both made a start on the tasty bottle of Chianti, clinking glasses as they gazed into each other's eyes.

"I had a really weird dream last night." Liz started the conversation tentatively as she was anticipating a challenge from Giles.

"Weird dream? Were you at the cheese again," smiled Giles.

"Well to be fair it started with a weird experience and then when I got back to bed I had this dream which has really shook me up." Liz started to explain the feeling she got when she went to the bathroom last night and as she put her feelings into words she almost felt embarrassed at how silly it sounded.

Giles unusually didn't scoff at what she was saying and seemed to be listening intently to the story. He didn't interrupt and allowed Liz to complete her explanation of the details of her dream. When she finished he took his time before he shared his initial observations.

"The mind is a complex organ, darling" he started cautiously.

He was careful in shaping his next words as the last thing Giles wanted was to add to Liz's grief by diminishing the importance of what she had felt. He worried about Liz's mental state since Rebecca's death. He could comfort her and be there for her physical needs but he did struggle to understand the impact of such intense grief on her ability to function mentally. He really didn't understand how to frame his advice without seeming patronising.

"Do you not think it might just be a coincidence, this dream? We have had a big upheaval with the move and leaving so many memories behind in

London," he asked tentively.

Liz had a puzzled look on her face as she absorbed his remark and tried to think how best to take this subject forward.

"I'm sure the dream was about our house. It looked so familiar from the outside and the detail just made me feel convinced that it was our home. But" she paused as she recalled the events of last night. "It wasn't present day. I mean, it was from the past. The clothes were old fashioned and there was no modern equipment in the house. All open fires and candles." Liz wanted Giles to believe her.

"Look Giles, I know it sounds crazy and I don't understand it myself. But the dream was so vivid and I remember it all. Usually when you wake from a dream you have a vague recollection but I can remember everything."

Giles took her hand across the table and squeezed it affectionately. "It's an old house and there will have been so many people who have called this place home. Perhaps you tapped into some form of memory of the past. I don't believe in ghosts but perhaps energy gets trapped in the fabric of a house and if you have the right receptors then it may tap into your subconscious."

"I definitely felt something on the landing last night though Giles." Liz grew bolder as her husband hadn't dismissed her story as complete rubbish and seemed open to discussing her concerns. "There was a sudden drop in temperature which was mad as it was so hot and sticky last night. And I'm convinced that I felt a breath on the back of my neck. Like someone was behind me and trying to get me to see them. It really scared the life out of me. But there was nothing there to see." She shivered as she recalled the experience. "You know what I mean? No weird lights or shadows moving around. One minute I was freezing cold and the next moment it was over and everything was normal."

"Look Liz, you know that I am struggling with this one as I don't feel anything strange in that house. It has a gentle and warm feel to me and I really don't want to contemplate that we have a resident ghost. You have got to be careful that you don't talk to Harry or Jo about this. The last thing we need is them getting spooked in their new home. You will promise me,

50

won't you?" Giles took a gulp of his wine as he launched into his pasta dish.

"Give me some credit, Giles." Liz was trying not to lose her temper at that remark. "The last thing I would do is unsettle the children. I want them to be so happy in our new home and give them a chance to heal. You are the only person I can speak to about this and I knew you would poo poo my story but I had to share it with you." Liz fumed at the thought that her husband might really think she didn't have her children's best interest at heart. She felt confused about last night's events and was trying to find answers.

"I don't understand the significance of the dream or even if there is any significance at all. The girl in the dream did look so similar to Becky so perhaps it was my mind making up things. Well perhaps that's my mind dwelling on what happened last year. But I don't know whether I believe that. Is that just the easy way out, pretending it was in my mind?"

"I'm sorry love. I shouldn't have said that. I know you do everything you can to protect Jo and Harry. That was bang out of order of me." Giles reached over and touched her cheek gently. "Do you feel scared in the house now?"

"No. That's the weird thing, Giles. I still feel a deep sense of belonging in that house. Perhaps it's just my mind working overtime. Don't worry about it. Just me being a bit crazy," she smiled across the table as she took a sip of wine. Her anger at her husband diminished as quickly as it had flared up. Perhaps now was the time to change the conversation away to something a little less controversial.

"Ok sweetie. Look I don't want you to hide anything from me so if this happens again will you promise you will tell me and perhaps we can work through it together." Giles looked at Liz intently as he secured her promise.

The couple relaxed into their meal as the conversation flowed onto the children and their first day at the new school which was fast approaching.

Liz's stomach was churning with emotion after her husband's response to her dream. She had doubts that he believed her. Was he just pacifying her? Would she share another experience if she felt it? I'm not sure I would, she thought as she gazed at her husband.

Giles was putting a brave face on things despite the real fear in his head that Liz had taken a further step in the wrong direction of recovery. That man has a lot to answer for, he thought. Destroying my family. Things were not the same since Rebecca's death and Giles felt incapable of getting his family back to where they had been before.

CHAPTER EIGHT – SUMMER 1860

Sarah brushed her hair wearily from her face as she picked up used tankards from the tables. She was exhausted after a busy night in the taproom. She had been on her feet all evening serving drinks and clearing tables.

It was a Saturday night which was the busiest of the week. Men who worked hard all week used this night to fill their bellies with ale. Other than church the following day, Sunday was their day of rest. Many of those drinking in The Crown and Hare tonight would pay for it with sore heads in the morn. Women didn't drink in the bar. This was men's territory and ruled over by Jack Whiting.

He wanted to be the centre of attention boasting of his own self-importance. He had become louder and more boisterous as the evening had worn on. Her brother Tom had taken himself off to bed some hours ago as, despite the day of rest ahead, he knew he would have work to do. He knew well how he would suffer if he didn't pick up the slack for his stepfather and master.

The only light in the dim hell of working the bar was Squire Cole. He was a gentleman and Sarah enjoyed serving him. He always smiled at her and often would slip a coin into her pocket. She was saving those coins. She never told Jack. She took those coins and hid them under her bed. If Jack knew he would hit her and confiscate them. For that reason she wouldn't share her secret with her mother or her siblings. This was her escape fund. One day she would leave with Tom and Hannah and never look back.

Whenever she was serving Squire Cole she kept her back to Jack. He could not see the attention she gave the major landowner. He would not see her smile sweetly as Squire Cole tipped another piece of her future into her pinny. Or so she hoped.

Jim, the pig man, was the last to leave as he staggered against the door frame in his stupor. Following him to the door, Sarah pulled the bar across and made sure the locks were all secure before returning to the bar. She started to wash the tankards, preferring to get this work completed before she dragged herself up to bed. She could see that Jack was slumped in a chair near the fire so was trying to complete her final tasks in silence. She could hear him snoring and watched a trickle of bile run out of the corner of his mouth as he dozed.

Sarah wondered why her mother had agreed to the match with this slob. He may have provided a level of financial security but Mary was a catch who could have held out for a better man than Jack Whiting. When John had died there was interest in Mary from across the parish and further afield. Mary Cozen was a beauty and had produced three children already so had proved her worth as a child bearer. Of course when Jack had come courting, he showed a different side to himself. One that swept the grieving widow off her feet and into his bed. Before she really understood the man, she was unfortunately married to him.

The oak bar needed a good scrubbing to remove the beer stains. Pools of residual beer gathered in patches and a bottle of whiskey sat in the midst of the chaos. Sarah pushed the cork into the bottle and set to cleaning up the spills.

While she worked she had her back to Jack. She did not see him wake.

He stared at her as she worked. He saw the way her breasts moved as she scrubbed at the stains. Her breasts were pert and inviting. Her hair gently caressed her lovely face. She really was a beautiful girl. The urge in him was rising. He needed to do something about it.

Suddenly Sarah felt her arm pulled behind her and felt wet slobber breath on her neck.

"Outside now," growled her stepfather as he pulled her out of the back entrance towards the outside privy. Her feet scrambled to find the ground as he dragged her through the house. Her arm burnt with pain as he forced her forward. Her clogs fell from her feet as she struggled to get any purchase on the cold floor. It all happened too quickly for Sarah to shout out. Even if she had, there was no one awake to hear her.

Jack slammed the privy door and pushed Sarah up against the wall. She was overpowered by the smell of stale urine. Her bare feet could feel the wetness beneath her toes. She recoiled from the smell and tried to move past him.

"Where do you think you are going, you whore" Jack drove his face into hers. His fierce eyes seemed to penetrate into her mind, almost hypnotic.

"You slut. You were all over Cole tonight; flouncy your hair in his face and pushing your breasts into his eyes. Do you really think he would look at a girl like you?" Jack was not waiting for her reply." You have airs above your station, my girl. You are just a barmaid and until you catch yourself a labourer to wed then you will behave under my roof," he continued. "And until then you will only put yourself out for me."

Sarah was stunned by this tirade and shocked by his last statement. Before she could act, Jack pushed her around so that her face was crushed up against the privy wall. He had his arm pushed into her shoulders making it impossible for her to move. It was then that the reality of what was about to happen hit her. Before she could scream for help she heard the sinister threat in her ear. "One scream out of you and Hannah will be next."

Sarah felt her dress pulled up towards her waist. He used his legs to push her open beneath him. His hand grabbed at her underwear and she felt the rip of fabric as he pulled them away from her. Her head was screaming "stop please stop" but she could not get the words out for fear of the consequences to her beloved younger sister.

Time stopped as she waited. Her blood beating through her body was the only sound she was aware of.

Then a ripping pain as he entered her. He thrust into her. Grinding his body against her, oblivious to the distress he was causing.

The pain was all consuming as he thrust himself into her time after time. She could do nothing as her face slapped against the wall and the pain across her shoulders stabbed her into submission.

When it was over, Jack grabbed at her hair and pulled her face towards his ugly glare.

"Remember if you say a word of this to your mother, I will kill you. And then your sister will be next" he threatened. "Got it? Now clean yourself up and get to bed, you whore."

He left her crumpled on the urine-soaked floor. Blood and semen seeped from her, carrying with it the shame of what had just happened. Sarah sobbed as she grieved the loss of her childhood and realised the awful future which now lay ahead for her at the mercy of her mother's monster of a husband.

CHAPTER NINE

The house was eerily quiet.

Liz was sat cross legged on the lounge floor working through yet another box. She was struggling to shake off the new dream from last night. The violence scared her. It was so vivid. She could smell the fear of that poor girl. It was so vivid she felt she could reach out and touch the girl. To comfort her, like she couldn't comfort her own daughter. She hadn't mentioned it to Giles this morning. In time she would but for now she tried to push it to the recesses of her mind and concentrate on the task in hand.

Pulling herself back to reality she turned to the new box. This one contained photo albums from their wedding and pictures of the children when they were small. Liz was a fan of old-fashioned photos. She disliked the modern way of downloading photos, which Giles and her children loved to do. It was so easy now to take numerous shots of every event whereas when the children were young Liz loved the excitement of the reveal. That moment when you picked up your packet of photos and found half of them were useless with heads and feet cut off. But in amongst the disasters could be a gem; a family memory to be treasured.

With her nostalgic head on, she took a sip of tea and opened up the first album on the top of the removal box. Her heart contracted as she looked at pictures of Rebecca taken soon after she was born. Her little crumpled face, with eyes scrunched up, tugged at Liz's soul. Rebecca was nestled in Liz's arms with a delighted Giles leaning in. His smile reached from ear to ear. The first trip home in the car, when Liz was so precious about her bundle of joy that Giles wasn't allowed over 30 mph. First bath, first visit with the grandparents. All those special first moments. This album covered Becky's first year of life.

A tear made its way slowly down Liz's cheek as she relived those wonderful memories.

Rebecca was a perfect baby, sleeping through the night within three months of birth. She was always happy and smiled at everyone. When Joanne came along, Rebecca was four years old and just starting nursery school. Every day she came home with another picture of her "bubba sis" as she like to call her. Harry was born two years later and Liz's family was complete. All three children loved each other deeply and were a great team. Their house was full of love and laughter.

Ok it wasn't all rosy, thought Liz, as she wiped away her tears. There were the usual family arguments. But these were just family squabbles and nothing too serious. Liz had gone back to work when Harry started primary school and a great network of family and friends had supported childcare after school and during the holidays.

Those who observed the Stamford family life might say that it was perfect. Both parents had great jobs. Money was never a worry and Giles and Liz loved the nicer things in life. Holidays abroad, the best school for the kids and financial security for their future retirement. The three Stamford children were bright and accomplished at whatever they put their hand to. They were beautiful children with an inner light of kindness that shone out of their faces.

But perfect lives don't always last.

Last year their world crashed down around them with Rebecca's death. The subsequent court case added to the emotional damage. This last year had been one which all the family were struggling to recover from.

Liz shut the last album and squeezed it into the sideboard. That was enough reminiscing for one day, she thought. As she packed away the albums she wished it was as easy to put the pain of loss behind you.

Mentally pulling herself together she decided it was time to grab some lunch. Giles was in Manchester today visiting some clients and his team in the business centre. He wouldn't be back until late tonight. Joanne and Harry were in school. From their enthusiasm over the last week, it sounded like they had made a great choice of school. Both of them had settled in well and were already sharing stories of new friends. Today was the first day that Liz had been completely alone in the house.

Giles had spent a number of days working from home over the last week, easing them both into the new environment. Liz secretly believed that Giles had rearranged his diary after she had told him about the dream. He did like to fuss over her and his attention probably wasn't needed. She felt a deep sense of contentment in their new home and even though she had been scared that night she didn't feel uncomfortable being alone in the house. Even the unusual dreams hadn't unsettled her. The house appeared to wrap its arms around her making her feel safe and secure for the first time in a year.

Liz grabbed a bag of salad leaves from the fridge as she contemplated what to have to eat. A plump avocado and balsamic vinegar made the salad leaves into a much more interesting option. Once she had knocked the salad together she pulled a chair up to the kitchen table to eat. Her favourite magazine was her lunchtime companion as she flicked through the pages. Liz had an eye on various household designs. Her mind was planning out the improvements she wanted to make to her new home. She had a good creative eye which could see the synergies between different styles to compliment a room. Giles gave her free rein to any design decisions as he had confidence in her ability which seemed to come so naturally to her.

As Liz ate her mind wandered whilst flicking through her magazine. She kept getting the feeling that she had seen something out of the corner of her eye but as she turned her head there was nothing there. She could swear she saw movement next to the Aga but it must be her imagination as when she turned her head there was nothing there.

As she stared into space the atmosphere in the kitchen seemed to change. All of a sudden a wave of sadness seemed to fill the room. The feeling hit Liz hard in her chest, making her heave with a dry sob. She gasped as she manically searched the room to try and work out the source of such an emotional feeling.

There was nothing there.

With the same urgency that the feeling of sadness had hit Liz, it departed. The atmosphere returned to normal.

At that moment Liz smelt a strong waft of flowers. A deep scent of nectar surrounded her. Strangely there were no flowers in the room and there definitely hadn't been a scent before the atmosphere had altered.

Very strange.

Despite the changing atmosphere Liz didn't feel scared or threatened by what she had felt. She instinctively knew that something sad had happened in the house before and for some reason she was being trusted with that emotion. Whatever this was had no intention for harm. It felt like some form of communication rather than trying to instil fear in Liz.

It's no good she thought to herself, she needed to understand more about the house and its history. Perhaps she would be able to trace the girl from her dream and explore her past and the circumstances which made her so sad. In her mind Liz was sure the girl was a memory from the past and not some imaginary presence of Rebecca. Giles had his doubts. He seemed to think this was her mind playing tricks with her grief. She didn't want to challenge Giles. If that's what he wanted to believe then she would just let things lie for now. Liz was ever the peace maker in their relationship and perhaps one of her biggest weaknesses was the fear of rocking the boat too much.

As she thought about the house and its mysterious past, Liz remembered that her mother was coming to stay next week. Jill Wynn had spent many years tracing her family history back to the 18th century. She was fascinated by the stories of her family's past and would be the perfect advocate to support Liz with her investigations. Liz nodded to herself as she thought how exciting it would be to trace the inhabitants of this house. Spending some quality time with her mother working on this together would do her the power of good. It had been such a hard time for her mother too. Sometimes it was easy to forget that Rebecca's death had wide reaching consequences, touching not only her family, but also her grandmother and her numerous friends.

CHAPTER TEN

The sun was blazing down as Liz slipped on her sandals and locked the front door.

She had decided to take a stroll into the village to pick up some milk. Other than meeting Joyce and Malcolm, they had not had a chance to socialise yet. They remained the newbies in the village and whilst a few villagers had waved as they passed the house, Liz hadn't really got to know anyone else yet. A trip to the shops would serve as a good opportunity to show her face and maybe engineer an introduction.

Liz was not the most confident at making new friends. That was Giles's forte. Once she had established a relationship, she was the best a friend could ask for. It was opening the door and starting the conversation which she had never been great at. When the kids were little it was always easy to mingle with fellow parents and she had remained close to a number of her antenatal classmates. Work was another natural place to develop friendships. Moving to the countryside removed all those traditional avenues of introduction from Liz and she would definitely have to take herself out of comfort zone to build her place in village society.

As she strolled down the hill towards the village, Liz was once again struck by how quiet it was. Bird song filled the air and a gentle hum of a distant tractor was the only sound of activity. There was an absence of any movement as the village slept in the summer heat. Liz decided to stop off at the Norman church and take the chance to explore its interior. It was a surprise to see the door to the porch unlocked; something which couldn't happen in London. Liz pulled up the ancient handle and pushed the huge wooden door inwards. Cool air hit her as she made her way into the small transept.

The church was simple in design with stone walls and floor dotted with plaques to those who had gone before. The sanctuary held the altar which was covered with a beautiful altar cloth of deep yellow flowers. The pulpit was constructed with dark wood panels and stood majestically gazing over the congregation. Wooden pews stretched out down the aisle and embroidered kneelers were neatly placed at intervals. These kneelers had been completed with love by the congregation over the years and added to the community feel of the church.

Liz took a seat on one of the pews and genuflected. She closed her eyes and offered her prayers in silent contemplation. The peace of the church surroundings embraced her. Liz had strong Christian beliefs but these had been tested over the last year. She had struggled with understanding why a loving God could take someone so young and innocent whilst those with evil in their hearts were not punished. In the peace of the church her mind questioned the fairness of her family's pain. The struggle played across her face as she frowned.

She was so deep in thought that she didn't hear the door open and the quiet movement of another visitor to the building. Slowly she raised her head from prayer and made eye contact with the new arrival.

"Hello there, I'm sorry if I disturbed you." The dog collar betrayed the newcomer's occupation. "Christine Abbott, vicar of the benefice. Pleased to meet you."

"Oh hello there, Christine. So lovely to meet you at last. Liz Stamford. We have just moved into Crown House. I was escaping the heat and enjoying the coolness of your beautiful church." Liz was conscious that she was rambling nervously so paused to collect her thoughts.

"I had heard that we had some new villagers and was looking forward to meeting you. I'm sorry I haven't popped in to introduce myself yet but it's been a manic week. So, welcome to St Andrews and hopefully we may see you and the family here at some point," Christine continued. "May I?"

Christine squeezed into the pew to sit alongside Liz as the two ladies spent some time getting to know each other. Liz instantly felt comfortable in Christine's company. She was easy to talk to and they were soon sharing family information. Christine and her husband, John, lived in the vicarage set back behind the churchyard. They didn't have children. Christine valued her role as the mother of her congregation. Perhaps this was some form of recompense for her inability to have her own child. You could see how well she was suited to that role as her demeanour was open and supportive and she genuinely seemed interested in people. There was nothing forced in her manner and it was easy to see how her parishioners could open up to her to share their emotional struggles.

"When I first came in, Liz, you looked troubled as if you were tackling a big issue. Anything I can help with?" asked Christine once their initial conversation had come to a natural end.

"I don't know whether you can help," replied Liz. The conflict of emotions played across her face. "I have tried to understand why bad things happen. Why God lets good people suffer. To be honest, I am struggling with my beliefs at the moment and whilst I felt peace here in the church, that's not always the case. I've just been so angry at times over the last year."

"That's understandable, Liz. If something bad has happened its natural for us to have doubts. God tests us at times and it's hard to accept why we are given such difficult challenges. But any burden we are given can be eased by sharing and letting others help us to cope and find a way through the darkness." As she spoke Christine took her hand and squeezed it gently. It felt the most natural thing to do despite the two women only having just met.

Liz felt a connection with Christine and at once knew she could share her dark story.

"My daughter was raped and murdered last year." Liz spoke those dreadful words which all too often she struggled to say out loud. Such a short sentence seemed too trivial to explain the depth of pain caused. The words hung in the air like a thunder cloud.

"Oh my poor love. You have been given a huge burden to shoulder. Did you want to talk about it?" Christine coaxed her to continue.

Christine felt that she was about to be trusted with feelings which hadn't been shared fully before. She recognised that she needed to draw on all her training to support her new parishioner through the telling of her daughter's story. She watched as Liz seemed to pull herself into a ball, drawing her arms across her chest and rocking forwards gently as she contemplated how to explain what had happened.

Liz took a deep breath and blew out through her mouth with a sigh. She felt ready to open up to this stranger. Over the last year, friends had tried to get her to talk and heal through sharing her feelings but she had shut herself down from their support. She just hadn't felt ready to accept any comfort. If she accepted comfort perhaps the pain would start to go away. Liz didn't want the pain to go away as then it would mean that she was getting over her loss. For some reason she figured that Christine wasn't motivated by a deep-seated need to comfort her or make her feel better. She was just prepared to listen.

"Rebecca was 20 and at university in Winchester. She was a beautiful girl and my best friend. We did everything together and I missed her so much when she went to university. She was doing so well and had everything in front of her. She was doing politics and history and was determined she would work in the government in the future. She was so driven and determined that one day she could have been Prime Minister. I have no doubt she would have made her dreams come true." Liz paused as a tear made tracks down her cheek.

Christine remained silent. Experience had shown her that letting an individual talk without interruption was the best way to support especially when dealing with raw grief. She held Liz's hand and gently rubbed her thumb across her palm in a soothing motion.

"It was Easter when it happened. Rebecca was home for a few weeks. She had gone up to Covent Garden to meet up with some friends from university and they ended up staying later than she expected. She had planned to get a tube back home but because it was so late she didn't fancy mixing with the drunks on the Central line. So she got a black cab."

"He took my baby and killed her."

Liz started to sob. Huge gulping sobs as she said those words. Tears dripped down her cheeks and her shoulders drooped as she allowed the grief to come to the fore. Retelling the story was painful and it was as if the events of that dreadful night came crashing down around her again.

Christine sat quietly holding her hand and waited. Platitudes were not required. Just silence and a recognition that she was there to support this grieving mother.

"He raped her. I can't get that image from my head. He must have hurt her so much. She must have been so frightened. Then he took her beautiful head and smashed it on the ground. Her last moments must have been so dreadful. Did she know she was going to die? Did she know that she had died? Was there a moment between living and dying?" Liz was crying softly as she spoke.

"Was she calling out for her mum? It torments me so much. I just can't get the thought out of my head. The pain of thinking about her last moments eats away at me. People talk about closure and moving on but I feel possessed by those last moments. It haunts me."

Christine put her arm across the trembling shoulders and allowed Liz to collapse into her. She rubbed her hand in gentle circles in an attempt to show her support. As she carried on with the rhythmical movement she tried to imagine what this family had gone through. She tried to put herself in their shoes and imagine the strength required to come out the other side of such a dreadful event. She was conscious of the huge responsibility she had been given to listen and try to give this mother some form of comfort.

Liz continued. "When they caught him, the police said he was responsible for over 20 rapes of young girls. But he killed my girl. Why? Why didn't they get him before he killed? I had to sit there in that court and see his evil face. He just looked at me and sneered. He didn't show any remorse for what he had done. He just stared at me. I wanted to grab his face and slam it against the wall. Smash his brains out like he did my beautiful baby."

"He got a life sentence."

After a dramatic pause, Liz continued "And so did I."

Silence filled the church as both women contemplated her words and the dreadful story behind them.

"I wanted to die when we lost Rebecca. I remember sitting there with the sleeping tablets the doctor gave me. It would have been so easy to take them and let the pain go. But I couldn't. I'm a mother and I have two other beautiful children. I couldn't leave them behind. So he has given me a life sentence too. I have to live with what he did every bloody day of my life."

Liz looked deeply into Christine's eyes as she continued her recollections of that awful time.

"We moved up here to try and heal as a family. My husband doesn't know how to deal with his pain. He throws himself into work and tries his hardest to look after me. He sees me as the fragile one but I'm not. I am so strong because I chose life rather than taking the easy way out." Liz didn't regret the decision she had made that fateful night when she stepped away from the precipice. Her family had needed her.

"Giles is struggling and doesn't know it. My daughter, Jo, is slowly learning how to live without her big sister but she still gets terrible nightmares and there is a little bit of her that's just not there anymore. And Harry is just Harry. It's hard to know how he is coping. He just doesn't talk about it. He has refused to from day one and I can't keep trying to force him if that's his way of dealing with it."

"That man will not win. I will keep going and my family will recover. This is a fresh start for us and I owe it to Rebecca to live and keep her in our hearts".

Liz drew herself back up to sit alone and took Christine's hand. She smiled through the tears as she finished. "I haven't spoken to anyone in such detail before. Thank you Christine for listening to me. I think that has helped me to say things that have been rushing around my head every day and just haven't come out before."

"Bless you dear girl. You are so brave. I am sure your Rebecca is looking down on you now and is full of pride for her mother. You have shouldered an immense burden which many people would collapse under." Christine smiled at Liz. "From what I can see you have the strength and power of a lioness. Your courage is outstanding. The lynch pin of the family who will do whatever it costs to protect her family from hurt. Even if that cost is to herself."

Christine continued, seeing an opportunity to help. "You say you haven't spoken to anyone before about how you are feeling. I think by opening up today you are making a huge step in the right direction. You are shouldering responsibility for the whole family along with your overwhelming grief."

Christine paused giving Liz time to think about the big step she had made. "You do need to share that burden and I am honoured that you have chosen me to help. Perhaps because we haven't met each other before, I am the right person. Someone who didn't know and love your Rebecca. Someone you can open up to without them being personally affected. Does that make sense?" asked Christine.

Liz stared into the distance absorbing what the vicar had said and began to feel a new kind of peace enter her. "I think you may have hit on something, Christine. I haven't wanted to dump how I am feeling on Giles as it's his loss too and I sort of feel like I shouldn't be grabbing all the attention." A sense of realisation hit her. "I do feel I am letting my family down as I just don't know how to support Jo and Harry. I can't cope with my own pain. I have been a coward in avoiding talking with them in case I feel worse. I'm frightened that if I start the conversation I could set back their healing process in a feeble attempt to do the right thing."

"Have you thought about grief counselling?" asked Christine. "It can work and it may help you to ease the pain. Grief never leaves you but little by little you can learn to live with it. The church has given me the opportunity to work with those who have suffered loss and I would be happy to work with you," offered Christine. "In time your husband and children may also be ready to speak to someone outside the family unit who can help them to accept the pain and find a way through the hurt. I also have a dear friend Malcolm Peterson who is a professional counsellor. I'm sure he could also help in time."

Liz recalled the name of her new neighbour. Perhaps he could be someone to help. She had warmed to his character when they met. He was like a gentle giant with a warm calming personality. Perhaps the fresh start in the countryside was also the chance for her to face the demons and try to find a way to live again. She already felt at ease with Christine and realised she was an excellent listener. Her role instilled confidence and trust. If she was going to start the healing process then Christine could be a good guide through the challenges ahead.

"I think I would like to try that Christine. I appreciate the offer and if you are sure it won't be too much trouble, then I would like to try." Liz smiled as she took those first steps.

"Why don't we pop back to the vicarage for a cup of tea and we can work through some dates to sit down a bit more formally" said Christine.

She could see the start of a new friendship with Liz. Both women felt at ease in each other's company. Christine didn't make friends easily as all too often people were put off by the dog collar. Other women seemed to think she would bombard them with her religious views. But in reality her approach to her ministry was all about friendship and kindness. Liz needed kindness in her life after the trauma she had suffered and Christine felt a need to support and protect her from those evil memories.

CHAPTER ELEVEN – SUMMER 1860

Sarah was on her hands and knees scrubbing the bar floor.

It was the task she hated most each week. Sticky alcohol residue combined with dirt from boots covered the flagstones. A wire brush was the only thing which would shift the stains. The effort required took all Sarah's strength and patience. As she scrubbed, the sweat formed under her armpits and dribbled down the back of her dress. Her long dark hair was tied back in a scarf but tendrils were escaping and sticking to her wet face. She hitched her skirt up at the front to add some padding for her knees. Her bones screamed with discomfort as she knelt on the stone floor.

She sat back on her heels as she assessed how much more work was needed. She had barely started but already felt weary. Sunday was normally her day of rest. Usually this job would be saved for the start of the week. Sarah had decided this was the right penance for her sins and a better use to her faith than attending church with the family.

Since her stepfather had attacked her, she could not face the thought of church. How could she stand in God's presence when she was a soiled sinner? She could not bear the thought of the priest seeing into her soul and judging her.

Her mother had questioned her when she tried to make her excuses. The family always attended the local church together. Sarah had blamed her absence on a headache which she could not shift. She had feigned nausea alongside an inability to raise her pounding head from the bed. She hated lying to her mother. Unfortunately it was the only way to avoid the humiliation of walking into the local church with all her neighbours seeing the shame which must be visible on her face.

The fact that her mother had not noticed the difference in her daughter over recent days, said more about the strain Mary was under rather than a lack of care for Sarah. Mary was not a cruel woman and she loved her daughters deeply. She had been ground down over the last few years and just didn't have the energy to seek out issues. Best to ignore what was troubling her daughter rather than ask questions she wouldn't want answered.

After church Mary and her two elder daughters would prepare the luncheon which normally included a freshly slaughtered sheep. The mutton would be tough but would provide the family with the most nutritious meal of the week and would provide the basis for many other meals throughout the upcoming days. Sarah had planned to start on the potatoes once she had finished the floor. She had not accounted for the amount of effort it was taking to make any headway.

Slowly Sarah struggled up to a standing position, holding onto a barstool. Picking up the bucket from the floor she swilled the dirty water into the sink behind the bar. Hot water was boiling on the kitchen stove so she would replace it and get back to work. She really wanted this finished before the children came back and rampaged through the house. As she turned she noticed the door to the bar opening.

Jack Whiting strolled into the bar in his Sunday best suit. Sarah was immediately nervous as the service had only just started so why had he returned so soon? Jack came over to stand in front of her gazing deeply into her eyes.

"I thought I best come home and check on my favourite step-daughter," he smiled at her.

The smile gave her the creeps. Why was he suddenly being kind to her? What was his true motive? It certainly wasn't out of any care for her.

"I guessed you made your excuses so that we could be alone together again," he sneered. "You only had to tip me the wink and I would have stayed behind with you."

As he spoke, Jack's fingers worked the scarf from her hair. Gently he wound a tendril of her hair around his fingers and lifted it to his nose; smelling her scent. Sarah froze. His fingers stroked the outline of her face; wound her hair behind her ears whilst touching her lobes with affection.

"God you look beautiful," he groaned.

Sarah could see his excitement rising.

Gradually his fingers started to move down her neck, shoulders and cupped her breast. Sarah recoiled. Without a care for her safety she slapped his hand away.

"Don't touch me," she winced as he grabbed hold of her breast.

Her reaction immediately led to that hint of kindness vanishing.

Animal rawness took over as he pawed at her bodice. She struggled to push him away. Without thinking of the consequences of her actions, she jerked her kneecap upwards connecting with his manhood. Jack gasped as the pain sliced through his groin, letting go of his victim.

Sarah turned and ran from the bar heading towards the kitchen. She was desperate to get away from him before he could recover. She knew the pain she had inflicted would make him more dangerous. Sensing him behind her before her eyes saw him. His face was red with anger, sweat breaking out across his brows.

"You stupid bitch," he snarled in her face as he grabbed hold of her head in a vice like grip. His hands were huge, making it impossible for her to turn her face away from the spittle which was splattering into her cheeks. "I try and be nice to you and look what I get in return. So you like it rough do you?" He grinned at her, licking his fat lips. His foul breath making her stomach churn.

He threw her face down on the kitchen table, pinning her face flat to the wood. With the other hand he pulled at her skirts hitching then up her legs. Sarah tried to cry out. All she could do was make a gurgling noise. She was struggling for breath as his hand flattened her nose against the table. Sharp splinters scraped at her cheeks.

He thrust into her.

He ripped at her flesh with his hand, driving her legs apart. Her body screamed out with pain as he thrust into her again. Her private parts were on fire as he violently pushed his member further into her. His fingers dug into her buttocks as he spent his juices.

Sarah lay prostrate as he wiped himself on her skirt and buttoned up his breeches. Without a word he pulled down her dress and left the room.

It was over.

It had all happened so very quickly.

Deep in shock, Sarah eased herself onto a chair. Her body screamed out in pain. She throbbed as she tried to find a comfortable position to perch in.

Sarah allowed the tears to flow. Her heart was breaking. Why was he doing this to her? What had she done to deserve it?

One minute he was trying to seduce her with kindness and then he snapped. The anger within him wanted to punish and hurt her. Was this how life was going to be from now on?

She felt so alone.

Sarah knew she could not tell her mother. If she did then Hannah would be next. She would not risk her stepfather turning his wrath on her baby sister.

As she wept, she felt a warming presence enfold her. A feeling of love and empathy which surrounded her. She could swear that she felt a cool breath on her cheeks. Raising her head, she expected to see her mother standing there.

The kitchen was empty.

She was alone.

CHAPTER TWELVE

Liz pulled open the Aga door, bending down as she positioned the casserole pot into the oven. The heat steamed into her face as she rushed to close the door. She had made a family favourite of beef and mushroom stew. The kids loved it and it was a good way of getting more vegetables into their diet.

As she stared at the hot oven Liz could not shake the feeling of distress which had suddenly hit her. A wave of fear had swirled around the room. Her hands felt clammy as she rubbed them on her apron. The atmosphere within the kitchen had gone from warm and cosy to fearful and cold. She could not put her finger on the feeling but she just felt that something horrible had happened. All of a sudden it dissipated as though it had never happened.

She shook her head, clearing her thoughts. In her gut she knew it wasn't one of her family causing that fearful vibe. The children were upstairs and she had only just spoken to Giles so she knew he was safe. Instinctively she knew this was a memory from the previous occupants of the house. It was some form of message. But how to decipher it? She really didn't understand what was happening but despite its strangeness, she still felt a great deal of comfort in the house. How weird was that?

Putting those thoughts to one side, Liz smiled to herself as she thought about Giles's phone call to say he was an hour away from home. He had made it away from the office in Manchester earlier than expected and the traffic all seemed to be working in his favour. With luck the family would be able to sit down for dinner together. Liz had always championed the benefits of a family dinner where the children could learn the behaviours which would stand them in good stead for the future. The ability to converse with others was a dying skill for many younger people as the attraction of the mobile phone interfered with their minds.

Liz was excited and nervous to tell Giles about her meeting with Christine and hoped that he would be supportive. She decided to wait until they were alone later to talk it through as she didn't want to open the discussion with the kids yet until she felt more confident in her own feelings.

Thinking of her children, she decided to seek them out and find out how their day at school had been. She was really impressed at how quickly they had adapted to a new environment. They put her to shame with their positive outlook on change and their ability to make friends so soon after joining the new school. They were both the sort of young people that others warmed too but it did take personal resilience to join into existing friendship groups.

Jo was bent over her desk with a pencil clamped between her lips. The intense look on her face was evidence of her concentration. She was deep in thought as she translated the set piece of poetry for her Latin homework.

Liz spent a few quiet moments just observing her daughter and smiling to herself. Liz had such a deep admiration for Joanne. She was developing into a special young lady. Their relationship had changed and matured since they had lost Rebecca. The two women had become so much closer and often they didn't need words to communicate what they were thinking. A sigh; a smile; a groan; all could signify their feelings without the spoken word. Joanne was more protective of her Mum since their loss and sometimes treated Liz with kid gloves, in a reversal of roles.

That was another area which Liz felt guilty about and with her new determination, after speaking to her new friend the vicar, she knew that it was time for her to step back into the mother role. Being a mum was a life full of personal guilt, she thought. Joanne was developing into a woman at a fast pace and would need her support and guidance especially when boys came on the scene.

"Hi, munchkin. How's the homework going?" Liz interrupted Jo's concentration.

"Oh not too bad, Mum. I think I have broken the back of this piece. The poems of Catullus should really be classed as soft porn" Jo giggled. "I do worry about what red flags are being raised on my internet surfing profile when I'm looking for translation support. Don't tell Dad though as he would have a hairy faced fit if he knew what I was reading. He still thinks I don't know what sex is. Bless him."

Jo had a couple of admirers in the past but none of them had managed to obtain the status of boyfriend. She had high expectations for a future partner and so far a boy who could achieve all those qualities was not on the horizon. Rebecca had a relationship with a guy from university for the last year of her life and it was blossoming into something special. Jo had loved to talk to her big sister about Josh. It had opened up a world of expectation especially about sex.

Not having her big sister to share her secrets with had left a big hole in Jo's life. She wished she could talk to her sister about the attention she was getting from a number of the upper sixth boys and how to handle it. She was trying so hard to remain cool and collected and not behave like an inexperienced teenager. The guys at school had this perception of Jo as a London cool chick which she was trying so hard to perpetuate.

"Sorry I can't help you out darling. I don't know a word of Latin and well soft porn has passed me by. I'm an old girl! I can't speak for your Dad though," she grinned noticing Jo discomfort at the thought of her parents in the act. "Anyway, tell me how school is going. Are you enjoying it?"

Jo wanted to be as honest as she could with her mum. At the same time she didn't want her parents to worry about how she was settling in. They had enough on their plate. "Mum, I'm not going to lie to you. I was a bit concerned when I started last week as everyone seemed a bit posh and stuck up. But first impressions aren't always the right ones."

"I know what you mean. It's a posh school judging by the cars I see in the drop off zone," laughed Liz.

"The thing is that most of the kids just seem really normal more than some of the weirdos in London. But on the subject of weirdos, I have started hanging around with a girl Hannah who is in my History set. She's well wacky and so confident in her style. She just cracks me up at times. So hard to keep a straight face when she mimics Mr Head, our History master. He is a strange one and doesn't seem to realise he is the butt of so many jokes." Jo paused for breath.

"I'm sure he does know," replied Liz. "I remember when I was your age and we were convinced that we were always one step ahead of the teachers. I think they let you think that so you get cocky and they catch you out. I guess it's all part of the job description." Liz was delighted to find out that Jo had made a friend already. Hannah sounded an interesting character. "Why don't you invite your new friend over at the weekend? I promise me and Dad won't embarrass you; although I can't voucher for Harry," laughed Liz.

"Ok Mum. I may well do that if she is up for it? Can she stay for dinner if she can make it?" asked Jo.

"Of course, my love. Just let me know details when you have arranged it and just check she doesn't have any wacky food habits to match her style. Anyway, let me leave you to finish off your homework." Liz started to back out of the room. "By the way Dad is on his way back from Manchester so dinner will be in about an hour if that works for you."

"Perfect Mumma Bear" smiled Jo, using the endearment for her mother which had been invented by Rebecca and adopted by the rest of the family.

Liz left Jo in peace and sneaked along the corridor to see if she could catch Harry out. Harry had a terrible habit of confusing homework with playing on his Xbox. As she got nearer to his room she heard the sound of gunfire and raised her eyebrows as she realised Call of Duty was winning over his maths homework.

"Hey trouble, how's your homework going?" asked Liz as she snuck her head around the door. The crash of the game controller onto the desk confirmed Harry's misdemeanours.

"Sorry Mum banged to rights!" Harry laughed. "I got side-tracked. I have pretty much finished my homework, honest. Just got a couple of chapters to read for English. Promise I will finish it before dinner." Harry gave his mum that big beaming smile which nine times out of ten got him out of trouble.

He is going to break some hearts when he grows up, thought Liz. He could charm the birds down from the trees with his cheeky smile. Liz could never feel angry with him for very long.

"Okay sport. Just make sure you finish off within the next hour. Dad should be home in time for dinner so it will be good to catch up properly then. I'll leave you to it" Liz winked at her boy as she retreated from the room.

Leaving the children to work, Liz decided to finish off a couple more removal boxes while the dinner cooked. The dining room had a huge wooden bookcase built along one wall and she hadn't got round to deciding which books would take front and centre and which would be consigned to Giles's office. Liz spent a useful half hour lovingly unwrapping her favourite writers and deciding the best location for each. She grimaced as she realised that Giles would probably rearrange them once he got the chance. Liz was laid back about the order of their special things whereas Giles liked to have a logical reasoning behind how he set things out. Whether it would be in terms of size and shape or genre, Liz accepted that some form of rearrangement would take place once her husband got round to noticing.

"You finished already darling," Liz asked Jo without turning round. Her comments were met with silence so she swung round on her heels only to find no-one there. "Well that's weird," sighed Liz." I could have sworn there was someone behind me." She had felt the movement of the air behind her and a distinct scent of another person.

As she stared into the space around her, Liz could smell a strong odour of flowers although there was nothing in the room which could be giving off that aroma. It was all very puzzling.

Liz was confused that she had felt a presence when there clearly wasn't anyone else in the room. It wasn't the first time today she had felt a presence in the house and with her recent dream it was all adding up to something unusual. She hadn't elaborated on the mysterious happenings with the rest of the family as she didn't want to unsettle the children. Giles was likely to be sceptical so it was best to keep things to herself for now until she understood better what was occurring.

The distant sound of tyres pulling into the drive brought Liz back to reality. She heard Giles open the electronic doors to the garage and reverse his car into place. Moments later Giles found her and pulled Liz into a bear hug.

"Hello there my darling. God I missed you today," sighed Giles as he nuzzled into her neck. "Did you have a good day on your own?"

Liz loved the feel of her husband as he enveloped her in his strong powerful arms. He looked amazing in his Paul Smith slate blue wool suit. The cut flattered his trim figure and it set off his backside which Liz felt was one of his finest assets. She squeezed his buttocks as she enjoyed the cuddle.

"Hi darling. You made it home in good time. Just in time for dinner. I had a really good day. Very productive. Let me tell you about it over dinner. Why don't you go and slip into something more comfortable and let the kids know while I serve up" smiled Liz gently slapping his bottom.

Liz made herself busy laying cutlery out on the dining room table and putting the vegetables on to boil. She could hear the noise of her family upstairs and smiled to herself as she listened to the enthusiastic cries of delight to see their Dad.

Soon the family were sat together enjoying food and sharing news of the day. Jo and Harry were chatting about their lessons with Giles, while Liz listened in, half cocked, having heard most of this in the car earlier. Liz and Giles had always tried to balance work life and home life. They had both held down responsible jobs throughout their children's school life and, unless they were away with business, then the chance to sit down as a family and share food was a vital part of keeping that balance in check. They felt that supper was an important family time. Everyone agreed that phones were banned from the table to allow conversation to flow.

Finally the school conversation came to a natural end. Jo updated her parents that she had invited her new friend Hannah round on Saturday. Hannah had agreed to stay for supper if that was ok with Jo's parents. Liz was delighted that the invitation had been accepted and was already planning in her head a menu to both impress and delight.

As they were on the subject of entertaining, Giles felt prompted to discuss the thoughts he had been having on his trip back that day. He was keen to get to know their neighbours Malcolm and Joyce. He had warmed to both of them on the initial meeting and felt that widening their circle of acquaintances would help the family settle in quicker.

"On that note, Liz, I was thinking it would be nice to invite Malcolm and Joyce over Friday night for supper. I'm working from home Friday so I can help out if that works for you?" Giles waited expectantly for his wife's views. Giles knew that his offer of help was superficial. Liz loved to entertain and would not want her husband butting in on arrangements.

"That would be nice. I'll give them a call tomorrow." Liz agreed that developing their social life in Little Yaxley was a great idea. They had a wide circle of friends in London and both adults had enjoyed regular dinner parties sharing gossip and news.

With the weekend plans agreed, Liz went on to ask Giles about his trip to Manchester. It was a long way to go in a day so she was keen to understand how their house move might impact on Giles's offsite visits.

"It was a useful trip, to be fair" started Giles. "It was good to catch up with John and his team. I got there in time for the morning huddle so I could get up to speed with the latest deals underway and get some feedback from the team about what we can do in Head Office to support their sales drive. On top of that John is working on one of the biggest deals this year with a large manufacturing company. We took their Executives out for lunch to talk through the key elements of the deal. Sometimes it just helps to push things over the line when they see the big boss getting involved. Not saying that John hasn't got the best relationship with them. It's just politics, I guess."

Giles was seriously underestimating his influence. He was a modest man in a business which was full of people willing to blow their own trumpet. This particular manufacturing company were extremely excited to meet the Head of Corporate Banking and his involvement would ensure the bank got this business completed with an extremely large fee package in place.

"So Liz, tell us about your day. We've all been waffling on for ages and we haven't heard what you got up to," asked Giles. He reached across the table to squeeze her hand.

"I'm really excited but I think I have made a new friend," Liz told them about meeting up with Christine. She kept the discussion light as she talked about the visit to the church and how she had warmed to their local vicar. "I think I will pop to communion on Sunday if anyone else fancies it?" Liz knew that Jo and Harry wouldn't be keen but Giles had often joined her at church in their London parish.

"Sorry love, but I really fancy a round of golf at the weekend. The weather looks promising so would you mind?" Giles was a keen golfer and tried to get a round in every couple of weeks. He had wanted to try out a few local courses before he made a decision about which one he would join.

"I certainly wouldn't want to get in the way of golf," Liz groaned. "Don't worry I'm more confident going for the first service on my own now that I have met Christine. They only have a service at our church every month as Christine covers about four churches so you have got the option of visiting other local parish churches over time."

Harry interrupted the conversation. He was literally squirming in his seat, an obvious sign that Harry was keen to leave. "Mum, is it ok if we get down from the table now?" asked Harry. "I really wanted to catch a programme shortly if that's ok."

"Sure thing, off you both go. Don't worry about clearing up. Most of this can go in the dishwasher." Liz could see Harry already sneaking towards the door to avoid the washing up. She knew she should probably insist that Jo and Harry help more around the house but while she was not working full time Liz tended to spoil the children. She was a soft touch.

Later that night Liz snuggled into Giles's back as they lay in bed. He had the kind of back that demanded attention. Liz was more than happy to oblige. Most nights they would fall asleep with Liz wrapped around his torso, snuggling her nose between his broad shoulder blades. As she stroked his shoulders she could feel the tension slipping away. Giles's job could be extremely stressful and she was reluctant to add to that pressure. Mentally Liz was weighing up the pros and cons of sharing the extent of her conversation with Christine. She hadn't wanted to speak of it in front of the children and after dinner the moment had passed as Giles sneaked off to watch TV with the kids.

"Darling, are you asleep yet?" she quietly whispered in her husband's ear.

"Not yet. You can carry on with that massage if you want as it's certainly doing it for me." Giles wriggled to ensure she had maximum access to his broad back.

As she continued to lay her hands on him, Liz slowly shared the thrust of the conversation she had had with Christine. She opened up on how she had spoken to the compassionate vicar about her intense feelings of anger and loss.

Giles allowed Liz to talk.

He sensed her cathartic release. His silence was intentional to support the process and provided Liz with the platform to release her pent-up emotions. Giles was staggered to hear the level of emotions Liz had shared with Christine.

The depth of feelings she had obviously not been able to talk to him about surprised Giles. She hadn't shared those emotions in the last year with anyone. He was not offended by her actions as he seriously could not imagine having this conversation any earlier. Giles really wasn't sure he could have handled it.

Despite their strong relationship, the only way they had managed to struggle through the last year had been to avoid talking their feelings. Giles had not encouraged Liz to share how she was feeling as he could not cope with the thought of opening that Pandora's Box.

Giles could feel tears rolling down his back as Liz came to a conclusion. Words were not required but actions were.

Giles rolled over and pulled Liz into his arms.

Gently he stroked her hair as she nuzzled into his chest. Placing his fingers under her chin he raised her lips to his and drank in her scent. His arms wrapped her in a strong embrace and he could feel his body respond to her nakedness.

Liz moved in his arms welcoming his desire as the couple made love.

As they drifted off to sleep, Liz saw the girl again through the mist of her mind.

CHAPTER THIRTEEN – AUTUMN 1860

Sarah was dreaming of that lady again.

She seemed familiar but her clothing was strange in design, nothing like Sarah had seen before. The image was so vivid that Sarah could smell her scent which was heady with a perfume she couldn't recognise. The woman hung about in the periphery of her eye line as Sarah desperately tried to bring her shape into focus. As she concentrated hard to see through the gloom, the lady seemed to fade into the distance. Sarah struggled back to consciousness.

Sarah had fallen asleep at the kitchen table with her head resting on her arms. She was exhausted and was struggling to bring herself back to the moment. How she could drift off during the day with all the activity going on around the pub and farm. There must be something wrong, she thought.

With a loud bang the kitchen door flew open and her mother strode into the room balancing a large wicker basket on her ample hip. The basket was stacked high with bedsheets. Today was washing day. Sarah, along with her mother, had spent the early morning stripping beds. The washing tub was a big wooden drum which had to be filled by hand with boiling water from the range. This task alone took a great deal of physical effort before the main work started. Between Sarah and Mary they had wielded the long wooden paddle used to beat the dirt from the sheets. The final effort involved feeding the wet cloth through the mangle to squeeze out any remaining water. Today had been chosen for washing day as there was a steady breeze and the late summer sun was still strong in the sky.

"Sarah, what in god's name are you doing," growled her mother as she dropped the basket in front of her weary daughter. "I turn my back for a moment and there you are with your feet up. Come on girl. Raise yourself and pull these sheets with me." Mary shook her head in frustration at her eldest daughter. She didn't know what had got into her lately. She had never been lazy before but recently she slacked at her regular jobs and showed so little enthusiasm. Her whole demeanour had changed.

Sarah dragged herself from the chair and wearily pushed her hair back from her face. She felt a wave of nausea wash over her as she stood up and swallowed the bile back down her throat. She couldn't understand why she felt so dreadful. She had no energy and the normal routine of housework and her evenings working in the bar just seemed to be draining her. Sarah was as strong as an ox and rarely sick so her current malaise was worrying her.

The two women pulled the sheets, folding and making a pile to ready them for storage. The spare bedsheets had been fitted to their beds whilst the washed ones had been drying out on the long rope tied between the stable and main house. At least this job only took place monthly. It needed a quick turnaround so the breeze was a vital component of wash day. The family would look forward to the smell of fresh sheets as they dropped exhausted into bed that night.

"What's wrong with you, Sarah," asked her mother with a faint sound of kindness in her voice. Mary Whiting was no longer the cheerful mother figure of old before John had died. She had become harder and didn't show the same level of affection for her eldest daughter since she had married Jack. It was rare for her to instigate any type of conversation about her daughter's needs so Sarah was immediately on guard to her mother's motives.

"I'm just tired, Mother" Sarah replied. "I am having some weird dreams at night which is keeping me awake. I keep seeing this strange woman in my dreams. She can't be real as she speaks with a weird accent and her clothes are very strange. It has been troubling me recently."

Mary groaned with frustration before she spoke. "Well don't tell your father about those silly fantasies, will you. He would love to use that as an excuse to place you in bedlam. I don't think I could cope without your help girl." Mary dismissed Sarah's concerns with no particular worry about her daughter's well-being. Her primary focus was on the impact any incapacity would have on her own workload.

Sarah was used to her mother's coldness. It disappointed her but knew it was a product of the relationship with that horrible man she called stepfather.

"He's not my father" challenged Sarah. "He's your husband and he's a bastard. I hate him and I really don't know how you can put up with sharing his bed. He stinks of sweat and beer and he makes my skin crawl."

The sting of her mother's hand across her face made Sarah wince. She knew she had pushed her luck to the limit. Sarah resented any comparison between her wonderful father and that monster. The name father should not be used for Jack Whiting.

"You mind your tongue, girl." Mary snarled at her eldest even though deep down inside she knew she spoke the truth. Mary was trapped in a relationship with a man she didn't care for but she had made her bed and she was damn well going to lie in it rather than admit the fact to her daughter.

"That man puts food on the table for you and you will pay him the respect he is due. When you find a man who will take you on and you leave this house for good then you will be entitled to an opinion. But until that day comes, you will watch your tongue."

Sarah kept her eyes down, avoiding visual contact with her mother. Inside she raged at the injustice of it all. If only you knew what he is really like, she thought to herself.

Thinking it was probably a good opportunity to leave her mother alone to calm herself, Sarah picked up the egg basket and slipped on her outside clogs. Sarah felt safe hiding out in the hen house mixing with her feathered friends. They didn't expect anything from her other than food scraps. They accepted her into their family group grooming her with their beaks. Her bond with the hens was reciprocated with a steady supply of eggs.

Sarah crawled into the tight space of the run and picked up her favourite hen. She stroked its dark brown feathers as she took a number of deep breaths trying to release the anger which had built inside her.

Since that first time in the outside toilet, Jack had continued to take Sarah whenever he wanted. Sarah had tried her best to keep out of his way especially towards the end of the evening working in the bar area. Most evenings she would stick close to her brother Tom whilst she cleared down the bar and washed up the tankards. But Jack was smart and found ways to get Sarah alone. Whether it was late at night or when he was out in the fields, he found ways to ensure she had to seek him out.

The threat of what he would do to Hannah was all the motivation Sarah needed to keep his dirty secret. She could not bear the thought of his dreadful hands touching her sister's nubile body. Sarah was already damaged beyond repair and she knew that any hope of finding a young man to make a future with would be unlikely. Her precious virginity had gone and to marry she would have to fool any future husband. That option was one that she struggled to entertain.

Since that first time when she felt she was being ripped apart by that dreadful brute, Jack had behaved in a strange way when he took her. At times there was a sense of gentleness in his actions. It was almost as if he was imagining she was her mother, in her youth. He liked to touch her hair and wind her curls around his fingers. He would gently pull her curls to his nose and drink in the smell of her. But all too often the encounters resulted in further violence as Sarah rebelled against his desires.

Sarah found his behaviour confusing. Despite the pain, she would rather he continued to hurt her and treat her with distain rather than show any affection which only messed with her head further. She was frightened of him. She could never know one day to the next how he would behave towards her. To add to the confusion, Sarah struggled to understand how he could want to hurt her and, at the same time, demand affection from her as he took her against her will.

Another wave of nausea made Sarah double over. This time she could not prevent the bile from rising and she spat out the acid onto the floor of the hen run. A shiver ran down her spine. Deep down she knew what was happening to her body even though she was trying so hard to ignore the signs. Her breasts were tender and her nipples engorged. Her tummy was starting to show a small bump. From her recollection it was some three months since her last courses. Having been brought up around animals and seeing her mother producing children for both her husbands, Sarah understood the facts of reproduction. She realised that her stepfather had got her in the family way.

She was terrified of the consequences of her dark secret.

Her mother should be the person she could turn to for support. How could she tell her mother that her husband had raped her eldest daughter and got her in the family way? Her mother would stand by Jack. Sarah could be thrown out of the family home to fend for herself. If that was to happen she would end up in the workhouse and her life would be over. If she told Jack what his rutting had done to her body, he would fabricate a way to throw her out and then her younger sister would become his next prey. It was a dreadful mess.

Sarah did not have many close friends. Her best friend Rachel lived in the village with her father who was the local carpenter. Rachel's mother had died some years ago in childbed so her friend had taken on the task of looking after her younger brothers and sisters. Rachel's father was devastated with the loss of his beloved wife and would not contemplate the thought of another woman in his bed. The lack of a new mother meant that the responsibility for the home and bringing up her siblings fell squarely on Rachel. Having time to meet up and talk was precious to both girls and usually only happened after church on a Sunday. Sarah was struggling to put into words how she could explain her position to Rachel. Could she be strong enough to tell her friend of her shame? Even if Rachel understood her plight, what could she do to help?

Sarah felt truly alone.

Her short life was over. None of the options before her gave any glimmer of hope. And now to add to that she was carry new life. It was not the fault of this tiny baby within her. Her baby was not responsible for the hatred which had conceived its life.

Trying to end this pregnancy was not an option for Sarah. She had heard tell of wise women who could bring an end to an unwanted situation but that cost money, which Sarah did not have. The money she was secretly hiding would not stretch to the cost of ending this baby's life. Added to that the rumour mill told of terrible stories of butchery, this often led to both the death of the baby and the mother. Despite the shame she could not put herself and her baby through that.

Sarah buried her face into her arms as she wrapped herself into a small ball. Tears started to fall as she tried to decide what to do. In her mind, the only option left open to her was to try and hide her secret for as long as she could and hope that something would happen to help her. Her mother was so tied up with her own troubles that she had not noticed the changes in her daughter's courses. She could pull her corset tighter to hide her fuller tummy. Perhaps she could get away with her secret for a few months more. Realistically she knew that the family situation was not going to change but avoiding a decision seemed the easiest option for now. She needed to be stronger mentally before she faced the truth.

CHAPTER FOURTEEN

"Giles, grab the door darling" shouted Liz from the bottom of the stairs. "I'm just browning the meat."

She heard the rumble of feet descending the staircase as Giles hurtled to answer the front door. It was Malcolm and Joyce who were slightly early but very welcome. Joyce had been delighted with the invitation to join the Stamfords for dinner. Their first meeting had been a resounding success and Joyce was keen to develop the friendship further.

As Giles welcomed their guests and got them settled in the lounge, Liz finished browning the lamb rack and popped the juicy meat into the oven to finish cooking. Liz was pleased with her menu for the evening. They would start with a warm goat's cheese salad. The main event was rack of lamb with Liz's homemade dauphinoise potatoes and French beans. The night would wrap with a rich chocolate tart which was indulgent and stacked full of calories.

Liz had fed Jo and Harry earlier so that the couples could spend some quality adult time together. Both teenagers were holed up in the games room with a couple of films to catch up on.

"Well hi there Malcolm and Joyce" cried Liz enthusiastically as she walked through to the lounge to greet her guests. She hugged them both placing kisses on cheeks. "So lovely to see you both and thank you so much for agreeing to come at such short notice."

"Oh we were delighted to accept," responded Joyce with a beaming smile. "I didn't want to hassle you too early as I know what it must have been like for you getting settled in. It certainly looks like you are doing well on the unpacking front." Joyce was surveying the room which showed clear signs of organisation. Joyce was ashamed to say that when they last moved home her family lived in total chaos for weeks.

"I am pleased to report that all vital boxes are unpacked and stowed and all that's left is a few crates up in the loft which I'm sure will probably stay there." Giles almost puffed out his chest with pride as he took the congratulations on the speed of settling the home into normality, despite the fact that the majority of the work had been completed by his wife, who shrugged theatrically. "Now what can I get you to drink? Malcolm? Joyce?"

As the couples enjoyed a pre-dinner drink they naturally settled into conversation which predominately centred on how the Stamfords were settling into the village and the children's first few weeks at their new school. Both couples relaxed in each other's company and the conversation flowed easily with no awkward silences. To the observer it would seem like they had been friends for years rather than this being their second meeting.

Liz interrupted the flow to invite their guests to the dining room. As she served out the warm salad she took positive vibes from Malcolm as he wolfed down the food and stretch out his belly in some form of tribal expression of satisfaction. Liz smiled to herself as she watched Joyce grimace with embarrassment at her husband's behaviour. She almost expected to hear a loud belch as Malcolm seemed to inhale his food. She could see where his impressive belly came from. He loved his food.

Once the rack of lamb had been served up, Joyce took centre stage as she outlined the history of the house as she knew it. The Stamfords were aware that the house had originally been the village pub but other than the estate agent blurb, they had little local history to support their knowledge.

"Well I remember doing some early research when we moved into our house which included going through the census papers for the parish," started Joyce. "Little Yaxley was mentioned in the Doomsday book and the church itself was built soon after the Norman invasion. The settlement has probably been similar in size over the years although a number of Norfolk villages were lost in the Middle Ages through the Black Death."

"So how long do you think there may have been a pub in the village?" asked Liz. She was fascinated about the house especially since she had experienced the recent weird events. Perhaps a better knowledge of the house's past may lead her to understand the messages she appeared to be tapping into.

"I guess there would have been some form of inn or coaching house on this site for centuries," explained Joyce. "I don't necessarily think this actual house has stood since the Middle Ages but there would have been some form of establishment on this land. I reckon it's probably 200 to 300 years old looking at the style of architecture." Joyce was surveying the timber beams as she spoke. "Also, if I remember rightly from the census, this land including the pub was aligned with Wood Farm which is way across the fields behind you. At some stage the two businesses were owned together."

"Oh exciting," smiled Giles. "Does that mean we bought a farm too without even knowing about it?"

"Sorry to burst your bubble, old chap" said Joyce. "I think the various bundles of land were sold off one by one over the last hundred years. The pub was sold during the Second World War and become a home. Although I do recall that various business activities took place since then as various owners used the land that came with the house." Joyce could see Liz and Giles were intrigued. "I must bring round copies of the census and show you both. I think I have them going back to 1800. It shows who lived in the house during each ten-year period."

Liz was already excited about the thought of trawling the records to find something of interest. "Thanks Joyce. That would be brilliant if you don't mind sharing those papers," replied Liz. "I have found some documents which seem to confirm the sale of the pub and subsequent owners, but I am really interested to understand who lived here in the past. Family history is so fascinating, and I can just imagine how many people have been born here, lived here and, I guess, also died here."

In her mind Liz was contemplating that she may be able to trace the girl in her dreams. It felt like a long shot but perhaps the answer to why she was getting these strange imaginings would become clear if she found out whether the girl actually existed.

"I tell you what" started Joyce," why don't I pop round one night this week with the papers I have and you can copy whatever you think will help. You never know you may find out some ancient scandal to rock the village". Joyce could not realise how close to the truth her joke was as the friends continued to gossip about the village and its inhabitants.

As they settled down to coffee later that evening, Liz reflected on a fantastic evening. Joyce and Malcolm were going to become close friends and she could not believe how relaxed they felt in each other's company already. They had covered a wide range of topics and despite having opposing views on a number of subjects the debates had been friendly and robust. Humour seemed to be important to them all and on many occasions that evening they had burst into loud guffaws of laughter.

Malcolm surprisingly moved the conversation onto the subject of ghosts. He told the story of how as a child he had seen the ghost of an old man standing at the end of his bed and it had frightened the life out of him. He had then got a walloping from his father for waking his parents up with his screams and for wetting the bed. From that night he had seen this old chap most nights until the family moved from the house. It was only when he was an adult that he plucked up the courage to tell his mother about the spooky events. She had been mortified that he had suffered all his childhood and hadn't felt able to tell his parents about what he had seen. At last she had understood the bed wetting and sleep issues of her child, which she had struggled with through his early years.

Once he had told his mother, she had set about understanding more about the history of the house she had brought her children up in. She had discovered that a previous owner had died in the back bedroom where Malcolm slept. This old man had been somewhat reclusive and had not been found for some months after he had died. Perhaps his loneliness had led to him revisiting the house each night.

"When I found this out from my mother I felt pretty angry with my parents. I spent my childhood scared stiff with these nightly visits" said Malcolm. You could feel the emotion he had dealt with over the years. "My parents had tried to make out I was just a difficult child. I think they thought I made up stories to cover my bed wetting. It almost gave me some comfort to find out I wasn't going mad but that I just had tuned into some strange memory from the past." Malcolm was brutally honest as he shared his feelings with his new friends. He wasn't embarrassed sharing the more personal details with them.

"I guess you believe in ghosts then Malcolm." Liz plucked up the courage to share a little bit about the dreams she had been experiencing since moving into the home. Malcolm's frank and open honest dialogue, including such personal revelations, gave her the confidence that he would not scoff at her thoughts. She was cautious to share only the briefest of details as she was aware that Giles was not keen on discussing these events.

"I have noticed some strange things happening in the house. Sometimes I swear there is someone else in the room even though my eyes tell me there isn't. And strange smells. I have smelt the scent of a flowery perfume which I know doesn't belong in the house."

"Really. Gosh I bet that scared the life out of you" Joyce jumped in.

"To be honest I'm not frightened by it at all. Thankfully no-one else has experienced it but I'm just intrigued. Is there a logical explanation for what I am sensing?" Liz looked across at Malcolm to see what his reaction would be.

"I would not be surprised if you are picking up on some residual energy," responded Malcolm thoughtfully. "As you say, so many people will have died on this site over the centuries and perhaps a presence is struggling to leave. There may be something holding it back to the house." Malcolm was thinking of the similarities with his previous experience.

He continued. "I certainly don't profess to be an expert on these matters. With my professional background, I should probably say that it's all in the mind but having seen a ghost before I have to admit to being a believer. And remember that not everyone is receptive to this type of energy. That's why so many people will dismiss the idea of an afterlife as they haven't personally witnessed anything to lead them to that viewpoint," sighed Malcolm. "It's so hard to accept what the eye hasn't seen. Personally, I like to think that makes me special rather than a freak," smiled Malcolm, sending Liz a wave of reassurance to her tentative approach to the subject.

"Oh, that's so exciting," Joyce squealed and grabbed onto Liz's arm. "Perhaps we can find something in the census that leads us to the mystery flower smelling ghost of Crown House. It will be a mystery for us to crack."

Joyce was a non-believer and liked to dismiss Malcolm's views on the supernatural with humour.

Sensing Joyce's views, Liz was happy to let the conversation flow on to other matters as she pondered on Malcolm's comments. Perhaps there is something in what he said and perhaps there is a mystery to solve. There must be some reason why the girl was coming to her in her dreams.

Liz knew that she had to investigate for her own peace of mind.

CHAPTER FIFTEEN

Liz was enjoying the peace of Saturday afternoon.

She was sat in the garden with a large glass of homemade lemonade and an excellent novel. Liz drank in the sounds of a lazy summer afternoon. Bird song filled the air and the hum of a tractor could be heard in the distance. Bees hovered around the plum tree surrounding the patio and on occasion a drunken insect would fall to the ground, its belly full of rich nectar.

Smiling as she looked out over the beautiful gardens and realised how lucky they had been to find this new home. For the first time in the last year she was starting to feel content and at peace with her lot.

Liz was enjoying some alone time. Giles was ensconced in the office catching up on his work emails. Liz accepted that the nature of his role didn't fit neatly into a 9 to 5 schedule and understood the benefits and flexibility he had to balance his work life commitments with the heavy demands of his work responsibilities. Although she did feel a bit sorry for him that this beautiful sunny afternoon was being spent indoors.

Jo and Harry were entertaining Hannah in the swimming pool. Liz could just hear the noises of the teenagers coming from the far end of the gardens. Liz had warmed to Hannah on meeting her. She was exceptionally quirky with such a happy demeanour. She had arrived in a bundle of enthusiastic energy and with the confidence of youth. Sporting pink hair, which Liz understood was a wig due to the restriction imposed at St Mary's. She was dressed in blue dungarees and a tie-dye t-shirt. A confused outfit which seemed to suit her perfectly.

It was like a whirlwind blown through the building as she breezed into the house and settled cross legged on the sofa. Hannah had run her eyes around the house taking it in the ambiance prior to rushing off with Jo to her room. Liz smiled to herself as she thought about this budding friendship and reflected what a unique addition to the wider Stamford household.

As Liz contemplated their house guest, Hannah walked across the lawn towards her. She had a beach towel wrapped around her waist just revealing her bikini top which true to form, was multi coloured.

"Hi Mrs S. Can I join you for a moment?" asked Hannah as she dropped with a sigh onto the garden chair. "Jo and Harry are doing competitive lengths so I made an excuse to get out in the sunshine." Hannah was not a great swimmer but had enjoyed the chance to cool down from this hot summer day with a brief dip.

"Of course, Hannah and do call me Liz. We don't stand on ceremony in this household. Help yourself to a glass of lemonade if you fancy one." Liz smiled at Hannah as she poured herself a glass and settled back in her chair.

"Liz, not sure how to broach this one with you so I'm just going to come straight out with it." Hannah stared intensely ahead as she gathered her thoughts. "I think you have a presence in this house. I felt it earlier when I was upstairs. I don't think you should be worried as it feels like a welcoming presence but I thought you should know." Hannah paused for dramatic effect as she examined Liz's reaction. She was slightly nervous of how her statement would be received.

"I haven't said anything to Jo or Harry as I don't want to freak them out but thought you should know," Hannah continued in a serious tone.

"Really," Liz turned to face Hannah and took her hand. "I have felt something too and have witnessed a couple of weird and unexplained events. What have you felt?" Liz gave Hannah encouraging vibes keen to learn more.

"It's a girl. I saw her on the corridor upstairs. She's not a recent passing. Her dress was old fashioned. I was gobsmacked to see her. She's a stunning looking girl. Long dark hair with the saddest expression ever." Hannah paused as she checked Liz seemed ok with what she was sharing. "She's searching for something. I think that's why she's still here. She needs some form of closure to let her rest."

Hannah didn't often share her perceptions of the spirit world as she was fearful of ridicule. Despite her quirky demeanour, she was reluctant to get a reputation as a ghost hunter. She had seen a number of presences but she rarely shared her perceptions with those outside her immediate family. She had got good vibes from Mrs Stamford so felt it was worth the risk.

"So, could you actually see the girl?" asked Liz. She was amazed, if she was honest. This strange new friend had started this crazy conversation as if it was the most normal thing in the world to discuss.

"It's hard to explain Liz," answered Hannah. "It's not like I can see the presence like I can see you. It's almost like my brain can see her and it tells my eyes what's there. Does that make any sense at all?"

Liz thought long and hard on Hannah's remarks. It sounded crazy but at the same time made perfect sense. "I think so Hannah," she responded finally.

"Sometimes I can see a presence which is evil and that scares the shit out of me. Excuse the language. Those evil spirits don't seem to know they are dead. They are like naughty children who want to frighten; using their energy to move things and make noises. Your ghost is not evil. She's sad. She can't settle but she's definitely not evil." Hannah smiled reassuringly at Liz as she finished her explanation.

"I really appreciate you telling me, Hannah. My husband thinks I'm imaging things and I haven't said anything to Jo and Harry." Hannah deserved an explanation. "I guess Jo has told you that we lost her older sister last year."

Hannah nodded without interrupting.

"Since losing Rebecca I have tried to protect them more than I probably should. I wanted this new home to be perfect for them so don't want to worry them with spooky goings on" Liz continued. "I have also felt something on the upstairs corridor. I even felt a breath on my neck outside the bathroom. It's weird but I can smell a presence when there's no one there in the house. I think its female too but to be fair I haven't actually seen anything. Just felt it." Liz sighed as she relaxed.

"Well I have seen a few ghosts before. My parents have grown to accept my skill but it can be a real pain in the butt," grimaced Hannah. "No-one wants a freak in the family but it's not something you can ignore. My understanding is that ghosts only appear to share some form of message. I think something must have happened to your girl which has prevented her from moving on."

"Let's keep it our secret for now. I just don't want the rest of the family to be concerned. My plan is to look back at the census for the last couple of hundred years and see if I can discover something from that. That could be my starting point and I will let you know how I get on with that."

Whilst Liz was delighted to find out that this new friend had perceived something unusual in the house she didn't want her to get too involved. It would take some explaining to Jo. She couldn't really work with Jo's friend without her daughter getting suspicious. At this early stage she was reluctant to spook the teenagers. At their age they were both very suggestable and could be really interested in a ghost story or could be frightened and have trouble sleeping at night. Liz was not prepared to take any risks with her children's mental well-being.

However, it was great to get the confirmation now from both Malcolm and Hannah that she wasn't just going a bit crazy. She had started to doubt her own mind; thinking that her grief for Rebecca could have been playing with her head and confusing her thoughts. If there was the presence of a young girl in this house then Liz was determined to understand what she was looking for. If she could help her then she would pile her energy into solving the mystery.

CHAPTER SIXTEEN

"This is a beautiful home, darling."

Jill Wynn, Liz's mother had arrived earlier that day for a long weekend. Jill was delighted to see her daughter in good spirits and kept taking a sneaky look at her as they wondered around the garden. For the last year Jill had worried herself sick over the pain and suffering inflicted on her daughter and her family.

Rebecca had been really close to her grandparents. Jill and James had spent many a morning getting the children prepared for school, allowing Giles and Liz to be at work early. This support had made the relationship with their grandchildren so special on both sides. Rebecca, Jo and Harry were devoted to their Nanna and Pappa and were devastated when they lost Grandad James a few years back to cancer. That dreadful time was the children's first experience of death and both parents had carefully navigated the children through the grief and hurt.

Jill felt the loss of Rebecca like a hard stone lodged in her heart which couldn't be shifted. She had been the shoulder for Liz to collapse on in the immediate aftermath. Despite her own grief she tried to keep the rest of the family together during the trial. She had been concerned when Liz and Giles talked to her about moving away from London. She wasn't sure that being further away from her support structure would be the right thing for her daughter. Just seeing her now in her new surroundings was bringing her some comfort.

Jill was a keen gardener and was explaining the various plants and shrubs to her daughter as they wandered. As they strolled, Jill felt her daughter's fingers wriggle into her hand like she used to do when she was small. Jill gently stroked her fingers as they talked and walked. Having a daughter was a special gift and, whilst Jill would never admit to favourites, her relationship with her only daughter was different from the way she interacted with her two sons, George and Michael.

As they came back full circle to the patio, the two women took a seat. Jill continued to survey the house, taking in the architecture and the clear differences between new and old.

"So, the house used to be a pub then darling?" asked Jill. "I love the flint in the walls; it looks so similar to north Norfolk houses which tend to be built with brick and flint. You remember my grandmother came from Norfolk. This house reminds me so much of the pictures I remember from my childhood." Jill had spent most of her childhood holidays in Norfolk and had a strong affection for the county.

"I know. It's fascinating thinking about how the house was used before. As you walk around parts of the building you can clearly imagine how it would have looked like at the time. And just look at the little outbuilding over there." Liz gestured towards the small brick building set off to the side of the patio. "That was the outside loo. You can kind of imagine the number of drunken old men who have made a mess in there, can't you? Remember how grandad got when he was old. I always remember you shouting at him when he peed on the carpet." Liz smiled at her mother as she remembered how she hated following her grandfather into the bathroom.

"Oh god don't remind me!" exclaimed Jill as she remembered her father and his inability to aim in the bowl. He had an outside loo at his old council house so never seemed to worry about perfecting his target practise.

"I know you have done a lot of work on our family history, Mum, so I was hoping you would be interested in the history of this house." Liz was keen to tap into her mother's interest in the past to see how much she could find out about the inhabitants of the pub. "Our neighbours have shared a copy of the old census for the area. I haven't really had a good look at the paperwork yet as I didn't want to spoil the surprise of sharing it with you. I think it goes back to the early 1800s."

Jill's interest was piqued. "Oh yes please darling. Go and grab the papers and let's spread them out on the table. Get a note pad too won't you. It is normally hard to read the writing so you will need to make notes as we go." Jill cleared the patio table of the remains of lunch making room for the women to start their investigations.

Over the next hour, Jill slowly deciphered the various photocopied pages which started in 1801 and detailed the occupants of the village over 10-year periods right up until 1911. It took some time to find the pub occupants as the names of the roads seemed to change slightly. Jill concentrated on the named occupation of residents to find the innkeeper and work back from that point. The writing was faded in places and it took a great deal of painstaking work to determine some of the names. Jill ended up using a magnifying glass to examine the intricate writing.

Jill was finally comfortable that they could identify the house on each of the census documents and detail out the individuals living in the premises including their children. Once they had started to detail the names out onto a blank sheet of paper it was easier to see any consistencies over the ten-year periods to understand the family connections. As they worked Liz had been updating her mother on the land which appeared to have been connected to the pub over the years so that she had a fuller picture. It was this discussion which prompted Jill to do some cross referencing with Wood Farm which was also included in the parish census documents.

"Look at the census for 1851," started Jill as she pulled the papers towards herself. "At Crown Inn you have John Cozen who is the innkeeper and is 30 years of age. Living with him is his wife Mary who is 27 and they have three children, Sarah who's 8, Tom who's 3 and a baby Hannah." Jill picked up the next document. "Then scroll forward to 1861. The innkeeper is Jack Whiting who is 38. But interestingly his wife is called Mary too and she is 37. They appear to have six children, Sarah, Tom and Hannah seem to be the right age as those in the previous census. Then there are three new children. Anne is 7, Arthur 5 and Emma is 2. That's too much of a coincidence isn't it? It must be the same Mary and it looks like she has married another chap." She paused as she gazed at the papers in front of her. "I bet her first husband died. There we go, that's our first job to see if we can trace a death certificate for John Cozen."

"Mum, look at the detail on Wood Farm." Liz wafted a new set of papers in front of her mother's face. "Back in 1851 Jack Whiting is the head of the household and it looks like his mother, Harriet lives with him. In 1861 its just Harriet registered at the farm so the new innkeeper must be that same Jack. That must be how the farm became linked to the inn as both owners got married." Liz could understand how her mum had got hooked on family history as she was buzzing with excitement as they completed the puzzle of these two families.

Having made that connection the two women looked in more detail at the census of 1871. They could see that Jack was still living at the inn. Tom Whiting appeared to be living at Wood Farm now with his wife Jane and small baby. At the inn they found Anne, Arthur and Emma still living with their father but no mention of Sarah and Hannah.

"I guess the two older girls would have married and moved away from home by then. They would both be in their twenties and girls married young in those days," suggested Liz. "I wonder what happened to the mother."

"I agree with you about the daughters, although people didn't tend to move too far away from the family home," explained Jill. "I wouldn't be surprised if we trawled the parish records and found those girls married to someone in the village," said Jill. "It's going to be a tougher ask that one as you will need to find marriage certificates to verify names. I tell you what we should do. Why don't we go for a stroll around the graveyard and see what we can find?"

Jill was keen to familiarise herself with the surrounding area.

"What a brilliant idea. I can show you the village while we are at it. The church is so beautiful, you will love it. Let me just tell Giles we are off out and grab my sandals."

Jill smiled to herself as Liz rushed off into the house leaving her mother to tidy up the paperwork and place it into some form of order. She felt a sense of satisfaction to see her daughter's pleasure in discovering something interesting about her home. This is just what Liz needed at the moment. The opportunity to find an interest in something other than her own family. Something she could focus on and research. It would no doubt help her settle into the village especially if their investigations led to a connection still living in the area. That was probably going to be unlikely in terms of the amount of time passed but Jill felt that giving her daughter a mission could be just what she needed.

As they wandered through the village, Jill took in the sights. They came across the odd neighbour working on their gardens and stopped briefly to exchange greetings. At the centre of the village stood the Norman church. The gates surrounding the entrance were garnished with a deep red rose bush which added to the picture-perfect view. Walking into the graveyard you could clearly see the history of the burial site with the more recent headstones standing clean and well-tended at the front left of the church. Dotted around the rest of the church were those stones aged and forlorn, a testament to a forgotten past.

Many of the headstones were difficult to read as the weather had taken its toll. Weeds grew between the graves covering many of the stones, adding to the difficulty in tracing the owners. Jill and Liz methodically swept through the graveyard trying to determine a pattern of deaths to a similar time period to try and narrow down the search. Away in the far corner of the church grounds they came across 19th century graves. With respect they tiptoed between the mounds trying not to stand or walk across the actual grave but getting close enough to run their fingers across the inscriptions.

"Mum look here," shouted Liz excitedly as she squatted down to take a closer look. "I've found Jack and Mary Whiting's grave. It's got to be them surely. Look at the dates. Mary died in 1875 and Jack in 1880. Those dates sort of tie in with the census so it would be too much of a co-incidence for it to be another couple."

"Agreed" said Jill thoughtfully. "I cannot see that being anyone else but the innkeeper, so I guess they lived in your house until they died. Although it was strange that Mary Whiting wasn't on the census for 1871. She was alive but where was she?" Jill saw another mystery in that story. "Just look here though. There's a small headstone just behind. Let me just clear away the moss and let's see if it may be related to Jack and Mary."

Jill brushed at the moss with her fingers, gradually revealing the name Sarah Whiting, born 15th January 1843 and died 17th April 1861.

"Oh Mum, that's so sad" sighed Liz. "She was only 18. That's no age at all. I wonder what happened to her." Liz touched the headstone tracing her fingers across the worn lettering. A shiver ran down her spine making Liz shoot round to look behind her. Nothing was there.

"Life was tough in those days," Jill reflected." Disease could kill especially when mixed in with a poor diet and hygiene. Though often you would find a number of the household dying at the same time if it was disease that hit" sighed Jill. "For women, childbirth was also a big killer although Sarah doesn't look to have been married. You know when I gave birth to your brother, George, I had a haemorrhage. I was lucky as I was in hospital and had first class support. But can you imagine in days gone by that a woman could literally bleed to death if that happened."

As her mother talked, Liz contemplated the information they had discovered. She was not ready to share her recent experiences with Jill as she wasn't sure what reaction she would get. Her mother would likely scoff at the thought of a presence in the house.

As they stood there by the grave a gentle breeze wafted around them carrying the sweet scent of flowers.

Suddenly Liz had an overwhelming feeling that the girl in her dreams was Sarah. She couldn't explain where the feeling came from but it hit her with a certainty that defied any evidence. Hannah had seen what she had described as a young woman on the corridor upstairs. All the evidence seemed to point to a girl dying young and maybe unable to rest in peace. Liz was even more determined now to understand what was troubling Sarah and why she couldn't move on.

As the two women strolled back towards the house, Liz smiled to herself. She had a purpose and was going to investigate this further. She would find a way of bringing peace to the house and finding some form of closure to the past.

CHAPTER SEVENTEEN – WINTER 1860

Jack and Tom shoved their chairs back from the kitchen table, scraping across the flagstones, as they made their way out after the mid-day meal. Sarah and Hannah set to work clearing the pots away to give their mother time to rest her weary feet.

Mary was with child again and the latest baby was lying heavy on her spine. Her feet were sore and puffy. The impact on her body of a seventh pregnancy was taking its toll; she was struggling to manage household duties. This put additional pressure on her two oldest daughters. Both girls were used to working hard. They were rightly worried about their mother. It was only two years since Emma had been born. As Mary got older the risk of childbed became a constant worry for the family. But not for her husband who kept getting her with child.

Hannah picked up the pot with kitchen scraps and made her way from the kitchen. The chickens would welcome the tasty morsels. Sarah squeezed herself between her mother's chair and the Welsh dresser as she balanced dirty plates in her arms. She winced as her bulk caught against her mother's arm. There was no way to hide the growing bump when pressed against another solid object. Mary slowly turned to look at her daughter and the colour drained from her face.

"Upstairs now," she shouted at Sarah.

Grabbing her daughter by the shoulders she manhandled her from the kitchen and pulled her towards the stairs. She did not speak until the women had made it into Mary's bedroom and she had pushed Sarah down on to the bed. As Sarah lay on the bed, her mother pushed her clothes aside so that she could examine her body. Having exposed her daughter's midriff, she laid her hands across her stomach feeling the movement of the foetus growing within her. A myriad of expressions crossed Mary's face; shock quickly replaced by anger.

"Oh girl. What have you gone and done?" Mary seemed to deflate as she looked at her firstborn and realised the mess they were in. "You are at least six months gone, girl. What the hell are we going to do about that? It's far too late to get rid of it now." Mary dropped her head to her hands as she thought about the trouble ahead. She had no idea that her daughter even had a suitor let alone that they were up to no good. The shame and reality of the situation was overwhelming.

Sarah stayed silent and kept her eyes fixed on a point above her mother's head. She could not move from her position on the bed or try to rearrange her clothing. If she lay completely still perhaps it would lessen the blow when it fell. She had known this time would come eventually. She could not have hidden her situation for much longer. Sarah had managed to conceal her condition for months now by letting out her corset and bulking out her winter dresses. As she lay there, Sarah waited for the verbal onslaught she knew was coming.

"You stupid, stupid girl. Why didn't you tell me sooner and we could have got rid of the problem? Who is the father?" she shouted. "When your father finds out he will go mad. I pity the lad when he faces Jack in a fury." Mary grabbed hold of Sarah's face as she shouted at her. "Well who is he?"

"I don't know, mother," cried Sarah as the pain of her mother's fingers scratched into her cheeks. Sarah knew that she could not share her dirty secret with Mary. She would not believe her. Jack would deny any involvement. There was no point in bringing any further disgrace down on her head.

"You silly slut," scream Mary with spittle splashing into Sarah's face. "How can you let a boy get you in this condition without knowing who is responsible? I thought you were a good girl with a sensible head on your shoulders. I thought I had a good eye on you," she shouted. "So, you found ways to sneak out and whore yourself out across the village. How am I going to withstand the shame? I have standing in this village. People respect me and your father. The shame will ruin our position in this community."

Mary was horrified by the reality that her daughter could not name the father. The shame of finding out that the daughter she had brought up to respect herself had allowed her body to be passed around. Would the youth of the neighbourhood be laughing at her family? If it had been just one lover then Jack would drag that lad down the aisle to marry Sarah.

Sarah waited for her mother to calm down. She could see the emotions playing across her face. Anything she said now would just inflame the situation further. She needed her mother to quell her anger before Jack returned to the house. She knew deep down that her mother would not throw her out in her current condition. No matter what she had done, she knew her mother would stand by her. Sarah needed Mary to find a way round this disaster and to protect her eldest from the wrath of her bullying stepfather.

Moments later she realised her mother was crying. Gently she reached across the bed to touch her. Like a child she enfolded herself in her mother's arms as her tears flowed.

Mary held her firmly in her embrace, rocking her gently. As she rocked, she crooned comfort like she would a baby. She could hardly believe how low her daughter had fallen. Her mind refused to imagine the horror which lurked at the periphery of her conscience. She didn't believe Sarah's story but there was no way she wanted to ask the question which was niggling at the back of her mind.

CHAPTER EIGHTEEN

The burgers hit the BBQ grill spitting with fury, hissing at the two men in charge of the cooking. The grill was already filling up with spicy sausages, kebabs and now the obligatory beef burgers.

Giles was sporting his novelty apron which the kids had got him for last Christmas. In bold writing it attested to Giles being King of the Blue Jobs. Like an orchestra conductor he waved the tongs around as he and Steve chatted. Steve was a colleague from the Bank and Giles's best friend. They had both started work together in the same business centre. Over the years their roles had moved in different directions but they remained close. Steve and his wife Maggie had lived a few roads away from them in London. As great friends they spent many weekends socialising. The couple had been excited to make their first trip out to see the new house.

As they supervised lunch the two friends dissected recent events at work. Steve worked in Head Office and was responsible for business strategy. They bounced ideas off each other agreeing the best approach for the next six months in the corporate business. With work chat exhausted the conversation moved on to the Stamford's new house.

"Wow, you get a lot more for your money out in the sticks, Giles," said Steve as he surveyed the garden. Giles and Liz had given the couple the tour of the house when they arrived. "Amazing that you got all of this for the same price as your old place. It's crazy to think what we could buy if we made the move too. How are you guys coping with being miles away from the action?" Steve knew he would struggle to get Maggie and the boys to make such a big move away from the city. Their lives were knitted into the fabric of London.

"You know I wasn't sure about it at first. It was really down to Liz, the move. But it hasn't taken long to settle in and now I just can't imagine living anywhere else." Giles responded. "I guess I spend a lot of time away with work but when I get to work from home it's just amazing." Giles grinned at his best friend. One of the only downsides of the move was not seeing his best mate as much.

"I can sit in my office and watch the wildlife. The other day a deer just sauntered past the window, bold as brass. When I was on our audio yesterday I was watching a woodpecker make his way across the garden searching for worms. You don't get that in the big smoke." Giles delighted in the view from his home office. He was already seeing an uplift in his own productivity as the relaxed ambiance aided his creative juices.

Steve turned to look at his friend's wife who was sipping on her wine. "How's Liz coping with the change? I reckon she's got a bit more colour in her face. She looks like she's put some weight back on too. I was so worried that she looked all skin and bones the last time we saw you."

Giles appreciated the support both of their friends had given them in those dreadful days after Rebecca's death. Maggie has been a close confident for Liz during the dark days. For Giles it had been good to have Steve as a friend he could talk to. All too often the machismo attitudes in banking made it hard for blokes to share their feelings.

"She is doing so much better, Steve. I think it's a combination of a new home, country living and not having dark memories around every corner," Giles was looking over at the two women as he talked. "She is still struggling but managing it so much better. The kids have settled in so well and without work, Liz can spend much more time with them. So, all around it's good." Giles turned the burgers brushing them gently with BBQ sauce.

"She's got a bit of a project underway too which is helping her to get to know the village. She's trying the trace back the ownership of this house to when it was a pub. Liz has also got friendly with the local vicar who is passionate about this stuff. So, I'm just encouraging her to focus her attention on that. You know what it's like if you have a purpose. Helps you not focus on the bad stuff."

Over on the patio Maggie and Liz had been having a similar conversation. The girls were sharing a full-bodied Merlot as they chewed the fat. Maggie had worked in the bank with Giles and Steve. In fact, Steve and Maggie had got together when she was his PA. That had put an end to that job for Maggie as it just wasn't the done thing to have a relationship with your boss. Maggie had moved departments and soon after they married and the two boys came along. Maggie had no desire to go back to work once her boys were born so unlike her best friend spent her days with her boys. Joshua was 18 and about to start university in Liverpool. Mark was two years younger.

Maggie and Liz had spent many weekends together enjoying their shared passion for retail therapy. Maggie had been a linchpin in terms of childcare for Liz. She had looked after Rebecca, Joanne and Harry after school when they weren't doing one of their numerous clubs and societies. Both sets of children got on well and over recent years the families had often had joint holidays in France; renting out a big cottage. Liz had pulled out her tablet and they were surfing the internet trying to find a suitable place for next summer. Steve had decided to take his crew to Florida this summer so the Stamford family were off to France on their own for a change.

At the top of the garden, Joshua and Mark were enjoying the pool with Jo and Harry. They had all gone to the same school in North London and despite the differences in age they all got on extremely well. After racing around the house showing their friends the delights of their bedrooms they could not resist a swim before lunch. It was one of those occasions when proper swimming practise was put to one side for a spot of fooling around. After their pent-up energy was spent, the friends sat on the side of the pool catching up on everything that had happened since they last met.

"You guys are never going to believe it," Harry jumped in after school discussion had been exhausted. "Don't tell the 'rents but this place is haunted." Harry loved the look on Mark's face when he came out with that bombshell.

"Serious?" gasped Josh "Come on. Deets please."

Jo look annoyed with Harry for sharing their secret. She glared at her brother as she urged Josh and Mark to keep quiet about what Harry had said. The last thing she wanted is for her parents to find out. Mum would have a hissy fit, she thought.

"Well something is living on the corridor upstairs. I can feel it at night. It's well spooky. When you go to the loo in the night its waiting there." Harry was enjoying the discomfort on his sister's face and the look of horror on Mark's. "There is no way we are telling Mum and Dad as I reckon they will proper freak out. The last thing we want is to move again." Harry was not frightened by the strange goings on. He loved his new home and had settled into school. He was not going to give his mum any reason to doubt the move.

"We honestly don't know anything for certain," Jo tried to take control of the conversation. "It's probably nothing. Just a weird feeling at night. But it's probably cos it's an old place. These old houses are creepy."

"Thank god we aren't staying over then," gasped Josh. "Last thing I want to do is meet some bloody ghoul in the middle of the night. How come your 'rents haven't felt it then?"

"They may have," Harry sighed. "I hadn't thought of that. They may be keeping it from us as they don't want to freak us out."

"Well either way, Harry, Keep the big fella shut. No one is to know about this unless Mum or Dad let on." Jo ever the sensible one was keen to put this discussion to bed. She expertly moved the discussion on to the latest Netflix boxset they were watching.

It was not surprising that both parents and children had felt different experiences within the house and were all trying their hardest to keep that knowledge from each other. It would be months before it became clear that the atmospheric changes had been felt by the whole family. Only then would they be able to share those experiences and validate the thoughts they had been having. Even those families with the best relationships will keep secrets to try and protect each other.

CHAPTER NINETEEN – WINTER 1860

Mary had sent the younger children up to bed early.

Tom had gone into the village to see Jane, his girlfriend. Sarah was alone in the bar which was quiet for the evening. Only a couple of regulars were supping on their beer so Sarah was able to keep her ear open to the conversation going on in the kitchen.

As expected, Jack had blown his top when Mary had broken the news of her daughter's condition. He had ranted and raved at his wife, blaming her for the situation. It was all her fault that her daughter had low morals. Mary had been shocked at how quickly he seemed to calm down after his initial burst of anger. She was not to know that his own guilt was the true reason why he was now listening intently to Mary's proposal.

"We need to hide her situation for as long as we can. If we could trust my sister to keep her mouth shut, we could have sent her away to stay with Vickie until the babe is born." Mary had spent the afternoon trying to figure out what to do so that she was prepared to lead her husband to a decision. "Then we could pass the baby off as a twin with my latest. But I don't trust Vickie to keep such a huge secret. Something will eventually come out and we will be shamed. The babe has to be born. She is too far gone. We need to find a way of hiding her until the babe comes." Mary stared at her husband willing him to support.

To her surprise Jack considered her comments and responded in a more reasonable fashion than she had ever expected. "Well if we can't send her away, can we not hide her away from the rest of the village and tell people she has gone to stay with your sister. We could even keep it from the children. They don't need to know she is still here and we will only need to hide it for a few months." Jack was thinking on his feet. The easier option was the best in his opinion. "Hannah will have to take over in the bar and pick up Sarah's work during the day. We could always make Sarah pick up jobs at night when everyone is asleep as long as she is careful and isn't seen." Jack seemed to have picked out an idea which may just work.

"But how do we hide her in plain sight and keep it from her brothers and sisters?" asked Mary.

"The storage room," Jack rubbed his head as he contemplated how his plan could work. "We don't need to use the room so could make up a bed in there and if she stays quiet and still during daylight hours, no one will know she is there." The thought of the girl just the other side of the wall from his bedroom excited him. It would serve her right for getting knocked up. "Then when the baby arrives we can pass it off as ours and maybe save her reputation. I don't want to be stuck with her as an old maid who is soiled. Once the baby is born then we get her married off as quick as we can. Someone must be persuaded to take her on. She's not a bad looking girl. Someone will take her on and not ask too many questions."

His audacity knew no bounds. He was responsible for Sarah's dilemma. Jack saw a way out which would save his face and get rid of the problem. He couldn't believe how easy it had been to manipulative his wife. Mary was worried he would throw the girl out but this idea meant he still had both women under his control.

The couple sat in silence for some time contemplating the crazy idea. The more they considered it the less crazy it seemed. This idea could work and could maintain their daughter's reputation and, most importantly to Jack, his reputation.

He was shocked that the girl had managed to get herself with child. It did not even enter his head that it was his fault. The workings of a woman's body were beyond him. He had planted his seed but that was as far as any responsibility lay with him. Once the babe was born they could pass it off as their own and Sarah would be out of his hair once and for all. He would find one of his farming community who would welcome a young nubile wife and wouldn't ask too many questions especially if she didn't bleed on their wedding night.

Jack smiled as he congratulated himself on his good luck. Sarah could have spilled the beans to her mother and he would have had to face the wrath of his woman. She couldn't have done anything about it as he was the man of the house. However, her wrath would make life more difficult for Jack. He enjoyed the pleasures of Mary's ample body and it would be a shame if she went cold on him because she was jealous of her daughter. Mary could not abide the thought of her young beautiful daughter's thighs around her husband's cock.

The fact that Sarah had no choice in this activity was totally lost on Jack. In his delusional head she welcomed his attention. He would wager she would be lost when the babe was born and he cut all ties with her. He smiled to himself at the sheer arrogance of his self-belief.

"Let's get the plan in place for the morn," started Jack as he called Sarah through from the bar. Leaving the door open so that the lingering villagers in the bar could hear, he made a show of explaining the situation. "Sarah, your Aunt Victoria is ill and cannot cope with the house and young'uns. She has asked that you go and stay for a few months to help out. Your mother and I have agreed that you go tomorrow morning. It's going to put a lot of extra work on Hannah and your mother but it's important that we help out family when they need it".

Once he was satisfied that the gist of their lies had been heard by those in the bar who would share the gossip around the village, he kicked shut the door and rounded on Sarah. He grabbed her by the arm and pulled her round to face him.

"Well you stupid girl, you get yourself with child and the rest of the family has to suffer for it. I cannot believe how selfish you have been and the upset you have caused your poor mother. I guess it was to be expected." His ruddy face staring deeply into her eyes. "You walked around here like you were too good for us. Airs above your station; looking down your nose at me when I married your dear mother and took on the running of this place to keep you out of the poor house. And this is the thanks I get." Jack was enjoying his tirade far too much. He was putting on an act for Mary but once he got started he couldn't help but get a smug satisfaction from his rant.

The tirade continued as Sarah kept her eyes averted to the ground. There was no point in defending her position as it was clear Jack was putting on a show for his wife. Any word from her would probably end up being met with a fist. Sarah bit down on her lip and took the venomous dialogue from her hated stepfather.

"In the morning your mother will send Hannah to the market for some essentials and once the young'uns have left for school you will move into the storeroom. The children will think you have left for Aunt Vickie's house. During the day you will keep still and quiet. I don't want to hear a peep out of you." His fists were clenched ready to strike out at any challenge from Sarah. "Your mother will be the only person you will see for the next few months until the child is born. We will take your bastard as our own when the time comes and you will be grateful. You will be thankful that you have kind and understanding parents who want to protect your reputation. Without us your life could be over before it has begun. There are not many whores like you who have caring parents who will hide your shame and give you a fresh chance at life."

"Yes father." Sarah looked Jack directly in his face.

She stared deeply into his eyes trying to drill her hatred into his thick skull. Any respect she had for that man was dead and buried. The only way she would get through the next few months of solitude was by harnessing that hate for this man. She would survive and once the child was born she would find a way of protecting it from this monster.

CHAPTER TWENTY

The Stamford family had been in Norfolk now for nearly four months and had settled back into a routine after their summer break.

They had spent two weeks in the South of France in August relaxing in the sun. Jo and Harry had loved lazing by the pool. It was a welcome change from their professional swimming. Both of them had developed fantastic sun tans. They looked incredibly healthy and Jo's hair had developed a beautiful shine with its exposure to the sun's rays.

Giles and Liz had spent time exploring Avignon and the Pont du Gard. They both had a passion for all things French and had mooched around the countryside enjoying the sights and sounds of Provence. Long lunches in chic cafes had given them both the chance to relax and enjoy each other's company and of course, the local wines. The car had been stacked with antique furniture on their return trip. Welcome additions to their new home.

It really felt like they were closer than ever and despite the children being with them, they behaved as if they were on a second honeymoon. Whilst Jo and Harry grabbed early breakfasts and set themselves up for a hard day by the pool, Giles and Jo took advantage of long lie ins. They made love each morning. Giles was more than relieved to get their sex life back on track. In those early days after they lost Rebecca sex was just not on the cards. Liz seemed to lose her libido and only wanted to be held. Her own grief made her oblivious to the needs of her husband. He sought the reassurance of love making to manage his own fears and stresses. The holiday had been another step forward in the couple's journey to recovery.

Liz placed the breakfast bowls on the kitchen table as she listened to the noises of her children and husband who rushed around upstairs. She knew they would be hurtling down to the kitchen shortly to grab breakfast before they rushed out the house. She loved the early morning panic especially as she no longer needed to prepare for a day at work. Giles was dropping Jo and Harry at school this morning before he drove up to Nottingham for a meeting. Spooning out granola and yogurt, Liz settled down to eat her breakfast.

"Mum, do you know where my football boots are?" shouted Harry as he charged into the kitchen. His hair was messy, testament to the fact that the hairbrush had not managed to get anywhere near him that morning. "I can't find them anywhere. You know I have footie practise after school today," he cried with frustration.

"By the back door, Harry darling. Where you left them at the weekend," laughed Liz.

She welcomed the noise and activity but also looked forward to the calm and quiet once they had all departed. She had plans for today which were exciting her. She was looking forward to putting her plan into action once Giles's car had departed.

Giles and Jo were hot on Harry's heels. Giles grabbed a coffee cup and filled it up from the cafeteria while he popped a slice of bread into the toaster. Jo copied her mother with a generous helping of granola topped with lemon yogurt.

"Darling, what are you up to today?" asked Giles as he spread his toast with a generous helping of olive oil spread.

"I'm going to have a go in that mysterious cupboard in our bedroom. I thought I would clean it out. It's full of rubbish. If I'm really brave and can face the cobwebs." Liz had a real aversion to spiders. "I should be able to see if we could use it for anything. I don't know if we could consider putting a dormer window in the roof and perhaps make it into a walk-in wardrobe. Either way until I get up the courage to clean it out it's hard to tell what use it is."

Liz had been thinking about the room for some time. She knew it was going to challenge her as she hated the dark especially when cobwebs were involved. The room seemed to draw her in. She wanted to find out what secrets it held especially the furniture under the old sacking. So, if she wanted to find out what was in there then she would have to be brave.

"Oh Mum, you will be screaming like a baby at the first spider," laughed Harry. Liz's fear of arachnids was legendary. Buying an old house in the country had tested that fear. Each time she cleaned a room the number of spiders swept up in the Dyson astounded Liz. These spiders must breed like rabbits, she thought smiling at the perverse analogy.

"Well just be careful in there, Liz". Giles looked concerned as he bent over Liz to give her a kiss before they left. "Just remember that the survey didn't cover that room so I don't know the condition of floorboards. Please watch yourself my love."

"I will darling. Don't fuss. If it feels dodgy at all then I will leave it. And I will keep my mobile on me so I can call for help if I end up being attacked by flesh eating spiders." She grinned at her son and ruffled his hair as the family made their way out. Liz stood sentry at the porch door as her family organised shoes, coats, and keys and made their way out of the door. She smiled to herself as she waved them on their way.

As quiet descended over the house, Liz grabbed a further coffee and made her way up stairs. The bedroom needed a bit of reorganisation to allow her to access the secret room and allow the maximum amount of natural light to support the torch light. The room was bigger than you would expect as it ran across the vast staircase up the middle of the house. It climbed high up under the eaves of the roof so that an average person could stand up in the highest part of the room. There was a steep slope towards the front wall so any attempt to use as a dressing room would need some careful planning. Liz was already thinking of the practicalities before she had started the task of cleaning up.

With hoover in hand and a mask over her nose, Liz started the painful task of sweeping away the cobwebs and dust accumulated over the years. It reminded her of the Dickens novel Great Expectations and the eccentric Mrs Havisham. The number of cobwebs were ridiculous. Liz needed to empty the filter twice as she worked her way across the space. It took a good couple of hours to get to a point where Liz felt she had made enough progress to investigate the furniture set away in the far corner of the room.

The main piece of furniture appeared to be an old bed. It had a wooden frame with slats supported by a solid base. It was low, almost touching the floor and not even the size of a regular single bed. At best it could be described as some form of cot rather than a bed and certainly didn't look comfortable. A lumpy dirty mattress covered the slats. Alongside it sat an old wooden chest with a large solid lock. Liz sighed with disappointment looking at the chest. She could not imagine it would be easy to find a way to open it. After a bit of fiddling it became clear that the chest wasn't locked. With a bit of leverage on the hinges it became clear that it may well open to reveal its contents.

Liz decided to take the chest down to the kitchen to use natural light to help investigate the contents. The chest was heavy and it took a fair amount of effort to ease it into the bedroom and then manhandle it downstairs. Liz was excited at the thought of delving into the past and at the same time felt a little guilty at probing into someone else's belongings. With reverence she carefully extracted the items one by one and examined them with fascination.

Packed at the top of the chest was a brown linen dress with a white pinafore. It appeared to be adult size and the style looked Victorian in period. It was worn in places which indicated it was not the owners Sunday best but the workhorse of everyday life. Beneath the dress was a pair of wooden clogs. The clogs seemed to fit with the style of clothes. They were chipped and worn well in places. The final piece within the chest was a beautiful knitted shawl. The shawl looked out of place as it had been made for a baby rather than as an accessory for an adult. Liz unpacked the shawl admiring the workmanship. It had been made with a great deal of love and effort both with the design and completion. Liz was no expert on handcrafts but could appreciate the intricate stitches which made up the border around the shawl. Tassels of wool, similar to pompoms finished off the design.

The chest was lined with a course sacking type material which appeared to be designed to protect the contents from the rough wood. As Liz ran her hand around the inside of the chest she felt a lump within the lining which she could tell wasn't part of the chest structure. She tried to find a break in the lining to investigate further but without success. Finding her sharpest kitchen knife, she gently made an incision in the fabric against the crease of the chest and managed to slit it open far enough to work her fingers into the gap. Inch by inch she moved her fingers along the bottom of the chest towards the lump until she managed to prise the object out through the slit. It was some sort of notebook. Although as Liz examined it further the term notebook was too modern a viewpoint. In reality it was a bundle of papers which were tied together with a piece of string. The papers looked in reasonably good condition despite their age. The notepad was made up of sheets of paper of random sizes as if the owner had grabbed paper when available and had formed it into a makeshift book.

Liz gasped as she looked at the front of the bundle and saw the name Sarah Cozen, the year of our Lord 1861.

"Sarah Cozen", Liz said out loud despite the absence of an audience. "Now that's confusing. I was hoping it would say Sarah Whiting. Oh, hang on". Liz quickly pulled open her special drawer in the kitchen which she was using to file the work both she and her mother had started, tracing the previous occupants of Crown House. As she worked her way through the papers the realisation hit her that Sarah was using her true father's name rather than the name on her gravestone which belonged to her mother's second husband.

Liz was excited and nervous at the same time as she gazed at the papers in front of her. This was an amazing find and could open up the secrets of why Sarah's presence remained in the house. The enormity of reading this story felt a heavy responsibility for Liz to burden. She felt that she was intruding on another person's private thoughts. She had strong principles about her own children's privacy and would not snoop in their personal belongings.

She had built her relationship with Rebecca, Joanne and Harry on total trust and expected her daughters and son to share any concerns they had rather than expect their Mum to find out by default. This approach had appeared to work well as both Joanne and Harry would share their troubles and aspirations with their parents especially when they needed help. She was sure there were some secrets they kept to themselves but let's face it, they were young adults and probably didn't want Mum and Dad to know everything.

Just at that moment Liz's thoughts were interrupted by the shrill of the phone. Shaking her head to bring herself back to reality, Liz reached out to grab the handset to find it was her newest friend, Christine calling.

"Liz, lovely to catch you in," Christine started the conversation. "I'm just putting a rich hot Columbian on the stove and I wondered if you fancy sharing it with me." Christine giggled at her double entendre. She encouraged Liz to drop everything and make the walk round to meet up with her.

CHAPTER TWENTY ONE

Within minutes Liz was knocking on the vicarage door holding a Tupperware box crammed with homemade biscuits. Christine was a sucker for anything sweet. Liz had developed a passion for baking but was conscious not to gorge on her produce if she wanted to keep her figure as she got older. A moment on the lips meant a lifetime on the hips in her opinion. The children and Giles were always on some form of health kick so any time that Liz could palm of her wares to a friend was appreciated by all the family. It took temptation away from them.

The two women embraced and kissed each other on the cheek as they wondered through to the vast kitchen. The centre piece of the room was a double Aga in racing green which was permanently switched on. It was the main source of heat and water for the huge vicarage. The kitchen was warm and inviting. The ambiance of the room was chaos; a mess of pots and pans intermingled with seedlings and plant pots. It was extremely disorganised which represented Christine's approach to domestic chores.

With the coffee poured and biscuits shared out the friends took a seat at the oak kitchen table which ran down the centre of the room. Mabel the wolfhound settled her large grizzled head onto Liz's lap and she unconsciously started to stroke her ears. Liz and Christine fell naturally into conversation exchanging stories of their summer breaks. Christine and her husband John had been to Southern Ireland with their camper van, so there were many amusing stories to tell.

"I've got something super exciting to tell you Christine." Liz waited for the holiday conversation to be exhausted before launching into her activity in the secret room. "I have spent the morning in this storage room linked to our bedroom. It's a really mysterious space as it wasn't on the plans when we got the house. I'm thinking we may develop it into a dressing room or something."

Christine could see the excitement on her friend's face.

"Anyway, the exciting news is that once I had fought off the army of spiders and cobwebs I found this old chest and in the lining of it I found what looks like a diary. I was just starting to look at it when you rang."

"Whoo, stop for breath," laughed Christine. "So, who is the diary owner? Any clues?"

"On the front it has the name Sarah Cozen but I think her real name is Sarah Whiting and she lived in the house when it was a pub in the 1860s. The diary is dated 1861. When me and Mum were looking around the graveyard before our holiday, I found her grave. If I remember rightly she died in 1861. She was only 18 years of age." Liz tucked her hair behind her ears as she picked up her coffee cup and took a refreshing mouthful.

"Oh gosh, that's young. Even for Victorian times that doesn't feel natural. Something must have happened to take her before she had much of a life. Do you know what? Why don't we have a shifty through the parish record books and see if we can find her. I know that vicars around here have a tradition of making an annotation in the record books as to the cause of death and it usually aligns to the death certificate."

Christine led Liz into the library which was dominated by an impressive bookcase across one wall. Large ledger books covered in deep red leather bindings stood in uniform position across the bookcase. Each one bore markings confirming the period of years it related to. At first glance the books appeared to go back for at least two hundred years. Reading her thoughts, Christine explained that the older records were kept in a less organised manner. Those records were in a more haphazard format. Fortunately, there was little call to access any older documents. The tradition of binding the parish documents and recording the detail of the death certificate commenced in 1800 when a new vicar had joined the parish who was an absolute stickler for order. His foresight was to prove invaluable to Christine and Liz.

After a period of browsing through the volumes, Christine found what she had been looking for and heaved the volume onto the impressive wooden writing desk which was positioned under the bay window. The desk positioning had been chosen for the beautiful natural light which shone across it in a pool of brilliance. Turning the pages with reverence, Christine reached the year 1861. After some careful examination of the detailed and ornate handwriting, she found what they were after.

"There we have it," she pointed excitedly to the entry in the ledger. "Sarah Whiting died 17th April. The cause of death is indicated as puerperal fever. Now that's very interesting," she exclaimed.

"Why interesting?" asked Liz as she leant over Christine's shoulder to look at the writing.

"Puerperal fever is the medical term for childbed fever. I don't understand why you would find this sort of language in a local village record. It's a bit over the top don't you think?" Christine looked across at Liz as they both examined the detail. "I wonder whether the doctor was trying to protect the young lady's memory or the family's reputation. She's clearly an unmarried mother. I know, let me check the births for that time period and see if we can see anything relevant there."

A further investigation of the ledger showed no evidence of a child born to Sarah Whiting. However, it did appear that a baby was born to Mary Whiting a few weeks before her daughter died. That infant had been a boy child named Jack.

"The mystery deepens then," sighed Liz as she took photos on her phone of the relevant pages. "Sarah seems to have been pregnant and dies from a fever contracted after the birth but there is no baby. Nothing registered as a birth or even a death. Could it be that the boy Jack was Sarah's baby but taken on by her mother to hide the shame of her daughter?" The plot deepened. "Hmmmm I think my next step is to have a read of the papers I found and see if there are any clues in that. I'll give you a shout once I have found out anything more and we can try and join up the dots on this one. I am so intrigued to understand what that poor girl must have gone through in her short life."

Liz's head was churning with thoughts as she strolled home. She was amazed that they had found such a detailed level of information over recent weeks but at the same time there were far too many gaps in their knowledge. She was intrigued about Sarah and determined to uncover her mystery. She instinctively knew the mystery was linked to their home.

Liz was snuggled into the cosy armchair in the conservatory later that evening. The children were in bed and Giles was watching a car show on the TV while supping a late night scotch. After the hectic evening rush, it was nice to enjoy the quiet ambience of the country. Occasionally the security light in the garden would come on as some local wildlife wandered across the lawns.

Liz picked up Sarah's journal. She was excited to start to delve into the material. She had been thinking about it all evening. Selfishly she didn't want to share the experience with the rest of the family. She wanted to keep the story to herself for now. Feeling an affiliation with Sarah, Liz wanted to keep her to herself for as long as she could. Only once Sarah's life and most importantly her death could jump from the page, would she share those secrets with those closest to her.

Liz turned the front page of the document and delved into the past.

"My name is Sarah Cozen. People know me as Whiting but that's not my real name. My father was John Cozen and he was a wonderful man. He was kind and gentle and we were a happy family. That all changed when I was nine years old. My life really ended then. My dearest father died. He got sick and died within a few days. Our world shattered. My mother went to pieces with grief. She was alone in the world with three small children. I have a brother Tom who was four at the time and baby Hannah was only two years of age.

My mother was running the inn and trying to look after us children. It was always going to happen that a new man would come into our family. A woman cannot run a business like ours on her own. She needs a master of the house. But why him? Oh yes, he was a charmer when he first started to walk out with mother. She was too easily led and before we knew him well enough, they were wed.

Mother had more babies with him. I now have two new sisters Anne and Emma and a brother Arthur. I love my new brother and sisters. Anne is a beautiful child. We all believe she was a gift from the angels to bring some peace to this household. When he gets angry and hits out with his fists, Anne can bring him back from the brink. She smiles sweetly and he is in her hands. She is an angel who tries to protect us all from his nasty ways.

But she couldn't protect me.

That monster took my childhood away from me. He took me. He hurt me and kept hurting me for months. I cannot tell mother as he told me that if I do then he will hurt Hannah next. And now I am with child. With his child. I am shamed. My life is over. And what hurts me the most is that my mother thinks I am evil. She does not know the man she is married to. How do I protect my sister? When this is over for me then he will want another little bud to deflower. What will happen to Hannah when that happens?"

A tear rolled down Liz's face as she finished reading. The intense pain of that poor girl radiated from the page. Reading the first few pages of the journal was already starting to join up the dots around the mystery of Sarah.

Liz dissolved into sobs as she grieved for the girl. Life is so cruel, she thought. The grief for Rebecca came flooding back like a wave. She understood why Sarah was coming through to her. The pain of her situation held such similarities with Rebecca. Both girls had been taken before their time; both girls had been violated by monsters.

As she sat there in quiet contemplation, Liz sent her thoughts and prayers across the years to Sarah. "You poor darling. I understand your pain and I want to help you rest in peace. Show me how I can help you depart this place and join your family."

Suddenly a heady smell of flowers filled the space surrounding Liz. It enfolded her in its aroma. The scent lingered for a few moments then dissipated.

The smell gave Liz comfort. She smiled as she thought about Sarah and the bond they were developing over the years.

Liz felt humbled that she had been chosen to help this poor girl. She was filled with determination. She would not stop until she had uncovered the mystery of Sarah Cozen.

CHAPTER TWENTY TWO – FEBRUARY 1861

Sarah struck the tinder box and fed the flame to the stub of candle.

She groaned as she realised that the candle nub would not see her through the hours of darkness. Once the house was still for the night, she would make her way down to the kitchen to find a fresh batch of candles to keep her going.

As she got heavier with child it was much more challenging to make her way down the stairs and to move around the house without making a noise. She had practised to find those steps which cried out with an ear-splitting creak when stepped upon. She had a picture in her mind of the route she needed to take to keep her presence unknown to her brothers and sisters. She would only venture out once her stepfather was snoring deeply as she had no desire to run into him.

Sarah liked to let herself out into the garden and spend time gazing up at the wonders of the star filled sky. As her current circumstances meant that she needed to keep silent during the day light hours she had adjusted her habits to that of a night owl. She would wander the silent house occasionally doing small household chores to help her mother out. When there was no work for her, she would hunker down in the kitchen beside the range for warmth while she worked on the baby shawl she was knitting.

The shawl was being fabricated with love. Over the last few months, Sarah had fallen in love with the tiny being growing in her belly. It was not the child's fault that its father was a monster. Sarah was absolutely determined that this child would be loved even if she could not acknowledge its existence. She would love the child from arms distance. She would maintain the pretence of sisterhood but would love the child with a mother's passion. Sarah knew she would protect it with her own life and if the child was a girl she would ensure that no man would abuse her beloved daughter. Should it be a male child then she would teach her son to grow into a man who respected women and treated them as gentle souls who should be loved and cared for.

Sarah cracked open the door into her parents' bedroom and listened intently to the sounds coming from the heavy wooden bed. Once she was satisfied that both parents were deeply asleep, she pushed against the door and tip toed from the room. On her stockinged feet she made her way down to the kitchen and reached her chilled hands out to the fire in the range.

The days had been so cold recently and all she had for warmth was an old blanket which she curled herself into for a crumb of comfort. The old pallet bed she slept on during the day did not give her much comfort. The mattress was hard and lumpy and with the size of her belly she struggled to find a place to ease her aching bones. To add to that, the cold wind blew in under the eaves, with icicles forming and dripping their cold liquid on her as she dozed.

As she settled herself down on her mother's rocking chair, she stretched her feet towards the stove and grimaced. The pain tingled as her feet started to defrost. She spotted her mother's work basket and noticed a pile of socks which needed darning. Lighting the kitchen lamp from her candle flame she got to work mending the numerous holes. These jobs allowed the night-time to pass as she kept herself busy. She knew that her mother needed the help as she too became heavy with child. Hannah had taken over many of Sarah's duties in the inn and supported Mary with the monthly washing duties. Sarah's contribution to the household was missed and she worried about the impact on her mother. Mary was carrying her seventh child. Sarah felt exhausted carrying her first so could only imagine the strain Mary Whiting's body was feeling.

Once the pile of socks had been completed and neatly folded ready for the morning, Sarah pushed herself out of her chair and made her way into the room Jack did his accounts. The rest of the family were refused entry to Jack's domain but her night-time adventures had driven her into the room to explore. Over the weeks holed up in the storeroom she had used her nights to examine the books for the farm and inn. Jack was making a decent living. She was filled with a passionate anger that her mother wasn't aware of his finances and certainly wasn't seeing the benefits of the income. Mother had never been close to the financial side of running the inn and had allowed Jack to take over from where John had left off. One day she would let it slip to her mother and try and galvanise her into action.

Unfortunately, she doubted her mother had the courage to confront her husband.

One of the additional benefits of snooping in Jack's desk was paper. Sarah was squirrelling away a piece or two every night for her secret project. She had started to write a journal. Sarah knew the risks of childbirth and she wanted to leave a record of her experience so that she could protect her sisters. She was unsure whether she could ever tell her mother what had happened to her. If her courage failed her journal would perhaps make her mother think about Hannah's welfare and protect her until she could leave home and find a man of her own.

She delved into Jack's drawers and found the precious parchment supply. She smiled as she thought about whether Jack had any idea why his paper supply was dwindling. She had been careful to leave no evidence of her night-time thieving. The parchment was mixed into piles of good quality and a rougher version. Sarah was careful to take the lesser quality material which would not raise as many concerns if the pile seemed to decrease in volume.

Carefully Sarah folded the parchment and slipped it into her apron pocket for later. She had taken to spending the time after breaking her fast to capture her thoughts in her journal. Once the noise of the house lessened, as Jack and her brother left for work and the younger children headed off to the village for school, Sarah would try to get into a comfortable position and sleep. Most days she would manage to sleep until her mother would come to see her with food from the supper table.

It was a thankless existence at present but Sarah understood that this sacrifice would enable her to continue her life without the shame of an unwanted baby. She knew the pretence would protect her and her baby from the consequences of her stepfather's action. Mary would love the baby as her own and the story would be circulated that Mary had given birth to twins.

The one decision that she and her mother had not yet discussed was how they would hide Sarah's baby until such time as Mary went into labour. Mary believed that she was due after Sarah's birth time so there was a need to hide the truth for some weeks. Sarah was concerned about the need to keep a new-born quiet. Her mother seemed to be confident that she had ways of making her baby come early to avoid the problem. Despite Sarah being with child, her mother was unwilling to share the knowledge learnt over six previous live births and a number of still births. She continued to admonish Sarah about her foolishness when she asked questions; accusing her of being too innocent to know the wiles of mothers.

From the kitchen, Sarah heard the chime of the clock which indicated it was the fifth hour. Her mother and father would soon be rising for the day. Sarah quickly moved back into the kitchen to clear up signs of her activity and slowly crept up the main stairs towards her mother's bedchamber. Once she was back in the room under the eaves, she carefully unfolded the parchment and using a knitting needle pushed a hole in the top left-hand corner. The journal was held together with a thick piece of twine and Sarah added her latest find to the growing book.

She could hear the sounds of her mother and Jack rising. Jack relieved himself in the chamber pot knowing full well that his wife would be clearing up his mess. He could have easily waited to use the outside privy, thought Sarah. Another example of the attitude of the man who did not consider his wife's wellbeing despite her being huge with the consequences of his rutting.

Before the rest of the house rose to break their fast, Mary would come and visit with Sarah to bring her bread and ale. Her primarily reason was to check on her well-being and to see if there were any outward signs of the child coming. Sarah lived for this period of the day. She missed seeing her brothers and sisters but it was her mother's company she valued the most.

Theirs had been a difficult relationship since her father had died. Mary knew that her eldest daughter did not approve of her choice in second husband. The current situation had made the two women rediscover a friendship and warmth between them. Whilst the time was snatched, it was possible to share news of the family.

Mary arrived soon after she had risen, carrying a small jug of weak ale and a husk of bread and dripping. The two women sat side by side on the pallet bed as Sarah chewed at her breakfast and Mary spoke softly sharing her news.

"I really don't know what has got into your sister Hannah." Mary showed her anxiety as she turned the conversation to Sarah's beloved sister.

Sarah's ears pricked up, suddenly fully focused on her mother's conversation. "Why what's the matter with her now?" she asked.

"I don't really know as she won't tell me what's troubling her. She has been sullen and moody over recent days. I know she is working hard in the bar each night on top of the help she gives me in the house, but I cannot get a kind word from her. She has been really stubborn with your father too. She just seems to snipe at him every time they are together."

"Perhaps it's all getting too much for her, mother. She probably misses my company and doesn't feel like she has anyone to share the burden of work with."

Sarah tried to make little of her Mother's concerns when inside her stomach was jumping in hoops. Could Jack have passed his unwanted attention onto her younger sister? Hannah was only eleven years old and barely had the shape of a woman. She had not started her courses yet and whilst she was doing the work of a full grown woman, she was still a little girl at heart.

"Mother, try and coax her to speak about what is troubling her. I hate to think of her suffering without her big sister to help her out. Perhaps she is being troubled by the changes in her body as she grows up. She may be too embarrassed to broach the subject with you and may need you to ask her questions to get her to talk. Oh god why am I stuck up here when my sister needs my help," Sarah sighed heavily, thinking about Hannah.

"I will try," groaned Mary thinking about another burden she had to shoulder.

When her mother had left to wake the rest of the house, Sarah fell into a deep melancholy. Her mind raced ahead thinking about her precious sister and the concern that the monster had turned to her. Surely, he would not risk touching another of his stepchildren, she thought. With her mother heavy with child and Sarah in a similar condition, Jack would be without female company. He had an unhealthy appetite. Surely, he would not find a child attractive? Would he have not learnt his lesson by now?

Sarah picked up her journal and started to share her thoughts with her secret diary. Now it was more important than ever to make sure that her sister understood the risk of being alone with her stepfather. Sarah had to save her beloved sister from the shame and disgrace she faced. If she found out that the beast had touched Hannah then Sarah would have no option but to share the knowledge with her mother.

It would break her heart.

A heartbroken mother had to be better than further abuse. Sarah wrote on. The pen travelled across the page with speed as she opened her thoughts onto the parchment with passion and anger.

CHAPTER TWENTY THREE

"OMG, Mum, I love the fact you don't work anymore," exclaimed Harry as he stuffed another piece of chicken into his mouth. "I'm not saying that we didn't eat well before. Of course." He grinned at his mother. "This chicken is to die for."

"Ah sweetie, flattery will get you far in life." Liz smiled as she enjoyed the praise. She got as much pleasure out of cooking as her family did from eating it. She knew that cooking was giving an outlet to her energies which normally she would have thrown into her professional work. She loved sourcing new recipes and was keen to try something new each week. Having the time to plan out menus and ensure that the family was getting a good balanced diet gave her a purpose. She didn't miss work at all but she had a deep-seated need to add value to the family unit and enjoyed their recognition of her skills.

"And most importantly, Mum, I am so happy to see you smiling again." Jo reached across the table and squeezed her mother's hand with affection. "Your smile reaches your eyes too. You know, I think we have got our mum back at last."

"Oh darling," Liz gulped "stop it. You will have me in tears in a minute. I am so incredibly lucky to have such wonderful children. Truly blessed. It's been a dreadfully hard time but I think we are starting to come out the other side. This house and the countryside are healing us all."

Giles had kept quiet up to this point watching his children supporting their mother. He had noticed the changes in Liz. She seemed to be more at peace than she had for months. He had found her singing the other day as she dragged the hoover around. That was a sound he hadn't heard for ages and it gave him immense pleasure. He knew that she still had sleepless nights. He had followed her downstairs many a night to observe her pacing the dark rooms almost searching for something. Perhaps the time was coming to broach the subject of grief counselling with Liz.

He had spoken to Malcolm in confidence who had shared some really useful insight. Liz needed to be ready to let go of the all-consuming grief before counselling could really help her. Malcolm had explained that Giles should not force her to get help but reassure her and lead her gently towards support. Liz had to be ready to talk before she would get any benefit from the experience. Until then she would not be receptive to understanding coping mechanisms which would help her sleep better and relax more fully. She also needed some help to let her two younger children spread their wings in due course especially when they made the decision to go to university like their older sister.

Despite what happened to Rebecca both parents would have to accept that they couldn't protect their children from all the dangers in life. It was going to be difficult to let them fly but it was an important rite of passage for the teenagers. Giles knew that Liz was getting some tangible benefits from her relationship with Christine. More formal professional support from Malcolm could enhance the strides she had already made.

Liz was enjoying life again. She loved spending time with Jo and Harry during the week; not just running them around as a taxi service. She had organised regular trips out for them as family to spend quality time together. Weekends were now packed with family fun.

Last weekend they had made a trip to the coast. A long walk along Holkam beach had led to a game of chase as they all darted in and out of the sea. By the end of the day they were wet and covered in sand but they were laughing and taking the mickey out of each other. Yes, Giles thought to himself, this move has definitely helped to start to heal Liz and the rest of the family would heal with her. She didn't realise the impact her emotions had on both her husband and her children. They were like flowers to her sun. When she shone they opened up and came alive.

As the family continued their dinner, Harry and Jo shared their excitement for the swimming meet the following day. Both Liz and Giles were attending. The children were representing their school at county level and both had a good chance to medal. It was the first big competition since Harry and Jo had joined St Mary's and was being held in Kings Lynn. It would be an early start for them as it was due to kick off at 9am.

Once the plans for the following day were agreed, conversation moved onto Liz's investigation into the house.

"Mum tell us a bit more about the journal you found in our secret room. Have you managed to read it all yet?" asked Jo. Her love of social history made the whole story of the house fascinating to learn about. She couldn't wait for her mum to finish the journal so that she could have a read of it herself.

"It is interesting stuff darling. The more I read, the more I get hooked on trying to understand the family who lived here. It's a story of such sorrow too." Liz decided it was time to share a brief outline of the journal's contents. "Sarah who is the author of the journal is the eldest daughter of Mary and Jack Whiting who owned the Crown and Hare inn during the 1860s. At that time this house was a pub and formed part of a farm as well. Well actually Sarah is not the daughter of Jack. Her dad died when she was young and her mother married again to the local farmer. That's why the pub and farm appear to be a joint venture at that stage." Having set the scene Liz could move the story on to the more difficult element of Sarah's life.

"The really horrible part of the story is that the daughter is pregnant and the father is Jack, her own step-father. Reading through the lines, he raped her and threatened her to not to tell her mother."

"Oh god that is dreadful," interrupted Giles. "How can any man want to rape his own child? I don't care that she is his stepdaughter. It's family. Men like that don't deserve families." Giles was shocked as he contemplated the depths of sorrow for that poor girl.

"That's sick," winced Harry. "How can you want to do that to your daughter? I have so many friends who have step-dads and you just can't imagine them having those sorts of perverted views." Harry shook his head with disbelief as he considered what had happened to Sarah who was not much older than his own sister.

"I know. It's really distressing." Liz continued the story. "It looks like Sarah was holed up the secret room over the staircase during the latter part of her pregnancy. While she's hiding away she seems to be writing the journal. Not sure why but it is proving an interesting support to my investigation. Hopefully it's filling in some of the gaps."

"How can she be hiding in the house without her mother knowing what's going on?" asked Jo, with a frown. She was trying to contemplate the lengths Sarah had gone to in hiding her condition from the outside world.

"That's what makes it even more upsetting. It sounds like her mum knows about the pregnancy but doesn't seem to have a clue who the father is. In those days it would be totally unacceptable for a girl to have a baby outside of marriage. It seems Sarah's mother is also pregnant at the same time. In the journal she states that her mum has agreed to pass the babies off as twins. I guess that's why Sarah is being hidden so that they can keep the pretence going. There's not much left to read but the bit I have got up to is where she is trying to decide whether to tell her mother who the father is. I think she is really scared that her sister may be the next victim of her evil step-father."

"Oh god how dreadful. I just can't imagine what she must be going through," said Jo thoughtfully. "Thinking of Sarah's mum and her situation, I guess in those days you wouldn't really get divorced if your husband did something like that," stated Jo. "It would be a dreadful situation to be in, knowing your husband had abused your child but not being able to do anything about it."

It was hard to view this story of the past through the lens of modern values and behaviours. Even with changing times and cultural differences, it was a shocking example of child abuse. A stepparent abusing the power of parental control to abuse a young girl under his protection.

"No, I don't suppose divorce was an option. The shame of it would be too great. And don't forget the man was in charge in those days. Sarah's mum would probably be kicked out of her home with her children if she tried to leave her husband," explained Liz. "Totally unfair but that was how it was in Victorian times. Women didn't have any real independence from their husbands and I guess abuse could easily be covered up." Liz reflected on the open and honest relationship she had with Giles. She could not imagine being subservient to her partner or that Giles would be happy in such circumstances. Her husband interrupted her thoughts.

"So how does this all fit into the information you and Christine found in the parish records," asked Giles. He was becoming more intrigued about the history of their home. He also valued the positive impact this investigation was having on Liz's state of mind. She seemed so driven and positive in her search for the truth.

"Well I think it's starting to come together but there are still a number of outstanding questions. There are so many loose ends which I'm not sure I can get from the diary or the records. Some days I wish I could just sit down with Sarah and ask her what happened. Although that is pretty wacky especially as she has been dead for over 150 years." Liz had not told her family about the unexplained smells and noises she had felt in the house. She didn't want to think that was all part of her highly suggestive imagination. It had been weeks since she had felt anything significant so was trying to put that to the back of her mind.

"I found out that Sarah died in April 1861 but there is no record of a baby born to her. I think there wouldn't be any physical record as the plan had been to pass it off as her mother's child. Her death certificate shows she died of a fever after childbirth so perhaps the baby died at the same time. But the strange thing is that there are no records of its birth or death. There is no record of twins growing up in the household after Sarah's death so it's a real mystery. What happened to the baby?" Liz put into words the issue which had been troubling her for days.

"That's so sad," sighed Jo. "To cope with your step-dad raping you then carry a baby in secret only to die in the end. Life can be so cruel, especially for women". Jo was a firm champion of feminism and had already set up an action group within her year group to discuss women's rights. She was interested in pursuing this focus on gender equality as part of her studies at university.

"Things have progressed so much for women since those days although there is more to do," agreed Liz. "I cannot imagine a life where you are totally at the mercy of a man; unable to make decisions about your future or your children and in many cases just a breeding machine. Popping out baby after baby until your body is wrecked. Me and your dad are a partnership. We decide important things together and I cannot imagine your dad ever telling me what to do."

Giles laughed as he responded. "Actually, your mum is the boss around here and don't you ever forget that kids. To be fair if I ever tried to tell your mum what to do, she would probably do the opposite out of spite." The family shared a moment of laughter as they tried to envisage their mum being under Giles's thumb. It just wouldn't happen.

"On a more serious note though," Jo tried to bring the conversation back to the investigation. "You said Sarah's mother had a baby boy around the time of Sarah death. She called him Jack which feels strange after what his name sake did to her daughter."

"Mum, could that baby be Sarah's baby? What if her own baby died and she took on her daughter's?" asked Harry. Her son threw another curved ball into the equation.

Liz paused for a moment before she continued as she considered Harry's suggestion. "That's the trouble. There are far too many unanswered questions and I don't know how you get to the answers. The truth is buried in the past and without that oral testimony we can only guess at what happened. I will finish the journal off and I have promised to lend it to Christine so that she can have a read of it. Between the two of us we may be able to make some sensible assumptions. I guess that's all we will get to. Some calculated assumptions about what might have happened."

"Well I think it's all really interesting, darling." Giles was in the process of clearing the dishes from the table and paused to rub his hands across Liz's shoulders. "Now let's get this kitchen cleared up kids. How about a film afterwards? I guess we should all get an early night with the swimming meet

CHAPTER TWENTY FOUR

"On your marks," the starter called them to their starting positions.

As the gun fired, Jo dived into the water and glided under water for a number of seconds. Her lungs were bursting with heat as she hit the surface of the water and pulled the air deep into her body. She moved smoothly into the crawl. The movement of her head from underwater to left then right as she pulled in breath to power her arms and legs. She moved with the poise and gracefulness of a dolphin through the water. There was hardly any splash in the pool as she reached the far end and flipped over to push away from the wall.

Jo could sense the presence of her main contender to her right side. She glanced across to see the distance between the two favourites for the 100-metre crawl. She could see Jenny was an arm's length ahead of her. She dug deeper as she raised her stroke rate. She could feel that her smooth movement was becoming a bit ragged and her heart seemed to be pounding as the blood rushed to her arms and legs. She could see the end of the pool rushing towards her as she put every last ounce of energy into kicking towards the end. Stretching her fingers out, she touched the wall as she threw her body forward.

Everything went quiet for a few seconds as the rest of the contestants reached the end of the race. Jo looked over at Jenny who was frantically looking to the electronic board for the result. It seemed an eternity before the name Joanne Stamford winner flashed onto the screen. Jo screamed with delight and punched the water with her hands in delight. She looked out to the audience to find Mum and Dad to share her delight. She could see Giles and Liz jumping up and down waving their arms around so figured they were pretty happy with her achievement.

"Well done, Jo," shouted Jenny over the noise of the crowd. "That was bloody close though. I thought I had you at the 50-metre mark so god knows how you managed to beat me." Jenny was drooped over the lane divider as she tried to recover from the furiously fast race. This new girl was fast. Jenny had never faced such competition in recent years. Perhaps she had become complacent being the favourite for so long.

"Thanks Jenny. It was too close to call so probably just fingertips between us. I feel absolutely knackered. It took everything I had to win that one so well done you too." The girls embraced across the lane divider. Jo was a good sport and her humble attitude would not allow her to gloat over her achievement.

Jo received the congratulations of the other swimmers as she pulled herself out of the pool. She sat on the side for a few moments to take in the noise of the clapping and cheering from the crowd. I could get used to this she thought. The adulation of the crowd was something else and made up for the early morning swims before school each morning to try and get herself ready for this event.

Picking up her towel she wrapped herself up and pulled the swimming cap from her head letting her long brown hair flow down her damp back. She had some time before the medal ceremony so fought her way through the milling swimmers towards where her parents were sat. As she got closer to them her mother squealed with delight and grabbed hold of her pulling her into her ample chest. Liz showed little concern for the damp patch forming on her cashmere jumper from Jo's swimming costume.

"Oh my darling, that was amazeballs!" Liz had hold of her cheeks and kissed her soundly on the lips. "That was the best swim I think I have ever seen from you, Jo. It was so close but you did it! I'm so proud of you darling."

Giles muscled in to take hold of her next. "You star," he shouted above the noise of the crowd around them. "I cannot believe you are the fastest in the county. What an achievement. Well done sweetie." Giles gazed around the people sitting alongside them, taking in the adulation for his brilliant daughter.

Jo beamed under their praise. She lapped it up like the cat with the cream. She was over the moon with the win. Her Physical Education teacher had high hopes for her but had told her that she would be fortunate to medal. In hindsight he was trying to take the pressure of her for her first county meet. It had the opposite effect on Jo. It had provided her with further drive to win. And she had nailed it. Not just a medal but a gold one at that.

All of a sudden, Jo felt a thump on her back only to realise it was her brother Harry who had launched himself at her. He was naked from the waist up, just sporting the school standard trunks. His own race was in the next fifteen minutes.

"Wow sis that was fab. You totally blew the favourite out of the water!" he cried. "I can't believe how easy you made that look. She thought she had you. You could tell she started to slow down in the last 10, thinking you were spent. But the way you sped up in the last 10 was amazing. She must have been gutted. Never take a Stamford for granted, eh sis." Harry was virtually bobbing up and down with excitement.

"Cor blimey, that was tough kiddo," sighed Jo as the adrenalin had started to dissipate and weariness came over her. "It took every last bit of energy to stretch out those last few strokes. I really thought she had done enough so it wasn't until they announced the result that I knew I had done it. And now I must pass the challenge on to you my young padawan." Jo gestured as if to pass on the virtual baton to her younger brother. "Go get em kiddo!"

"I'll do my best sis. I will be lucky to medal though as there are some pretty good boys in this race. Most of them are a good year ahead of me so I am just looking to test myself. I don't think I have a chance of a medal." Harry gave his family one of his beaming smiles as he bounded off to the warmup pool to get some last minute practise in. His modesty was not shared by his parents. They were looking forward to another win or at least a medal.

"Miss Stamford," called the umpire. "Medal ceremony in 10 minutes please. If you want to get changed then you best get a wriggle on."

"Ok thanks," shouted Jo as she left her parents and rushed into the changing room to take a quick shower and change into her school tracksuit. She had only just managed to drag a hairbrush through her tangles before she was summoned for the ceremony.

Both parents were bursting with pride to see Jo stand on the podium to receive her gold medal. Smiles stretched wide across their faces as they watched their daughter take a bow to the crowd of onlookers.

Jo stood there with her chest puffed out enjoying the moment with a smile fixed ear to ear. The Mayor of Kings Lynn presented her with her medal and a bunch of dried flowers. Jo looked out at the crowd and focused in on the rest of her school team who were cheering her name. The transition from newbie to school hero was complete, she thought. Her nature was such that she could delight in the momentary hero worship but with the full knowledge that by next week it would be just fish and chip paper gossip.

Once the medal ceremony was over Jo joined her parents to watch Harry's race. As he predicted there were some strong contenders who seemed overly confident as they strutted up to their lane block. Harry gave the crowd one of his cheeky smiles as he stepped onto his block and waved to his family. The crowd took to Harry immediately as they recognised his enthusiasm.

The race started as the swimmers dived into the clear blue pool. Harry was struggling to stay with the favourites. This race was over 200 metres which gave Harry the chance to adjust his stroke, giving him additional power. He had the ability to preserve his energy for the final 50 metres, when others were fading. At the halfway point he was sitting in sixth place which was in line with his coach's expectations. In the second 100 metres he dug deep into his reserves and his pace increased. The lad to his left hand started to fade which gave Harry further confidence as he moved past him. The fourth and third place swimmers were an arms-length ahead and both seemed to be struggling as Harry took the biggest breath in and dunked further under the water. As his face hit the surface once more, a quick glance confirmed to Harry that he was in third place. Ahead of him the two favourites were fighting it out and deep-down Harry knew he couldn't catch them.

Two more strokes and he touched the end of the pool coming in a very credible third place. Harry smacked the water in celebration and then fist bumped Joseph who won the race. He was over the moon with his performance and knew that this would be seen as a big success by his team coach. Today's success would set him up for more first team activity in the months ahead. Jumping out of the pool he almost skipped to the changing rooms full of joy at his performance.

After a quick shower he pulled on his tracksuit and went to find the rest of his family. The meet was over for both him and Jo. Mum had promised that they would find a pub for a spot of lunch on the way home. As he walked towards his family he smiled to himself. Both Mum and Dad looked so relaxed for a change. He was delighted that they were doing things again as a family. It was great to spend time with his parents and he was just pleased to see them enjoying life again.

His Mum was glowing. There seemed to be something special going on with her and he would love to know what the secret was. She looked different. There was lightness in her face. The worry lines which had seemed to be a feature for so long had gone. Her eyes seemed to have come alive again.

All is good, smiled Harry.

CHAPTER TWENTY FIVE

The volume of numerous conversations hit them like a wave as Giles opened the door into the village hall and ushered his wife in ahead of him. The noise was deafening. The hall was teaming with people all finding their tables and jostling for prime position near the front. Giles scanned the room looking for Malcolm and Joyce and found them towards the back of the hall. As they made their way through the throng, they stopped to exchange pleasantries with several villagers. Funnily the Stamford family were still seen as the newbies to the village despite them moving in months ago. Most residents, who had lived in the village most of their adult lives, believed a few months didn't count for full resident status just yet.

"Well hi there you two." Malcolm folded Liz in a bear hug as they came across their new friends. "So lovely that you could make it tonight. I hope you have brought your thinking caps with you," he laughed.

Malcolm had the amazing ability to make a person feel at ease immediately and he gave the best hugs. It wasn't just his professional training but a deep human connection with others. He tuned into others emotions and always seemed to know when to nurture, when to listen and when to provide the shoulder to lean on. Giles and Liz knew they had made a friend for life in Malcolm.

Joyce moved in to welcome Giles and Liz with an equally huge hug. The couples settled down to their table rearranging chairs. The noise of chairs scrapping on the floor was now the predominant sound as the crowd started to settle in for the night. Tonight was one of the regular quiz nights held in the village and the first one which Giles and Liz had made it to. It had a reputation for being great fun and a boozy night. Residents were encouraged to bring their own drinks and snacks so the sound of bottles chinking and crisp packets rustling were adding to the noise levels.

The quiz team tables were laid out in a horseshoe approach facing the quiz master at the front of the hall. Teams appeared to be made up of mainly 6 or 7 people and Giles estimated that there must have been nearly 80 people in the room, hence the crescendo of volume. The room seemed to be full to capacity which was good news for the organisers. Quiz entry donations would keep the village hall running for months.

"Its years since we have been to a quiz night," mentioned Giles as he cracked open a can of beer and took a deep gulp. "Is it just the four of us tonight then?" As he spoke Giles scanned the room looking for familiar faces.

"No, we are a six," responded Joyce. "We have some new friends for you to meet. Dave and Sheila live in the cottage right at the opposite end of the village from us. We have known them for years. Dave is a teacher and a font of all wisdom so there is usually a fight to get him on your team. Today is our lucky day as we have grabbed him before anyone else could," she giggled.

As Joyce was telling them of Dave's quizzing skills the couple in question approached their table. Dave was in his early fifties with the stereotypical appearance of a geography teacher, despite the fact that his subject was history. It was clear that he and Joyce bonded over a shared love of the subject. He had ruddy cheeks and a bald head which gleamed under the spotlights. A tall man with a full figure, he wore brown corduroy trousers and his beige shirt was protected by a knitted tank top. By contrast Sheila was small and petite with a well-groomed chestnut bob and trendy jeans and Joules sweatshirt.

Malcolm proceeded to introduce them to Giles and Liz. Both couples relaxed easily in each other's company and conversation flowed as they waited for the quiz to start. Within moments they were chatting about families and their respective jobs with ease. Having Malcolm to facilitate a conversation helped as he orchestrated discussions bringing each person into play with a nod or a question.

The quiz master Sid was a young lad who had a large contingent with him on two tables at the back of the room. Sid was in his early thirties. He was tiny in stature but huge in personality. Full of life and laughter, he held the audience's attention as he set out the rules for the evening. Surprisingly he stunned the room to silence as heads went down and quizzers started to fill out team names on their papers. For a young guy he had the ability to take control of the evening. It was him and his questions which stood in the way of any winners. Sid held the key to that success as he explained the format of the evening. That format included six differing subject rounds and a picture round to be completed throughout the evening.

Round one was a music round. There was a good selection of modern songs and golden oldies. Liz was surprised at how well she contributed to their answers. Whilst their team all whispered their answers across the table in eagerness to be the first to grab the answer, it was mostly Liz who pulled the gem out of the bag. Her eclectic taste in music gave her a broad range of knowledge.

"Wow Liz, you are on fire," shouted Joyce over the surrounding noise. "Music is your round that's for sure." Joyce was celebrating her decision to invite Liz and Giles. A wise choice especially as she had little passion for modern music.

"I reckon that's a clear 10 out of 10," added Sheila. "Next up is the history round and seeing that's Dave's subject we could be onto a win tonight." She turned to Liz as she continued. "It's so lovely to meet you and Giles. I can't believe we haven't run into each other before now."

"Yes, lovely to meet you guys," responded Liz. Liz and Sheila were sitting next to each other and were chatting between rounds exchanging family information. Sid had organised the format so that there were good breaks between the rounds to allow his able assistant Suzie to complete the scores and, of course, to allow the teams to drink and chat. "Joyce told us that Dave is a teacher. What about yourself? Do you work?"

"I run my own business actually," Sheila smiled as she explained her passion. "I have a small shop in Norwich selling wool and all things knitting related. I always loved to knit as a child and when the kids left home I wanted to find something for me. I spent most of our married life at home bringing up our two girls and this just seemed like the perfect opportunity to put my hobby to good use. Do you knit Liz?"

Liz giggled as she remembered her childhood attempts with needles. It had been a disaster to put it politely. "To be honest I tried as a kid but wouldn't know where to start now. I really admire those that can create wonderful things with their hands. I'm not the most practical in that respect." Remembering her recent find she continued, "I must show you this shawl I found in our place. Think it was left by a previous resident. It's so beautifully knitted I'm sure you will appreciate it."

Sheila nodded.

"And to work for yourself, that must be so liberating. Before we moved to Norfolk, I worked in an accountant's office in London organising everyone's lives. It was constant rush and stress. I can't say I miss the job but I do think I will need to find some work even if part time soon." Liz was enjoying the chance to take a career break but knew that sooner or later she would need to stretch her brain cells into a new challenge.

"I do love the independence of running my own business," continued Sheila. "Although it can be stressful at the same time. There is always something that needs doing to keep me on the right side of the law. Whether its tax returns, VAT returns or just doing the books. I am lucky though. It's the sort of business that I can manage on my own and as it's not teaming with customers every hour of the day, I do get the chance to do the paperwork during the day. You must pop in and see that shop when you are next in Norwich." Sheila was hopeful of a new customer. It was never too late to take up the art of knitting and she was passionate about teaching others the basic skills.

"I will do that," smiled Liz. "I am still getting used to the city so would be good to explore some new areas."

Anticipating another new recruit Sheila spotted her opportunity and move in. "The other thing you may be interested in is our weekly hobby craft meeting in the church hall. We meet up on Wednesday afternoons and have a reasonably good attendance from the local villages. We knit and do other crafts and there is always someone on hand to support those new to a discipline. If you fancy learning to knit then I would love to help." Sheila took the opportunity to take out her business card for the shop to share with Liz.

"Whiting's Knitted Wonders, that's a name I have seen before." Liz was racking her brain to connect to the unusual name. "Is that your surname, Sheila?"

"Certainly is. Not the most inventive name for the shop but I thought it had a decent ring to it," she responded.

"Oh of course, I know where I have seen the name before." Liz was excited as she started to share the reason with her new friend. Unfortunately, it was at that point that the next round of the quiz started so their conversation was interrupted for the next 15 minutes.

"Ok Dave, you're up now," laughed Malcolm. "It's the history round. We are playing our joker on this, so no pressure!"

Liz could hardly contain herself as the questions rolled on. Dave was doing a sterling job of answering them so she could sit back and ponder on the questions she wanted to ask of Sheila. As the round concluded, Liz leaned into Sheila to continue their chat.

"So, Sheila, tell me, is the name Whiting a common name for Norfolk as I came across the name in some investigations around our house."

"Well it's not overly common but it has got history in this village. I think Dave can trace his ancestors back for hundreds of years." Sheila lent forward with intent as she was intrigued with what Liz had to share. "Actually, I do believe that one of Dave's family used to own Wood Farm which is behind your house. I think it was his great great grandfather Arthur Whiting if I remember."

"Dave," Sheila shouted across the table to grab her husband's attention. "Scoot over here. We need to pick your brains during the break."

Dave was fascinated to understand the connection between his ancestors and the new family in the village. He vaguely remembered his grandfather talking about the family's standing in the village, being the owners of one of the biggest farms in the area. He also recalled the connection with the old village inn, although he couldn't recall all the information.

"Tell you what," Dave said. "I have a box of old papers in the loft. I am more than happy to lend them to you so you can have a look and see if there is anything of use." Dave had to be honest that despite his love of history he had never invested anytime in his own family history. He'd never even been through the papers from his ancestors, just assuming it was old copies of deeds.

"That's so kind of you, Dave. I would love to take you up on the offer. Let me know when is best for you and I will pop round and pick it up." Liz was virtually bouncing with excitement. Could there be a hidden nugget in that box which would tell her something about Sarah and her family.

Dave knew it would be a bit of a job to find the box in his very untidy loft so agreed to drop it round later the following week. Liz would have to contain her excitement a little while longer.

The quiz carried on for a further four rounds by which time the group were all feeling a bit tipsy. It had been an excellent evening getting to know Sheila and Dave. Malcolm and Joyce were on good form and the evening was filled with laughter. Over the course of the evening the three couples had rotated their seats which gave them all the chance to talk over the crescendo of the quiz night.

Late in the evening Liz found herself sitting next to Malcolm and having a heart to heart. It was amazing that you could hold conversations with the buzz of the activity across the hall but somehow Malcolm found the opportunity to probe Liz on how she was feeling. She was vaguely aware that Giles had spoken to Malcolm about Rebecca which meant she didn't have to go through the awkwardness on both sides of introducing the subject of the death of a child. It was clear from his questions that he understood her struggle to manage leaving her memories of London behind.

"I do feel like I am making steps in the right direction, Malcolm," started Liz. She felt relaxed with this man. Malcolm had an incredible power to relax his friends. It must be one of the reasons why he did the job he did. "I know it's a long journey but I am finding positive thoughts in each day. Before we moved I really felt I was struggling to function on a day to day basis. I think I was sucking the joy out of everyone too so I definitely know that any improvement in me is helping the rest of the family. It's the right thing for all of us."

"I'm so glad to hear that, my dear." Malcolm gently placed his hand over Liz's. "I totally understand if you say no but here goes. Would it help to have a grief counselling session with me? No pressure but I do find that counselling can really support recovery and works especially well once the immediate stage of grief is coming to an end and the person is able to talk about the impact on their life and their family."

Liz took her time to respond as she absorbed the offer. In some ways it felt strange to contemplate talking to Malcolm about her feelings but on the other hand she was feeling ready to examine the turmoil going on inside her. Malcolm was such a gentle man and she felt that his approach would be totally professional despite their newfound friendship. She had talked at length to Christine. However, the discussions with the vicar were those you would share with a friend rather than any form of physiological support.

"I think I would like to try that, Malcolm. I would like to keep it professional though so I am paying you for the session if you don't mind. I could talk to you as a friend but I wouldn't want to abuse that relationship. Does that make sense?" Liz was keen not to offend Malcolm with her response to his offer but at the same time she would not place him in an awkward position around the financial side of his work. Ultimately he did this for a living so she didn't want to call in favours.

"I understand, Liz and I agree that we should deal with this as I would any private client. I know I have a couple of free sessions available next week so let me text you some available times tomorrow and we can go from there."

Malcolm was delighted that Liz had agreed to meet. He would update Giles confidently before they parted that night. Any conversations between them would, of course, remain confidential but he knew that Giles was keen to support his wife and this first step was a big one. Liz would need the help of her husband to take this path.

"Excellent idea, thanks Malcolm. I know this is going to feel a bit strange but I think I'm ready to try," agreed Liz.

She smiled to herself as she thought about what was in front of her. For so long she couldn't even accept that Rebecca had gone. Feeling ready to talk about her feelings with someone outside the family felt like a huge step forward. She had spoken to Christine about her anger and loss but this meeting with Malcolm felt like a momentous turning point in her journey to recovery.

CHAPTER TWENTY SIX

A few days later, Liz perched on the edge of her seat in Malcolm's study as she waited for him to return with the cups of tea.

She felt sick with nerves and was on the cusp of running from the room and forgetting the whole business. Strangely she had felt confident this morning. Giles had been so supportive before he left for work and encouraged her to approach the session with an open mind. As soon as she had left the house the doubts hit her. She felt she was grappling around in the dark trying to find an excuse to cancel.

"Oh, come on Liz, grow a pair." She didn't realise she had actually said that out loud until she heard Malcolm cough outside the door to the study. She blushed at the thought as he entered.

Ever the professional he avoided her eye to allow her time to recover her embarrassment.   Malcolm moved quietly around the room arranging the drinks and sorting out his seat. His method of calming slow movements was designed to create an atmosphere where the counselee could relax.

Liz was close to running out. Fortunately Malcolm's calming influence worked wonders in relaxing her. Gradually she felt herself slipping further back into the cosy chair and crossing her ankles as she stretched her legs out across the carpet.

Malcolm opened a notebook on his lap and cleared his throat as he looked intently at Liz and took in her gradual relaxation. He knew that he would need to take this session carefully if he was to help his patient.

"Liz, I know this is incredibly hard for you and I want to start by thanking you for coming today. I'm sure you had reservations about the session and I want to say at the outset that my role is to support you in understanding your journey through your dreadful loss. If I can do something small to help then that will be the success we both want." He paused. "I'd like you to try and relax. Anything we talk about within this room is totally confidential and will not be shared with anyone else. You have my word that this session is just for us to work through your feelings together."

Liz nodded as she listened intently to Malcolm. She had her hands gripped to the side of the chair and could feel her breath rasping through her lips as she tried to remain calm. She remembered to use her yoga principles, breathing deeply through her nose and expelling through her mouth. Over time she could feel her heart rate settling.

Malcolm's voice was measured and supportive as he coaxed her to open up. "Shall we start by exploring how you currently feel about Rebecca's death, shall we? I understand it's been just over 18 months since that day," started Malcolm as he smiled encouraging at Liz.

Liz took her time before answering, examining her thoughts and putting them in some form of order. She gulped down the bile which was threatening to rise. Taking a sip of tea she swallowed down the acid in her throat.

"Ok. How do I feel? It's hard to explain that Malcolm. There are days when I feel like I have a huge weight on my chest and I just want to scream out loud with pain. But then other days I just feel down and struggle to want to get out of bed in the morning." Liz hated those days when opening her eyes hit her with a wave of memories. "On the good days, I feel calm and contented and can think about all the good things in my life. But on those days I feel incredibly guilty that I'm not feeling sad and it sort of feels like I'm forgetting my baby. Does that sound crazy?" Liz was wringing at her hands in her lap as she paused. She didn't know she was doing it; just a normal reaction to the level of stress she was feeling.

"Liz, that all sounds extremely normal especially as your loss was so unexpected. Murder adds longevity to the stages of grief and does make it more difficult to move through the various stages of grief." Malcolm was keen to talk her through the process. If you could ever envisage grief as a process. "Generally experts believe there are four stages of bereavement. Let me talk you through them, if that's ok?"

Liz nodded in agreement. She was starting to relax even more and found listening to Malcolm quite therapeutic.

"Firstly, there's the acceptance that the loss is real and that the loved one has died. People don't always recognise that this is a specific stage. For many people actually accepting that someone has died is so difficult, especially when someone is taken suddenly. That acceptance will naturally lead to the pain of grief. As you candidly described it, it can be that weight of grief that hurts to your core. The third stage of grief sees the bereaved adjusting to life without the person who has died. The final stage comes when you feel that you are putting less emotional energy into grieving and channelling that into something new. Does that resonate with you?" He waited a moment before continuing. "Do you feel able to talk to me about those stages and where you think you have been and are now?" Malcolm reached across the space between them and took her hand in his to give it a gentle squeeze of encouragement.

Liz remained silent for a few moments as she collected her thoughts. "When we first got the dreadful news of Rebecca's murder, I fell apart. I abandoned Giles to deal with it all. Giles had to identify her body. It must have been hell for him to do that. For him to see our beautiful girl all beaten and cold must have broken his heart." Liz found it hard to imagine the pain of that experience. "I feel dreadful that I let him down in those first few days. I didn't think about his grief or the hurt of my two other beautiful children. I was selfish and could only think about what had been taken from me. She was my firstborn and was so precious to me that I just couldn't think about anyone else."

It was evident that Liz was carrying a huge amount of guilt.

"I don't know that we would have got through the first month without my Mum. She was in pain too. Rebecca was her precious grandchild and she was still suffering from losing my dad to cancer a couple of years before. She took Henry and Joanne and gave them all the love in the world to help them through the trauma."

Liz paused for breath and to collect her thoughts. Malcom decided not to interrupt but allow Liz to continue.

"That first month I just don't really remember much. I think I was on some pretty heavy sedatives. I used to just sit in her room and cry. We couldn't have the funeral for over a month as they needed to gather all the forensic evidence for the court case. I guess we were lucky as they got the bastard within a few days. He had left his calling card all over her beautiful body so the police could catch him quickly." Liz dry sobbed as she thought of the damage that man had done to her beautiful child.

"I think in that first month I was going through the early stage of grief you talked about, Malcolm. I didn't want to accept that she was gone. I wanted to believe it was some sort of nightmare and we would all wake up and it would be over and my little girl would be asleep in her bed. Trouble is that every morning the realisation she was gone came back and hit me smack in the face again." Liz took a deep drink of her tea and glanced over at Malcolm. He smiled again reassuring her and encouraging her to continue.

"I think the funeral was the time when I realised that nightmare wasn't ever going to end. I had to say goodbye to Rebecca. We were so overwhelmed by the love and support which got the whole family through that day. We had some really special friends around us who helped organise the funeral and were a shoulder to lean on during the day. So many of Rebecca's friends from home and from University came to the funeral. It gave me a massive reality check. I think that's when I really realised that it wasn't just me that had lost my daughter. To see the grief and suffering in that church showed me that Rebecca was loved by so many. Her father lost his daughter, Harry and Jo lost their sister, my Mum lost her granddaughter and all these people in the church had lost someone special to them. I do feel incredibly guilty about my behaviour. I let Giles down. I let my kids down and I let my Mum down."

"You have to forgive yourself for that time, Liz," Malcolm interrupted. "There is no set behaviour for grief. It affects us all in different ways. Whilst there is a natural progress through those stages we talked through earlier, there is no standard for how it hits you. There is no model for how to go through it without impacting those around us. From a neutral perspective you may have helped Giles, Jo and Harry deal with their own feelings. They needed to support you and sometimes that need to care for others gives people a purpose which allows them to move more swiftly though the cycle of feelings."

Liz thought on what Malcolm had said. His words hit home as she recognised how her family had pulled together during that period. "I must admit I hadn't thought about it that way, Malcolm. I do see the care and support they wrap around me. It's almost like I can see them watching me;

judging my mood and waiting to pick me up when I fall."

Liz frowned remembering that time.

"After the funeral I tried to get things back to normal for the kids. We fell back into our normal day to day life in the city. I went back to work but I really couldn't deal with it. Giles threw himself into work and probably had the best year ever in his career but it was killing him. The kids worked hard at school and stayed over at friends a lot. Perhaps too much. Perhaps they found it easier being out of the house although their psycho of a mother was constantly checking up on where they were and whether they were safe."

Liz paused.

"Then the trial started. That took over our lives for a month. I sat in that court every day of the trail with my Mum by my side. Giles didn't want to. He came for the verdict but he didn't stop me from going. He was worried about what I would hear. But you see I needed to hear it. It felt like I had to know what Rebecca had gone through, even though it tormented me. I sat through the coroner's report, the forensic evidence; all those intimate details of the damage the rape did to my little baby; and how he smashed her head in with a brick to end her beautiful life." Liz paused for breath as a tear gently fell down her cheek. Malcolm kept the silence as he let her regain her flow of thoughts.

The room was filled with silence as Liz regained her composure. Malcolm had heard some dreadful traumas during his career but this story was rocking him to the core. As a father of a young daughter he struggled to imagine the pain this family had been through.

"It was his eyes that got to me the most. He sat there in that court and just stared at me with piercing blue eyes. They didn't have a crumb of regret in them. He never once apologised for what he did. His only emotion was regret that he got caught. But when he looked at me, it was as if he was sniggering at my pain. He was getting his rocks off seeing me like that. During the trial I was constantly angry. I gave up my job as I just couldn't function. My employers were great but realistically they couldn't let me take that time off to be in court every day. They tried to encourage me to take a sabbatical so I would have something to go back to. I just knew I couldn't go back. Going back was doing all the things we did as a five rather than a four."

Malcolm made encouraging noises without breaking Liz's flow.

"I was a pain to live with as that anger slipped into day to day life. But I needed to channel that anger. It was a way of me accepting that Rebecca was gone. I think I needed to hate her killer. When people talk about forgiveness for those who hurt you I just think that is total bollocks until you have been through what we did. I will never forgive that bastard and if I could have half hour in prison with him, I would stick a knife in his heart without hesitation. I just hope he rots in hell for what he did."

"I guess he was found guilty eventually," asked Malcolm. He was not shocked by her reaction to Rebecca's killer. To some extent he could empathise with her views. "How did that make you feel? When the verdict came in?"

Liz was back at the end of the court case in her mind. She could see the judge summing up, the jury returning their decision and the tears of pain from the family as they witnessed the end of the case.

"I accepted the verdict although if it was still legal, I would have called for the death penalty for his crime. He got life but in reality he could be up for parole in 15 years' time. That's not enough. In 15 years my Rebecca could have been a mother herself. She had her life ahead of her and he took it. For that he gets 15 years of tax-free living at her Majesty's pleasure. That's not justice is it?" groaned Liz.

"I understand how you feel, Liz. I guess the punishment doesn't fit the crime especially from a mother's point of view. That's why I think the grief of losing a child is magnified when murder is involved. It makes it so much more difficult to accept the loss and to get through the pain of loss. Do you feel comfortable if we move on now? Can you tell me why you and Giles decide to uproot the family and move to Norfolk?" asked Malcolm, keen to move the conversation on from the anger of the murder trial.

Liz recognised the transition to discussing a happier time. She was ready to talk about the future. With honesty she started to explain the rationale for uprooting the family to Norfolk.

"We talked long and hard as a family about the decision. The children were involved as we were asking a great deal of them. They were giving up their friendship groups and school to move so it was important that they had a say in the decision. As a family we agreed that a new home was what we needed to repair our family unit. The memories in the London home were sad ones. The sad memories just ate into the happy times and I think we knew we couldn't stay there. When we talked about moving house it just seemed natural to want to move away from London and try and find a different pace of life. It was so hard for me to leave Rebecca's bedroom behind. I'm sure it was the same for the rest of the family. It does feel illogical as Rebecca was no longer there. But I could still smell her in that room. Every time I sat in there it felt like I was picking at a blemish. I was opening up the pain and anger. I had to let her go. Moving house isn't about forgetting Rebecca but about moving on as a new family without her. Does that make sense or does it sound harsh?" asked Liz.

They had reached the crutch of Liz's problem. She wanted to live again after her daughter's murder but felt guilty. She needed to forgive herself and learn to live her life to the full without her precious daughter. Malcolm was optimistic that she was ready to do that.

"No that doesn't sound harsh, Liz. It's probably something that many families do. It can be hard to start anew in a fresh town but at least all your new friends don't carry around the knowledge of what you guys have been through as a family. You can be accepted as the family unit you are now. So, I can really understand how this has been a good step in your journey to recovery. Having not seen you at your worst time, it's hard to judge, but you do look more at peace since the first day we met. Is the move the catalyst for that change?"

Liz thought long and hard before answering.

"I think so, Malcolm. I think we are all happier. The kids are blossoming at their new school and have settled into new friendship groups. Giles is just Giles. He loves his work and I guess working from home with that beautiful garden is a blessing."

Malcolm interrupted her flow. "What about you, Liz? You have spoken about the rest of the family but how do you feel?" scrutinised Malcolm.

Liz smiled as she thought about his question. "I feel happy again. I can see joy in each day. I still have the pain which is ever present but there are more days that are good than bad. When you talked about the final stage of grief about spending more time on positive stuff rather than thinking about the pain, that really resonated with me. I have thrown myself into my investigation of the house. I think that has given me a purpose; almost like a new job."

Malcolm was aware that Liz had started to show interest in the history of the house and the village and was keen to understand more about how this interest was helping her accept and move on with her life. "Tell me more about your investigations and how you think that's helping you," he asked.

Liz talked to Malcolm about the story of the family she was working on and how Sarah's journal was adding more fabric to the story. "I think I can feel Sarah in the house."

It was at this suggestion that Malcolm raised his hand to stop Liz's dialogue. "I really would like to explore that comment. What do you mean by the word feel? Are you seeing a presence?"

"Oh god. I do hope you won't laugh at me, Malcolm." Liz had been extremely careful in sharing details of the strange happenings in the house as the last thing she wanted was for anyone to think that she was imagining things. She hardly believed herself at times so what would an eminent psychologist think?

"The first time I felt her was soon after we moved in. I felt her on the landing as I went to the bathroom in the night. It was just a cold presence and a breath on my neck. It frightened the life out of me but she wasn't trying to scare me. She was trying to tell me something. And then the dreams started. They seem so vivid. I can sense her joy and more importantly her fear. During the daytime hours I can walk into a room and I know she is there even though I can't see her. I can smell her. She smells fresh and flowery and it's just not a smell that's normally in the house. What do you think? Am I imagining it?" Liz looked at Malcolm with concern.

Malcolm considered what she had told him carefully before he spoke. "I know we have talked about my belief in ghosts before when we came to dinner so I certainly wouldn't dismiss your views. It's interesting that you can feel her but not see any apparition. I guess if she is haunting the house there must be a reason why she is there. Some unfinished business maybe."

"That's what I'm really intrigued about," explained Liz. "Her story is not a happy tale. I found a journal in the room above the stairs; the one that was hidden by an old wardrobe. I'm not sure if Giles told you about it. The journal is building a picture of Sarah. It's a sad story. She was raped by her stepfather and is expecting his baby. She's being kept hidden in the house to try and avoid scandal. But from the work I have been doing with Christine, I cannot find a baby born to Sarah and she dies soon after giving birth."

Liz collected her thoughts. "I sort of think that the baby died and she is trying to find it. There's no record of the baby's birth or death too. I sometimes just wish she could tell me what she wants and then at least I could help her rest. Perhaps she has come to me for help as I have lost my child. I understand a mother's loss and the pain she must have felt. I know I'm probably jumping ahead of myself but it sort of makes sense in my head," sighed Liz.

Malcolm's face lit up with excitement. "Wow that's fascinating. You could be right on that one. If the baby wasn't officially buried on church land then perhaps she is trying to find a way back to the child. And who better to support her in that quest than a mother who has lost her own firstborn". Malcolm almost forgot the purpose of their counselling session as he got excited with the thought of an actual ghost hunt.

"You don't think I am going mad then," smiled Liz.

"As a psychologist I would never use the term mad," Malcolm spoke seriously before cracking a smile. "To be honest with you I definitely don't think you are going mad. I believe you are probably more suggestive to her presence because of your grief. I don't think it would hurt you to explore this story further and I'm sure I would be happy to help you in any way. In terms of your grief cycle, I think you have already recognised that Sarah's story is helping you to find a purpose outside your family. It is a bit like finding a new job to channel your energy. Have you talked to the rest of your family about what's happening?" asked Malcolm.

"Well they know about the research and the journal but I haven't told them about the dreams or sensing her presence." Liz paused as she thought back to the conversation she had with Giles in Norwich. "I lie. I did try to tell Giles after I felt her on the landing but he just doesn't believe in that sort of thing so I have left well alone. He would definitely think I have gone lala. And I don't want to frighten the kids. I love this house so much and selfishly I don't want to have to move because the kids are scared of a ghost."

It was amazing that all four members of the family had felt something unusual within the house and all of them were avoiding talking about it for their own reasons.

"Interestingly one of Jo's friends came round some weeks back and she told me she saw Sarah on the landing. Hannah's like you. She can sense the paranormal. Despite being so young she seems very perceptive and mature so I trust that she was telling me the truth. I also know she won't tell Jo as she doesn't want her to think she is some kind of freak. Sorry, that sounds a bit derogatory and I didn't mean it like that but she is quite quirky, Jo's friend. It's so easy for children to mock those that are a bit different from the pack and she is definitely different."

"I understand why you wouldn't want to tell Jo and Harry. I do think it may be worth sharing with Giles now. I think he can see how you are recovering gradually and I think he wants to help. Perhaps talking to him will share the story and let him get involved too. I agree that when you first moved into the house the time probably wasn't right. Let him in and let him know the full picture. I think it will help you both to share this experience together. As you mentioned earlier, at times you have shut Giles out of your feelings. Perhaps this is a way of allowing him to see your need to solve this mystery as part of your healing process. Does that help?"

Malcolm had spoken to Giles on a few occasions where he had shared his frustration that Liz didn't want to let him in emotionally. Talking to each other about something which would challenge both their personal beliefs would probably do the couple the world of good.

"I will try," said Liz. "I guess I have enjoyed keeping it secret as it made me feel special that Sarah has chosen me to reach out to. I do need to trust Giles not to mock what's happening. I will speak to him about our session today and lead the conversation into Sarah's story."

As Liz walked home she smiled at herself as she reflected on the session with Malcolm. She had been worried about talking to him but his approach had been supportive and gentle which had coaxed her to share more than she had with anyone else. Liz felt she had an element of control over her grief. Things were starting to get better; step by step.

CHAPTER TWENTY SEVEN – MARCH 1861

Sarah shifted her bulk in her mother's rocking chair as she strained to see the stitches she was working on.

Her mother had left some of the children's underwear for darning tonight. She couldn't get comfortable since the baby's head had turned. It was pushing its feet up under her rib cage, kicking as if to announce its presence, soon to arrive in the world. Each day it became more and more challenging to heave her bulk down the stairs in the dead of night to occupy her fingers and support her mother. Sarah could hardly believe that she could get any bigger as the baby strained to fit itself in her huge belly.

During the daylight hours she struggled to sleep deeply. As soon as she managed to find a position on the lumpy pallet, the baby would start to turn circles as it enjoyed the additional space. Sarah was also worried sick about the impending birth. Her mother had shared little information about what to expect. Sarah had seen animals give birth. That was all part of country life. Her mother had always used the services of the local midwife who lived close by in the village. Mary had insisted that her daughters were too young to witness the birth of their siblings. So her mind was boggled over how this huge baby was going to make its way out of her body.

Suddenly Sarah heard a loud scream from upstairs. It was a deep throated howl of pain. It vibrated through the still air. There was only one person who could be making such a noise, thought Sarah, it was her mother. The noise resounded through the quiet house with enough volume to waken the dead. She could hear movement from the upstairs rooms and panicked. She knew she needed to get back up the stairs and into her room before any of the children were woken by the sounds of their mother. As she levered herself out of the rocking chair she could hear voices. Her father was shouting, obviously not pleased that his sleep had been disturbed. He banged out of his bedchamber and Sarah heard him crash down the stairs and into his office where he had a day bed.

"What an inconsiderate bastard," Sarah whispered. "All he cares about is himself. Who is going to go for the midwife?" Sarah knew she had to make it up the stairs to check on her mother. As she waddled across the kitchen, the door flew open.

"What the hell?" exclaimed Hannah. "Sarah what are you doing here?" Her eyes dropped to Sarah's belly as her mouth opened in shock. "Oh Sarah, look at you. What happened? Where have you been? I thought you were at Aunt Victoria's." She fired the questions at Sarah in quick succession.

Sarah panicked as she looked at her younger sister. There was no way she could hide the truth any longer. Now was not the time for lengthy explanations. Their mother was in need of their help.

"I never went anywhere, Hannah darling. I wanted to tell you but Mother insisted I was hidden to spare my shame. I'm so sorry I couldn't tell you." Sarah reached out to her sister as they embraced. "I will tell you more later but first we need to help Mum before the rest of the house wakes."

"Mother called to me to bring water and fresh cloths. The baby is coming quickly. There's no time to go for help so we will have to do this together."

Hannah was scared at the thought of being responsible for her mother's labours. She also had an overwhelming feeling of dismay to find her sister here in the kitchen. However finding Sarah at home would at least ease the responsibility for what lay ahead over the coming hours of labour. The shock of seeing her sister's condition would have to wait for now.

The sisters sorted through the linen cupboard to find the cloths they used for their monthlies. Hannah drew a large bowl of water before they headed up to their mother's room. There wasn't any further time to talk as both sisters were called into action to support their mother's advanced labour.

Mary had a cushion clamped between her teeth to stop the sound of her screams which were wracking her body. Her back arched as her body was blasted by another contraction. Mary pulled at her nightdress and Sarah quickly understood the intention. Carefully she sat on the edge of the bed and pushed her mother's nightdress up to her waist. There was no embarrassment between the three women as the sisters set about the business of bringing their latest sibling into the world.

Mary inched her way up the bed to grab hold of the headrest for support. "Hannah, grab that sheeting on the floor over there and put it under me. I can't afford for the bedclothes to get covered in blood." She gasped for air as the next wave of pain washed over her.

"Sarah it's coming now," Mary cried. "You will need to help me by supporting the head when it comes out. Hold it carefully as it will be slippery with blood." She panted with the effort of pushing the baby, alongside trying to direct her inexperienced daughters to help her.

Sarah glanced down and could see the crown of a baby's head emerging from between her mother's legs. With great care she placed her fingers underneath the head as it slowly made its way out of the birth passage. Inch by inch the baby worked its way into the world until the whole body was revealed. Sarah grabbed a linen cloth and used it to wipe the baby's face.

"Tie the cord," Mary gasped as she fell back onto her pillows. "Once it's tied then use a knife to cut the cord. Quickly Sarah, Hannah."

Together the girls followed their mother's instructions. Sarah picked up the baby and held it in her arms whilst she rubbed gently on his front encouraging the little boy to take his first breath. After a few moments the baby let out a small cough and then a wail. Sarah smiled as she gazed at her baby brother. He was perfect. So small but with a good pink colour. His tiny hands and feet kicked out at his new world. She passed him over to her mother who settled the babe on her breast.

As the baby took its first pulls on the breast, a further wave of pain hit Mary. The afterbirth made its way out of Mary. Hannah gathered this up and covered it in cloths to be buried in the yard later.

As Sarah gazed across at her mother and new brother she smiled. This was the true beauty of God's creation. Seeing this small human child take its first breath was a blessing. Her brother did not have any idea of his future before him. He was an innocent who would have his life moulded and shaped by his parents in the months and years ahead. And soon this little baby would have a brother or sister to grow together as twins.

At this stage, Sarah had given no thought to the logistics of her baby's birth. She had not thought about how her parents would manage the birth of one baby not coinciding with the birth of the second. Perhaps that was naivety or just a complete lack of reality. She had been shut away from the family for so long now that she had no idea of the conversations her parents must have been having about the future. And now that Hannah was aware of the situation it was clear that things would change. Would she still need to remain hidden or could she re-enter that family unit.

Sarah could see that her brother had slipped off the nipple and was asleep. Mary appeared to be sleeping also. Carefully she lifted the baby from her mother's chest and gently clothed him in a blanket, wrapping a clout around his tiny bottom. She placed him into the family cradle which stood ready at the foot of the bed. Mary had worked her way further down the bed and had rolled onto her side completely relaxed. The effort of giving birth had drained what little energy she had. Healing sleep took over.

All was quiet as the two sisters embraced with all the emotion of the birth and of finding each other again after their months of separation. The house remained silent. The other children had slept through the disturbance. Jack had clearly gone back to sleep, ignoring his wife's travails.

"Come, Hannah," suggested Sarah. "We can sit on my pallet and talk for a while. I cannot see any more sleep for us this night. If we leave the door open we can listen out for the baby and let mother sleep."

The sisters settled down on the pallet with Hannah laying her head on Sarah's ample lap. She could feel the movement of the baby and the reassuring noise of its heartbeat. Before all this happened the sisters would lie together at night whispering their secret plans for the future. They held nothing back from each other and were loyal to their father's memory. The girls shared a dislike of the man who was trying to replace him; but failing in his attempt to come anywhere near that blessed gentleman, John Cozen.

"I have hated these last few months since you went to Aunt Victoria's. Or should I say moved into the storeroom," corrected Hannah. "I don't mind the extra work. You know I am not scared of hard work. I have tried so hard to balance helping Ma in the house and working the bar each night." Hannah sighed as she was hit with a wave of fatigue.

"I'm so sorry that my absence has impacted on you my dearest sister," replied Sarah as she ran her fingers through Hannah's long hazel hair caressing the length. "I have missed you so much. Mother came to see me early every morning with food and ale but she couldn't really stay for very long. I have had to grab what news I could in the time we had together. So many nights spent in the kitchen on my own."

"I wish I had known. I could have crept down to see you, "sighed Hannah.

"God I know. I was so desperate to steal into your bedroom at night and just look at you. I couldn't risk it. Jack would have killed me if he caught me trying to see you. Both Jack and Ma were determined to keep my condition secret so they can pass my baby off as theirs."

Hannah was trying to comprehend how her sister could have hidden herself away from the family so successfully for the last few months. "It must have been so hard for you all alone. But you are not alone anymore. I know about you now and they can't stop me from seeing you. I really don't care what Jack thinks anymore. That man makes me feel sick to my stomach."

Hearing those words sent a chill through Sarah. She could feel the sweat break out across her forehead as she listened to her sister. She watched the emotions flying across Hannah's face as she started to tell her tale.

"He keeps finding a way to get me on my own in the bar. It started off with him just making lewd comments. But last week he grabbed at my breast. He stank of beer so I think he had been at the ale for some hours. How does Ma put up with him? He's just a smelly horrible lecher."

Sarah was devastated to hear Hannah describe Jack's behaviour. After all she had endured in silence over months of time, for him to now turn his attention to her young sister. Hannah was only eleven years old. She was not near to womanhood and as far as Sarah was aware, had not started to bleed yet.

"Oh god Hannah. Please tell me he's not started on you too. He promised that if I kept quiet about what he had done to me that he would leave you alone. He threatened to hurt you if I told Ma. I haven't told anyone what he did to me, even knowing the state I have been left in."

Sarah clutched onto her sister's hand as she stared deeply into her eyes. She understood that now was the time to bring her beloved sister into her confidence. It was too late to keep the secret any longer. This man needed to be stopped before he ruined any more lives.

"He took me by force one night in the outside privy. He hurt me so much, Hannah. It was disgusting. He was drunk but he knew who I was and what he was doing. I was so scared that he was going to kill me. He kept hitting me while he stuck his smelly old cock in me. Then he whispered in my ear that if I told my Mother about what he had done then he would do the same to you. He told me that Ma wouldn't believe me and that he would say I asked for it. Flaunting myself at him and trying to compete with my own mother."

She shivered remembering those dreadful nights. "He is just a horrible dirty old man and I cannot believe Ma is happy with him. I think she is trapped like we are. At the behest of a bully who delights in putting the fear of god into his adoptive family. I hate him so much, Hannah. Oh, why did Pappa have to die and leave us at the mercy of this animal?"

The sisters held each other as Sarah quietly sobbed in Hannah's loving embrace. It was a huge relief to share her dreadful secret with another. This could not happen again and Sarah knew that she had to protect her sibling from the hurt and pain she had endured. It was frightening how alone she had felt in the last year, bearing the shame of his actions.

"The worst part of this horrible story is that Jack is the father of my child." Sarah paused as she realised the magnitude of her statement. Saying those words opened a door that could never be closed again. "The pain and humiliation I had to deal with. The look of disgust on my mother's face when she found out I was with child will stay with me for ever. She was ashamed of me. I just wanted to scream at her and tell her it was that brute of a husband who did this to me. I needed my Ma but she was ashamed of me."

Sarah cried, big heaving sobs of hysteria.

Hannah held her sister as she let the pain out. She was stunned by what Sarah had told her. This was an evil truth which would never leave them. Hannah was determined that she would protect herself from that monster. He could so easily turn his attention to her next. Perhaps once the baby was born she could persuade Sarah to leave home and take her younger sister with her. Perhaps she could marry and take Hannah with her to a new safer home. Where they would go and how they would arrange their escape was impossible to imagine at this point. But they need to flee from Jack's clutches.

Unknown to the sisters who were sharing this terrifying story of abuse, they were overheard. Lying in her bed, sore from the pain of childbed, Mary Whiting listened. The truth which had been staring her in the face for all those months had become a reality. She knew in her heart that Sarah was a good girl. She had never given Mary any cause to worry before.

Mary had turned her face away from her own intuition. She should have trusted her gut feeling when she discovered Sarah's condition. She had ignored the signs out of fear that it might well be true.

A tear rolled slowly down her cheek as her heart shattered into pieces.

CHAPTER TWENTY EIGHT

The house was quiet.

Liz was reclined on the sofa in the day room enjoying the peace. Joanne and Harry were out with friends after school and not expected back until later. Giles was in London but on his way home by train.

The last few days had been stupidly busy. Liz had felt desperately tired. She was concerned that she may be going down with something as she struggled to get through the day without a nap. That was so unlike her as she was usually full of enthusiasm and drive. Mentally she felt so much better than she had for such a long time but physically she felt drained.

Next to the sofa she had positioned the box which Dave Whiting had lent to her at the weekend. She hadn't had the opportunity to have a look until now and was intrigued to see what treasures it held. Dave had explained to her that the box contained papers from Arthur Whiting who had owned Wood Farm in the late 1800s and included some old journals and letters from family members.

Liz was intrigued to see if she could find anything about Sarah. Arthur would have been Sarah's brother albeit they had different fathers. He would have been very young when Sarah died but it was worth a look to see if she could have some family testimony to the events leading up to Sarah's death.

Unfortunately Sarah's journal, which Liz had found in the storeroom, had stopped abruptly a few weeks before the baby had been born. Liz felt there was a huge hole in her knowledge covering the period leading up to Sarah's death which probably held the clues as to why her presence was still wandering around the house so long after her death.

Painstakingly Liz sorted through the box reviewing a number of legal documents which appeared to outline the ownership status of Wood Farm. It looked like Arthur had become the owner of the farm upon his father Jack's death in 1880. Liz remembered that when she had reviewed the census documents with her mother it indicated that Tom Whiting had been living at the farm back in 1871. It would appear that blood had proved stronger than family ties. Jack had left his property to Arthur his actual son rather than Mary's son, Tom. Perhaps Tom took control of the pub upon his stepfather's demise which would explain how the two businesses become separate once again. There were no documents in the box covering the Crown and Hare Inn which seemed to support Liz's theory.

Buried deep in the box laid a bundle of letters tied together with string. Liz picked at the knot trying to loosen the string without breaking it. After a number of attempts she was able to complete the task and take a look at the yellowing envelopes. All of them were addressed to Arthur Whiting at Wood Farm. The handwriting was beautiful with sloping loops and twirls. Handwriting was a lost art, Liz thought to herself. Kids now a days didn't really learn to write beautifully since the introduction of the keyboard. Not all progress is good, thought Liz.

She opened the top envelope and gently eased out the sheets of parchment. The letter was from Arthur's sister Hannah. As she delved through the pile of correspondence it transpired that all the letters were from Hannah and appeared to cover a period from 1870 to 1875. Hannah was living in a village in Suffolk with her husband and children, along with her mother Mary. Mary was the reason for the numerous letters between the siblings.

As she read through the letters a picture seemed to be forming. Mary Whiting was not a well woman and seemed to be suffering from some form of illness of the mind. She appeared to have moved in with Hannah and her husband so that she could be cared for rather than risk her being placed in some form of asylum. The letters documented Mary's decline as little by little her mind seemed to be wandering away from reality. It was distressing to read the heartache this was bringing to her children and especially to Hannah who was providing the majority of the care.

It seemed strange that her husband was not the principle carer for his ailing wife. According to Liz's records he outlived his wife by some five years. Perhaps the need for a woman's touch had driven the responsibility for Mary to her eldest surviving daughter. How times had changed, she thought. She could not imagine Giles abandoning her in a time of need.

One of the letters detailed Mary's obsession for her lost garden. She appeared to be distressed that she was unable to sit under the old oak tree.

Hannah had tried to persuade her mother to use their garden for some relaxation but her mother had scoffed at the offer and just said it wasn't what she needed. She needed the old oak tree for comfort. Hannah felt this was further evidence of her mother losing touch with the real world around her. She couldn't remember her mother ever having time to sit in the garden at The Crown and Hare Inn. She was always too busy to waste time relaxing in the sunshine. It seemed an odd memory for her mother to be fixated on.

After reading a number of letters, Liz came across a significant development. It was dated June 1875 and detailed that Mary Whiting was facing her fast approaching demise. Hannah had written:

"Mother has become more alert over recent days and seemed to recall happier days when we were all living together. She is talking about the younger children and asking about their welfare. Please write and send me news of Emma and Jack will you. Is Emma still courting? I am trying to keep her thinking of happy memories but she does keep turning to Sarah."

The letter continued. "She misses her so very much, as we all do. She says she needs to beg forgiveness from her for the wrong she did her. I think she is confused now as she said the baby lived. We know that's not true. I think she is just getting confused with her Jack who was born weeks before Sarah's babe died. When I tried to reassure her she got really angry and started to bang her hand into her forehead. I had to restrain her before she did herself more damage. All she kept saying was that it was her fault the baby died and that Sarah needed to forgive her for her sins."

Liz finished the letter and sighed as she contemplated this mother's last few days on earth and her pain for her lost child. She could empathise with Mary Whiting. No mother should bury her first born child.

Just at that moment the smell of flowers overwhelmed the room. "Oh Sarah, are you here with me. You darling girl, can you hear me?" Liz gazed around the room to try and make out any change in the atmosphere. It was the smell that told her that she was not alone. She couldn't put her finger on it but the room felt different. There was an overwhelming feeling of sadness mingling with the scent of flowers.

Liz scanned the room to locate the location of the smell and spoke to the air surrounding her. "Your mother died asking for your forgiveness, Sarah. I wish you could tell me why? What did she do that needed your forgiveness? I so wish I could help you make peace. I won't rest until I find a way to help you, lovely girl."

As quickly as the smell arrived, it dissolved and the atmosphere in the room went back to normal. Liz knew this was yet another signal from the past; evidence that she was getting closer to the truth. She remained determined to resolve the mystery of Sarah's baby.

CHAPTER TWENTY NINE

It was later that night that Liz plucked up the courage to talk to Giles.

Malcolm had advised her that now was a good time to let Giles in on her feelings and experiences since they had moved to their lovely new home in the country. She was nervous that Giles would laugh at her relationship with Sarah and dismiss it as foolish fantasies. Giles was a very practical, down to earth type who called it as it was, rather than as it seemed. The conversation would have to be handled carefully to ensure that he listened to her. Picking the right time was important.

Liz chose to broach the subject as they were getting ready for bed that evening. Their normal evening routine included watching the News at Ten and then making their way to bed to read before sleep. Jo and Harry were tucked up in bed after an exhausting evening out in Norwich. Liz knew she would not be disturbed and could have Giles complete attention. Their mobile phones were always left downstairs to avoid the screen sleep interference.

"Darling, I need to speak to you about something," Liz started. She was sat cross legged on the duvet as Giles was hanging out his shirt for tomorrow's meetings.

"What's troubling you, Liz?" Giles could tell from her body language that Liz was struggling to start the conversation. He finished what he was doing and sat down opposite her on the intricately carved wooden chair which they had picked up recently from the local antique shop.

"You know that I have been doing research on this house and the young girl that died here."

Giles interrupted before she could continue. "I know. I'm really impressed with what you have found out so far and I can't wait to hear more. It's really given you one hell of a project. I guess once you get stuck in then you are hooked."

"Hooked is a good word for it, my love. But I think it's more than being hooked. It's become sort of personal. I haven't told you before but there is more to this research than I have let on". Liz began to relax as the conversation developed.

"Oh right. What do you mean by personal?" Giles looked puzzled and somewhat concerned.

"I'm not just doing this work to find out more about our home. I'm also doing it to help Sarah. Please don't laugh at me. But…." She paused as she looked seriously at Giles, daring him to crack a smile. "I have felt Sarah's presence in the house. At first it was quite scary. I got a cold feeling on the landing upstairs during the night and I even felt her breathe on my neck. But over time I have become more settled with her presence. Most of the time it's just a sense of her being in the room and the scent of her perfume."

Liz stopped and examined Giles's expression to see if she could read any indication of disbelief or humour in his face. To her surprise, her husband looked intrigued and she could tell she had his complete attention.

"I think she is still here in the house because she has unfinished business. That's what's been driving me to try and understand as much as I can about the history of this place and more particularly her family."

Giles was gripped. He had a gut feel that there had been more to this search than Liz was letting on. He had been worried that this was all related to Becky. He had thought that the death of their own child had become intrinsically linked to the death of this girl nearly two hundred years before.

"Don't look so surprised, Liz. Your face is a picture. I guess you thought I was going to laugh at the notion," smiled Giles.

Liz had seemed to go a puce colour as her face told the shock in finding out that her husband did actually believe this wild fancy.

"I believe you, darling. I think I have felt something weird especially on the landing. I didn't want to say anything especially as I didn't want the kids to get freaked out."

"Oh my god. What are we like?" They laughed together and the tension that had built up dissolved.

Giles probed further. "So what makes you think there is something to find that you haven't managed to uncover yet?"

"My gut feel is that it's something to do with the baby which, according to the records, does not exist. Sarah is pregnant with her stepfather's baby. Her mother is pregnant with the same guy's baby. But only one baby is registered in the parish records and that is supposed to be Mary's child, Jack."

"Which was the evil step-father's name wasn't it?"

"Exactly. If that was Sarah's baby, I seriously cannot believe that she would name it Jack after the bastard who got her in that mess. Sarah dies of childbed fever so she definitely gave birth. Perhaps the baby died during the birth but then why isn't it recorded somewhere." Liz's excitement about the subject shone from her face as she explained her thinking to her husband.

"Is it possible that parents in those days didn't have to register a baby's birth if it was born dead?" asked Giles.

Liz looked surprised at his suggestion. She really hadn't contemplated that scenario. Giles may well have a point. And if he did that would add a further layer of complexity to the investigation.

"That's a possibility. I hadn't thought of that. If that was the case why is Sarah still hanging around? That doesn't make sense. Wouldn't there be some form of burial for a baby though even if it wasn't registered?" Liz remembered that in the graveyard there was no mention of a baby in the same grave as Sarah. In her head she was starting to tie the various loose ends together.

"And today I found something out from that box that Dave shared with me. There was a pile of letters from Hannah, who was Sarah's younger sister, to their brother Arthur. It appears that Mary Whiting, the mother, had some form of mental breakdown and is living with her daughter rather than in the family home."

"Gosh the plot thickens," sighed Giles.

"In her last days she seems to have been fixated by Sarah and a dying need to beg for her forgiveness. That doesn't sound like the actions of a woman whose grandchild died during birth. She seemed to feel responsible for the baby's death or Sarah's death. There is definitely something more to this than meets the eye. What we need to figure out is the missing link and how we can solve the puzzle. Perhaps if we can do that then Sarah will be able to rest in peace at last."

"Wow what a mystery," exclaimed Giles. "Would you like me to get involved and perhaps have a look through what you have found so far? I'd love to help. Why don't we spend some time at the weekend looking at what you've found?" Giles was excited to think there was some deeply hidden mystery attached to their new home.

"I really would appreciate that Giles. Maybe a fresh pair of eyes is what I need to unlock the secrets of Crown House."

Liz remained concerned that they just wouldn't discover why Sarah's presence remained in the house. The documents she had looked at gave a reasonable account of the story but there were huge gaps. Liz didn't think she was missing anything from the papers she had looked at to date but having Giles to review and then be able to bounce ideas off may well support progress.

She was determined to uncover the mystery surrounding Sarah. If she could only understand what haunted the poor girl then perhaps she could help her to rest in peace

CHAPTER THIRTY

Liz sat in the surgery waiting room reading the numerous posters on the wall which covered a range of illness and preventative actions. She knew there were a couple of patients ahead of her in the queue so she picked up a Norfolk Life magazine and started to flick.

She had made the decision to see the doctor a couple of days before as she really could shift this bug. She felt exhausted and had actually vomited this morning. Liz wasn't in favour of wasting the doctor's time over trivial illness but she was concerned that she may pass the bug onto her children who had some important swimming races coming up.

The door opposite opened up and a middle-aged man popped his head around scanning the waiting room. "Elizabeth Stamford" he called out. Noticing Liz rise to her feet he made eye contact and continued. "Please do come in."

Liz followed Doctor Fox into his surgery and settled herself down in the seat next to the doctors cluttered desk space. The surgery also boasted an examination bed with screening curtains for privacy.

"What can I do for you today?" Doctor Fox smiled encouragingly at her. The lead doctor in the practise, Joseph Fox was renowned for his kindly manner and thorough examination approach.

"I really hope you don't mind me bothering you but I think I have some sort of bug which I just can't shift. I feel sick constantly and I'm exhausted. Strangely for me, I am sleeping really well but when I wake up I feel as tired as when I went to bed," explained Liz. She couldn't understand how tired she had felt recently. For the last 18 months she had survived on so little rest and now that she was getting a full 8 hours sleep she felt dreadful.

"Right, well let's do some basic tests and see if we can find out what's going on with you shall we."

Joseph Fox proceeded to check her blood pressure and undertake a number of observations of her breathing and pulse. "I think it might be worth is taking some blood and seeing if that tells us anything. Can you roll up your shirt sleeve and I will take a sample if that's ok."

Liz wasn't great with blood tests so averted her eyes whilst the doctor went about his business. She usually fainted at the sight of her own blood. Funnily she could cope with other people's blood. It was just her own which freaked her out. The doctor continued to ask her some background questions as a distraction as he took her bloods. His approached did take her mind of what he was doing and made the process go without a hitch.

"Can I ask when you had your last period, Elizabeth?"

Liz stared at the doctor not realising her mouth was wide open like a guppy. Seriously? She had not thought about that subject or had to worry about the inconvenience of that situation for a long time.

"Oh at least a year ago," responded Liz. "They were fairly erratic for the last couple of years before that. My previous doctor explained that it was the early menopause."

Dr Fox considered her response before framing his following remarks. "You are quite young to be going through the menopause but it's not unusual. I guess you are taking sensible precautions. Or should I say, is there any chance that you might be pregnant?"

Liz gulped again as the reality hit her like a sledgehammer. "Oh god. I can't be, can I? I seriously didn't think of that possibility but now you say it the signs are there. Oh god. What I am going to do?" Liz dropped her head into her hands in a moment of despair. All of a sudden Liz knew that the obvious answer was pregnancy. She had been convinced her child rearing days were long gone so that eventuality had been the last thing on her mind.

"Ok then, first I would like you to give me a urine sample and we will do a simple pregnancy test and then we will have a feel of your tummy. Can you pop out to the toilet and do a sample for me then come back in when you've done." Dr Fox passed her a sterile test tube and motioned Liz towards the door.

Liz's hands were shaking as she came back into the treatment room after squeezing out a urine sample. She felt sick at the thought of what this test might show her. She seriously had not contemplated the thought of pregnancy. She and Giles had recently had an active sex life and over the past few months she could honestly say they hadn't been sensible and been much more spontaneous. She hadn't even contemplated that they were taking any risks. She had just assumed that she was menopausaland safe.

The practise nurse was in the treatment room with Doctor Fox and took charge of the sample as Liz settle down on the bed for her examination. The doctor's hands were cold on her tummy as he gently felt around her womb. She felt her stomach contract at his touch.

Gill the practise nurse re-entered the room; her beaming smile told Liz all she needed to know. "It's a positive result, Mrs Stamford. You are pregnant," confirmed Gill as she offered the pregnancy test stick to Liz for her overview. "Congratulations."

Time seemed to stop as Liz tried desperately to absorb the news.

Dr Fox interrupted her thoughts. "I do think you may be 12 to 14 weeks pregnant, Elizabeth. Just from a feel of your abdomen. I think we need to get you a fairly urgent scan at the Norfolk and Norwich so we can get a good idea. In view of your age there are a number of additional tests we should consider once we know how many weeks along you are. If you don't mind waiting I will give the hospital a call and see if we can get you in over the next couple of days."

As Liz sat in the waiting room her mind was churning. At 45 years of age could she really face the thought of giving birth again? Or more to the point carrying a child to term. The thought of an aching back and swollen ankles certainly didn't appeal. And how would she tell the kids. They would be horrified surely. It's hard enough thinking that your parents might be having sex but the embarrassment of the whole world knowing they were at it was beyond comprehension.

"Mrs Stamford", Gill the practise nurse interrupted Liz's machinations. "I hope this works for you but the hospital have a cancellation at 1pm today and will see you then. You probably know the drill but if you could drink a good pint or so of water before you head over there. If you head to Level 3 in the West Block and report to reception, they will be expecting you."

Liz turned the key to the front door as she let herself back into the house. She dropped her handbag on the sofa as she threw herself down onto her favourite comfy armchair. It had been a long tough day and there was more to come. She had gone straight to the hospital from the surgery only stopping to grab a sandwich and a huge bottle of still water so that she could fill her bladder. Despite the cancellation appointment, she had been hanging around the hospital for a couple of hours ahead of having the ultrasound. She was exhausted and her mind was churning with thoughts about the next steps.

"Hello, darling, where have you been? I thought you would have been here when I got home." Giles stuck his head out of his home office as he heard his wife arrive home.

"Hey there. I didn't know you were at home this afternoon," answered Liz. She was surprised to see her husband. Liz had craved some time alone with the news before she had to face telling Giles.

"I just had some meetings in Ipswich this morning and the afternoon session was cancelled so I thought I would come home and have lunch with my lovely wife. Who blew me out!" Giles grinned as he ruffled her hair. "You ok?"

"We need to talk," said Liz. "I've been at the hospital this lunchtime. That's why I wasn't here."

Giles crouched down next to his wife with a look of real concern. "Tell me. What's the matter darling." He clutched fearfully at her hand as he waited for her to speak. In his mind a vast range of dreadful illness was swirling around. He felt sick to his stomach to think that anything could be wrong with his wife. Could this family take any more bad news?

"I'm pregnant."

Her words dropped like a bombshell into the silent room.

Giles's face was a picture of disbelief as he stared at his wife. "Pregnant? How? Are you sure?"

Liz smiled as she took in his expression. It really was a picture. But it must have been very much like her expression when Gill showed her the test results. Shock and disbelief.

"I went to the doctors this morning as I have felt rotten for days now. I just thought it was a bug but it looks like there is life in the old dog yet. Or new life to be precise. The doctor felt I was a few months along so sent me to the hospital for an urgent scan. I didn't come home in between or you could have come with me. Sorry darling."

Liz continued to examine her husband's face, trying to gauge his immediate reaction. She watched his expression slowly turn from fear to shock and then to a huge grin.

"Hey, don't apologise my love. Wow. Another baby. How do you feel about that?" Giles had a huge smile on his face which to the neutral observer was evidence that he seemed pretty pleased with himself. He clasped at his wife's hand as he waited patiently for her reaction, hoping it matched his own.

"At first I just felt sick with the thought of it. But then I saw the baby on screen and she looks perfect. It was love at first sight," Liz gushed and grabbed the scan photo from her handbag waving it at Giles.

"She? Did they tell you the sex then?" Giles took the scan photo and stared deeply at the new edition to the Stamford family. The grainy picture of the small human; huge head with tiny limbs curled into a foetus shape. When the other children had been conceived they hadn't had the chance to have a photo of the baby in the womb. This was such a special photo for them both.

"I did ask the sonographer what they thought but it's too early for them to say with total confidence. She thought it was a girl but couldn't commit. I just have a gut feel she's a girl. It's sort of fate isn't it if she is. Nothing will ever replace our darling Rebecca but perhaps this is God's way of giving us a gift to help the pain of loss." Liz started to cry silently as Giles grabbed her into one of his famous bear hugs.

The couple held each other tight, delighting in their news. The real and present dangers of Liz's age and the likely impact on her body would come later. Now was a time for celebration.

"Oh, come on you guys," shouted Harry as he threw his school bag down on the floor. "Get a room" he laughed. Harry made exaggerated movements pretending to stick his fingers down his throat to vomit. He laughed as he took the mickey out of his parents' affection.

Jo followed Harry as both children watched their parents extract themselves from the cuddle. Both of them could sense the atmosphere in the room was different. Serious faces took over as they wondered what news was about to be shared. They could see Liz had been crying but their dad was smiling. Mixed messages were flying at them.

"Good day at school guys?" asked Giles. He hugged both children with more passion that they were used to which caused two concerned faces to stare at their parents.

"Ok Mum, what's wrong," asked Jo. "You look like you've been crying so come on tell us what's happened." Jo was extremely perceptive of her mum and could see she was distressed. Although adding to the confusion her face was starting to crack into a smile.

Liz looked across at Giles for his agreement before she spoke. He nodded his consent. "We've got some news for you both. I hope you won't be too shocked but I'm pregnant. You are going to have another baby brother or sister."

Liz dropped the bombshell again and waited.

Harry looked embarrassed. He looked at his Dad and then at his Mum. Finally he looked at his sister for support. He really wasn't sure what to say so was desperate for Jo to take the lead. His mouth opened and closed with shock as he was trying to form a sentence.

Jo simply burst into tears and threw herself at her mother. Liz held her and let her cry, feeling desperate for the pain she had obviously inflicted on her daughter. Harry continued to look confused.

"Oh Mum, that's the most wonderful news in the whole wide world," cried Jo as she managed to find her voice. "A baby. That's just what we all need. She is going to be so precious and I love her already." Jo extracted herself from her mum and launched herself at Giles, continuing to weep happy tears.

"Oh darling. I'm so happy that you are ok with this. It's been a shock to me and your Dad as it's not something we have planned."

"Gross." The only words Harry could find just at that moment.

Liz continued undeterred. "We don't know whether it's a girl or a boy yet. The scan seems to show everything is ok but because I'm an old girl they will be doing some more tests to just keep an eye on things." Liz took her daughter's face in her hands and looked at her full of love. "I'm going to need you to be so grown up and help me out when the baby gets here."

"You try stopping me," squealed Jo. "And it's a girl. I'm sure."

"Harry, you ok mate," asked Giles. Harry looked a bit lost, out on the extremity of the family group.

"Well other than the fact that it's just so gross that the rents are still having sex at your age!" laughed Harry. "Actually it will be cool having a younger brother or sister as I'm no longer the baby in the family. Takes the pressure of me. But seriously Mum, I am so happy for you. Just as long as it doesn't disturb my sleep."

"Come on," Giles pulled Harry in. "Group hug."

The family cuddled as the news was absorbed.

It was going to be difficult adjusting to a baby late in life. Adjustments would be required to balance the needs of a baby alongside the demands of growing teenagers. The baby would just have to fit into their busy life. The family was a strong unit and Liz knew they would all support each other to make the changes required.

The baby was a gift. Perhaps it was what they all needed as part of their journey of recovery. As Liz basked in the love of her family she could smell the slight scent of flowers behind her.

Liz smiled.

CHAPTER THIRTY ONE – 2ND DAY OF APRIL 1861

Sarah awoke to a grinding pain in her back.

It felt like something or someone was rubbing against her spine; grinding bone on bone. She gasped as a wave of nausea hit her. The pain grew slowly in intensity. Gasping she struggled to a sitting position and pulled herself up to sit on the edge of the bed she was sharing with her mother.

Since Jack had been born last week, there seemed little point in hiding away as the wider family were now aware of the situation. Jack senior had moved out of the bedroom whilst his wife recovered from the birth so it had made sense for the two women to share a bed and support each other. Hannah had been a support too, fussing over the new baby and ensuring her sister was resting. Sarah could not believe the size of her belly. In the last few week she felt that her body was no longer her own. The downward pressure as the baby prepared for birth made any form of movement challenging.

The rest of the children approached with caution, unsure what to make of Sarah's huge belly. There was a reluctance to ask questions of their sister. Their father bellowed his way around the home striking fear into his children. It was clear that he was raging about the situation and the children intuitively knew not to question their father. There was time enough for questions once the baby was born and things got back to normal. Although what normal would look like was one of those questions everyone was too frightened to put into words.

Sarah looked across at her sleeping mother and quickly checked on baby Jack tucked into the family cot at the end of the bed. All looked well. Jack was now almost a week old and seemed a contented baby who suckled well and slept in between. Mary had been up a few hours before dawn to feed the baby and was now taking advantage of his sleep to rest up.

With this in mind, Sarah decided to leave her mother in peace and see if anyone else in the household was abroad yet. Jack and Tom would probably have left for the farm by this hour. Hannah would probably be supervising the younger siblings to break their fast ahead of their lessons at the schoolhouse.

As she heaved her bulk into a standing position, Sarah felt a twinge between her legs. Suddenly liquid was trickling down her leg and she pulled at her nightdress to look. She was scared that she was bleeding but the liquid looked translucent. As she tried in vain to wipe herself a stronger grinding pain griped across her abdomen and up her spine. She gasped with the shock of the contraction as it took over her body for about ten breaths. She gripped hold of the bedstead as she tried to steady herself. She didn't want to cry out and wake her mother. She bit down on the sleeve of her nightdress to muffle her cries.

As soon as it came on, the pain slowly left. She took in big gulps of air trying to build up the courage to move away from the bed. She knew the baby was coming. The shock of the pain hit her as the reality built. Sometime this morning she would give birth to another human being.

Gently she eased herself out of the bedroom and was able to call down the stairs to Hannah. Hannah was swift to answer her cries. She had been preparing the morning meal and dropped everything when she heard her sister call out to her. Together the sisters walked up and down the landing between the two bedrooms. Having seen their mother in childbed a number of times they knew that this could be a long process and staying mobile for as long as Sarah could stomach may ease the babe into the world. Hannah rubbed affectionately on her back as the sisters walked back and forth.

The pain came in waves and they started to count the circuits of the landing between the pains to try and establish a pattern. Counting her progress was helping Sarah to focus on something other than the growling pain which seemed to be grinding on her bones. It felt like the pain was the only thing she could feel at the moment. She had stubbed her foot on the stair post but that pain just wasn't registering with the gripes in her belly. Sarah felt she was no longer in her body but watching from afar. The whole situation did not seem real. The pain was all consuming.

Down the stairs they could hear the sound of the younger siblings clearing away their breakfast bowls and then the noises of the children readying themselves for the day ahead. The normal day to day sounds were of some comfort to Sarah as she tried to clear her mind of what lay ahead of her.

A baby cried. It was the cry of a new-born desperate for attention and food.

The girls heard their mother stirring and then the soft nuzzling cries as Jack latched onto his mother's breast.

Hannah left her sister's side for a moment to get her mother's attention to Sarah's travails. With the baby in her arms suckling, Mary was at her eldest daughter's side within a heartbeat. It didn't take Mary long to assess her daughter was far advanced in her labours.

"Come my girl. Let's get you back in the bedroom. Can you sit on the bed so I can have a look at how far along you are? I will be quick." Mary used her experience of childbearing to examine her daughter who was swollen with the pressure pushing down on her. "When did the pains start girl?"

Sarah gripped the blanket as the next pain hit her like a wave. She panted for breath as she was buffeted by the wave. As she crested it and came down the other side she was able to answer her mother.

"The pains started soon after the cockerel started this morning. Just after daybreak I think. Me and Hannah have been walking the landing for about an hour I think before you woke." It was difficult to determine the length of time she had been labouring. In her mind it seemed like days.

Her mother gently felt between her daughter's legs to assess her progress. "I think you are coming along fast Sarah. I can feel the baby's head. Hannah, will you get me the sheet cover for the bed, some boiling water and the towels. This baby is making its way into the world. We won't have to wait long." Mary knew it was unusual for a first baby to come this fast. It appeared that this baby was determined to make an entrance in a hurry.

Mary's face remained serious as she helped her daughter into position. Sarah found the least uncomfortable position, kneeling up on all fours to ease the pain which was grinding against her spine.

Mary's stomach was churning with the thought of the arrival of her husband's bastard. How was she ever going to deal with the knowledge of this child's conception? Since she had overheard the sisters talking on the night of Jack's birth she had been sick with anger with the man she called her husband. Things had not been good between them for some time despite the many babies she had borne. The thought that he had raped her daughter to satisfy his evil ways was disgusting. The fear that he may turn his attention to Hannah next was consuming her mind. How could she protect her daughters from their evil stepfather? What sort of future could this baby have with the stain of incest hanging over its head?

Hannah returned and supported her mother to prepare the bed for the baby's arrival.

"Hannah, I want you to sit at the top of the bed and help your sister. She will need to hold onto you for support so you must be strong for her. I will deal with the baby." Mary did not want Hannah to witness what was to happen.

All too soon Sarah felt an overwhelming need to push. She put all her strength into easing the baby's head down her birth canal; pausing for breath between the rolling waves of pain.

As time passed, the three women worked silently at their allotted tasks. Hannah held her sister in her strong embrace as Sarah worked. She would not witness the birth as she concentrated on supporting her older sister.

Finally the baby pushed its way through the birth canal. As it made its way into the world, Mary gazed up at her daughter with love. The birth cord was hanging out of Sarah along with the baby's head and shoulders. Swiftly, Mary wrapped the cord around the baby's neck and pulled it tight. The infant opened its eyes as it struggled for its first breath without success. Within seconds the light went out of the new-born eyes as the rest of the body was expelled from Sarah.

The baby was dead.

With speed Mary cut the cord and wrapped the limp body in a towel. Her hands were shaking as she held the dead child to her chest. She felt sick to her stomach knowing what she had done but in her heart she knew this was the only option. She was saving her daughter from shame and humiliation at the hands of the monster she called husband.

"Mother is it over?" cried Sarah. She came to lie on her side as she searched her mother's face for confirmation. The pain had left her body as she expelled the afterbirth. Exhaustion was her friend as she eased her body into a comfortable place.

Mary glanced at her daughter realising the enormity of what she had done. She struggled to look Sarah in the eye. Now she had to share the heart-breaking news with her daughter.

"I'm so sorry my darling girl. The baby is dead. It was born with the cord around its neck so it never had a chance. I am so sorry." Mary passed the limp body over to her daughter who took the bundle in her arms.

Sarah looked down at the beautiful face of her child and could not believe how someone conceived with such violence could look so angelic. Tears ran down her face as she held the baby to her chest and gently rocked back and forth. Her fingers gently worked open the towel so that she could examine the body. It was a girl and she looked perfect with tiny fingers and toes. Her body was limp and flopped across her arms. She had a fine head of light brown hair which Sarah stroked. She tried to work her finger around the baby's little hand but the poor thing could not grip. It had departed and would never know the joy of holding onto her mother.

Sarah's heart was breaking as she looked at her mother and tried to understand what had happened. "Did I do something wrong, Mother? Why did she have to die? Is it a punishment for my sin?" Her confusion flashed across her face as she sought some answers.

Mary was filled with self-hatred and doubt. She had not planned this to happen. At some point during the birth she had decided on the course of action and despite her daughter's grief she had to stick to the belief that this was the only way. It was for the best. This child could not grow up and find out the circumstances of its birth.

"Oh darling girl, it's not your fault. We could not know this was going to happen. It's just a dreadful accident. The poor child never knew it had been born so she didn't suffer. She's with the angels now and at peace. Come. Give her to me and I will take care of everything. Hannah, stay with your sister and comfort her."

Mary was crying silent tears as she took control of the situation. She could see the shock portrayed in Hannah's face as her younger daughter struggled to understand what had happened.

Sarah bent over the child and kissed its eyes, nose then mouth. She stared intently at the baby to fix it in her memory. Reluctantly she knew that she could not hold on to the dead child any longer and with one final glance handed the bundle over to her mother. As she let go of her baby daughter she collapsed into Hannah's loving embrace.

Mary fled the room with the bundle. Her heart was breaking as she had watched Sarah say farewell to her daughter. She heard the wail of grief as she walked away. Was that Sarah screaming for her child or her own shame escaping as she carried the object of her guilt away?

Pain hit her with its full force.

Those times when Jack would angrily slam her against the wall whilst in his cups, the pain felt intense. But this pain was beyond comparison. She had murdered the child. If anyone found out she would face the gallows. In her heart she knew she deserved to hang but what about the children. She couldn't leave them in the care of Jack Whiting. If anyone examined the perfect body of the little girl they may doubt it was born dead. Mary could not risk the questioning and examination of the evidence. This baby needed to be buried and quick.

Mary let herself out of the kitchen door and found that all was quiet in the backyard. There was no sign of Jack or Tom. It would be an hour before they came back for their lunchtime food so she had time to deal with this dreadful problem. In the outbuilding she found a small shovel and made her way across the yard to the orchard.

Standing guard to the entrance of the orchard was a magnificent oak tree. It had probably stood there for hundreds of years watching over the land. It had big knobbly roots near the surface which were running across the land like veins. As if by chance there was a dip right in front of the tree which looked ideal for her purpose. With love, she laid the girl-child on the ground and set to work with the shovel. The ground lent a hand. A recent rain shower had softened the mud allowing her to make headway at speed. Once she had dug out enough earth, Mary gently laid the child still wrapped in the towel under the oak tree and scooped the remaining mud and leaves over the top.

Once she had finished, Mary fell to her knees and clasped her hands together in prayer. She couldn't remember the right words so cried out with love and pain.

"Dear God. Watch over this poor child and take her into your loving embrace. Watch over my Sarah and bring her peace. Forgive me for my sin. I know I will face judgement when my time comes but until that day comes I swear I will always protect my children from evil."

The future stared ahead of her.

For years she would carry the consequences of her actions. She had murdered the poor child, her first grandchild. It was a dreadful wrong and she knew she would be punished in the next world for her deadly deed.

It was a moment of clarity which had led her to take this action. She had spent the previous week dealing with the dreadful news that this baby could be both sister and niece to her new son Jack. The thought of this secret coming to light would destroy her family and their reputation. They would be shunned by the village. It could even mean the end of their businesses. The shame would drive them from the village. Mary had been born in the village and had never known another community.

No matter what part Jack had played in this evil matter, she had to put things right for the family's sake. She would take responsibility for making sure the awful secret could never be revealed.

The moment the baby's head had been born she knew she had to make sure the poor mite never drew breath. She had to live with that guilt for ever.

She now had to deal with Jack and the rest of the family. They needed to believe the baby was born dead. The family would gather round to protect Sarah from gossip. Perhaps in time she would find a boy to marry and have another child who would help her to forget this awful time in her life.

Despite the horror of what she had been driven to, Mary knew she had done what any mother would do to protect her children.

CHAPTER THIRTY TWO

"And the blessing of God Almighty, the Father, the Son and the Holy Spirit be among you this Christmas time and remain with you always. Amen." Christine raised her arm to complete the blessing of her congregation.

Across the full pews the congregation bowed their heads in a final personal prayer.

A cacophony of conversations broke out as neighbours wished each other a peaceful day as the Christmas service came to an end. Thoughts were turning excitedly to presents and, of course, Christmas lunch.

Liz, Giles, Joanne, Harry and Jill Wynn made their way back down the aisle towards the heavy wooden church door. They greeted a number of new friends including Joyce and Malcolm along with Dave and Sheila Whiting. It felt so good to be sharing their first Christmas with new friends. They stopped to wish Christine a very merry Christmas as she stood at the door, seeing her congregation off. Liz and Christine embraced; a sign of the close friendship which had developed in the last six months since the family had made their home in Little Yaxley.

The family made their way out of the village towards their home. It was a bright crisp morning with the remains of a frost on the grass. Liz could feel the crunch under her feet as they strolled across the village green. Harry and Jo were in a rush to get back home and sped off ahead. Giles placed a comforting arm under Liz's arm to steady her as the ice on the road was slippery. Liz smiled at his gesture of chivalry. His protection of her wellbeing was touching to observe.

The world was silent. The adults indulged in their own private thoughts as they made their way home to enjoy the festivities.

Back at the house, Liz went to check on the turkey which she had put on just before they left for church. Pulling the tin foil open she could see that the plump turkey was coming along nicely. The fragrant smell of stuffing combined with the bird juices filled the kitchen. A bit of basting was in order but other than that all preparations for dinner were on track. Liz and

Jill had been up early peeling potatoes and preparing vegetables.

The pop of a Champagne cork broke the silence. Giles quickly positioned a glass under the exploding stream of fizzing bubbles. He carefully poured glasses for all and carried these through to the lounge where everyone was gathering. It was a family tradition that presents were exchanged after church and ahead of lunch. When the children were little they had been allowed their main presents early in the morning. Sometimes this was incredibly early especially as the children crawled into their parents' bed in an effort to wake them to get permission to go and see if Santa had been. As the children had grown their patience had developed and they were keen to wait for Nanna and Pappa to join them.

The log burner was well established and spread its warm heat inviting the family to settle on the huge leather sofas. A real Christmas tree was a novelty for the Stamford family. In London it had been difficult to get a decent tree so they had been used to a fake one which currently resided in the dining room. The tree had been decorated by Jo who, with an eye to detail, had designed a theme of beautiful red and gold baubles and golden pinecones. The smell of pine needles along with the scent of logs burning filled the room. Jo supplemented the pungent odours by lighting the many candles on the hearth to add to the ambience.

Liz had settled on the sofa as she sipped her Champagne. A small glass wouldn't do the baby any harm she thought as she gazed at her family. Giles was enjoying organising the kids who were scrambling under the tree to find their presents to Nan. Both children still had a Santa sack which had been used since they were babies. Despite the fact that they no longer believed in Father Christmas some traditions just couldn't be broken. She smiled across at her mother who was sat beside her, as both women enjoyed the warmth of the family setting.

"Oh darling, is that a new perfume you have on", asked Jill. "It smells beautiful. A wonderful smell of summer flowers." Jill sniffed the air around her daughter inquisitively.

"Really? Can you smell flowers Mum?" Liz had her usual Prada perfume on so knew that the scent her mother had captured was not from her.

"I could. But that's strange. It's gone now. How weird is that?" Jill looked confused. Luckily Jo and Harry were screeching with delight as they opened their presents and didn't overhear the conversation going on across the room.

"It's Sarah. She was with us briefly," explained Liz.

Her mother continued to look confused as she looked at her daughter who sat there serene and happy. Jill was delighted that Liz and Giles were expecting another child. She was concerned about the toll it could take on Liz's body but she seemed to be healthy and most importantly content. Her comment about Sarah was confusing. Was this evidence of pregnancy mind getting to her daughter?

"Sarah? Who is Sarah," she whispered.

"You know. Sarah from the journal. She visits us quite often now. You can always smell her as she comes through. It's a distinct smell. I'm just so pleased that you felt it too. Giles and I have felt her so many times recently but of course, we haven't spoken about it to the children," Liz continued in a whisper.

"Ok," Jill said hesitantly. "Not sure what to make of that. It may be something to do with your pregnancy darling." Jill was sceptical as she tried to close off the conversation. Jill turned her attention to her grandchildren effectively closing down the conversation. She was not interested in listening to any sort of new age theories.

Out of respect for her mother, Liz decided to drop it. She could have challenged her mother as to why Giles was feeling Sarah's presence too but sometimes it's just best to let sleeping dogs lie, she thought to herself.

"Mum, it's your turn now. Look this present is for you from all of us." Jo and Harry placed a huge oblong parcel in front of Liz as Giles hovered just behind them.

All three were gripped as they watched Liz carefully open the beautiful wrapping paper. As was her way, she was trying hard not to rip it so that the paper could be recycled. As the last of the paper fell away, she could see the back of a picture frame with the heavy duty string attached for hanging.

Carefully she turned the frame over to review the picture.

Staring back at her was the most beautiful water colour of Rebecca. She was standing in front of a corn field with poppies dotted randomly across the landscape. The picture captured the absolute essence of her first born. The look of determination was alive in her beautiful face. Her smile shone into her eyes. She appeared so alive as her hair flowed in the breeze. Rebecca was wearing one of her favourite dresses and her feet were bare, with her toes curling into the earth.

Liz burst into tears as Jo and Harry fell into her arms.

"This is seriously the best present I have ever been given, darlings. It is so beautiful. Who did it?" asked Liz as she dried her eyes. She couldn't get over how the artist had captured Rebecca's essence; bringing her back to life.

Giles lent over and planted a kiss on her lips. "It's a local artist we found via Joyce. He took a number of photos we had of Rebecca and placed her in this setting. We wanted something that represented Rebecca still in our hearts and in our new home. Do you like it sweetheart?" Giles was over the moon with Liz's initial reaction.

Jo had come up with the idea. She wanted her sister to share their new home. Having the picture centred in the local countryside was an excellent way of combining both worlds. When they first met the artist, Giles had been really impressed with his back catalogue. He felt confident in entrusting him with this precious job. That confidence had paid off.

"It is amazing. It's like she is here with us. I just can't get the words out to explain how much this means to me. Thank you all so much. I will treasure it always." Liz pulled Giles in to join the family hug. "Can we hang it on the wall over there? The frame goes so well with this room too. It's marvellous."

"I'm so glad you love it darling. We were a bit worried that you might find it too difficult. It was a risk and I'm over the moon it paid off". Giles smiled at Jo and Harry who had been involved in the planning. "We nailed it kids! We will hang it in pride of place above the fireplace."

Giles picked up the painting and took his time trying out differing positions on the wall. As he did so, Liz watched. She smiled with contentment. It was so different to last Christmas when the family had struggled to have any fun. The move out of London was already a success. As a family they were healing and remembering their lost Rebecca with happiness.

Jill ushered the rest of them to the table.

The table itself was a work of art. Joanne had been responsible for the display and she had outdone herself. She had followed a similar colour theme as the Christmas trees. Her attention to detail included artistic displays for each napkin, designed in the shape of a different animal or bird. She had saved the stuffed turkey shape for her father who cracked a smile as he examined it.

On the table sat the starter course of smoked salmon on a bed of rocket. Liz had taken a break from the cooking to join the rest of the family and multiple conversations broke out as everyone enjoyed the fleshy salmon covered liberally with lemon juice.

It was another family tradition to take time over Christmas lunch. There was usually a break between each course to allow digestion. Most years this extended lunch ended up lasting well into the early evening. This year Harry had organised a Christmas quiz which would start after the turkey course.

As Jo cleared the plates away, Jill and Liz were back in the kitchen putting the final touches to the main event. Roast potatoes were nestling in the warmer, all crispy just how the family loved them. Vegetables included the obligatory sprouts, broccoli and cauliflower cheese. A roast wasn't a roast without cauliflower cheese, according to Harry.

Liz bent over the cooker as she gently levered the turkey pan out. It was a big bird which she had bought from the local farmer. She had been told that they were the best turkey's money could buy. He certainly looked a fine specimen thought Liz. Clear juices spilled from under the bacon which had crisped across the top of the bird.

"Ok Giles, I'm ready for you to carve," shouted Liz to catch his attention. Giles was deep in conversation with Harry.

Her husband was very traditional and he delighted in dividing up the bird. Harry and Giles were leg men. Jo loved stuffing and Liz was keen on the crispy skin. It was his responsibility to ensure everyone got some of their favourite parts of the bird. He performed the task with the persona of a mime artist carving the meat with a flourish.

Everyone was back in their places at the large dining room table. Plates were stacked with generous helpings of food. Wine glasses were filled with a vintage Chateauneuf du Pape. Apple juice for Liz, which was murder for her. Chateauneuf was her favourite wine but her pregnancy put an end to that for this year at least. A small price to pay for the new joy in their life.

Giles caught everyone's attention by lightly tapping the wine glass with his knife. "Guys can I have your attention before we start eating."

"Oh dad," groaned Harry who was desperate to get started.

"Just a few words from me. Sorry Harry. I will be quick. I just wanted to thank your Mum for this lovely spread. She has produced a fabulous meal despite spending the first hour this morning with her head down the big white telephone. Sorry Jill," Giles spotted his mother in law's grimace at the analogy. "And of course, not forgetting your Nan who has worked so hard on producing this lovely meal too." He paused then continued in a more serious manner.

"I would like us all to raise a toast to our first Christmas in Norfolk. This house provides us with the perfect family setting and I hope that this will be the first of many in our lovely new home. It will be the last quiet one too with our new arrival next year. Now eat!"

"To us" resounded around the room as glasses were clinked in celebration. "Happy Christmas everyone."

As the family toasted the season a faint waft of flowers crossed the room and faded away. Liz smiled and raised her glass in salute.

CHAPTER THIRTY THREE – 17TH APRIL 1861

Mary sat beside her daughter's bed.

Her face displayed the anguish of the last few days. She had neglected her duties and even the well-being of her baby son to stand vigil over her beloved firstborn.

Sarah had been struck down with a fever within a few days of giving birth. It started soon after her milk came in. With the death of her child, the pull of the milk in her chest added to Sarah's consuming grief. Mary had considered placing Jack to her daughter's breasts but Sarah just pushed him away in disgust. She seemed to have lost her will to live. Over the last few days she was slipping in and out of consciousness.

Mary had insisted on paying for a visit from the doctor despite the potential shame it may bring down on the family. The doctor would know the true reason for her fever. Jack had called a doctor in from Norwich, some miles away. He would not be known in the village and was being paid to hold his tongue. Jack was behaving strangely and was far more amenable than he had been for years. Guilt perhaps, thought Mary.

The doctor had confirmed Mary's own fears. Sarah had childbed fever and was probably caused by an infection during the birth. He was not convinced that everything that should have been expelled from the young woman's body had come away. In view of the state of the patient, he was not willing to suggest any action to rectify the problems in the womb. In his opinion the girl would die and there was no point in prolonging her suffering.

Mary knew that she was saying farewell to her daughter.

It was too soon after the latest additional to the family had entered the world. She was consumed with grief but also racked with guilt. Why had she not seen the way Jack had been behaving with her beautiful girl? Or had she seen it? Had she just ignored what was happening in front of her eyes? Had her need for family security cast a veil over her eyes? Was it some form of sickening jealousy? Seeing the vibrancy of Sarah against her own haggard demeanour was a comparison hard to bear. Over recent years she had been feeling her age. She knew her body was sagging through repeated childbirths. Her looks were a thing of the past.

She was responsible for the death of her own grandchild. In a moment of madness she had snubbed out the poor babe's chance of life. She would have to live with that knowledge. Out of guilt for what she had done, she also felt responsible for the illness of her daughter who was wasting away in front of her. If she had protected her from evil then perhaps Sarah would have enjoyed the expertise of a midwife when her first child was born.

Sarah stirred. She let out a long exhale which woke Mary from her thoughts. As she looked over at Sarah, she could see her eyes trying to focus.

"Mumma," Sarah whispered through her cracked and sore lips. "Promise me."

Sarah seemed to drift away again as Mary gently stroked her hand encouraging her to talk again. It was some moments before Sarah weakly opened her eyes again.

"Promise me you will protect Hannah," Sarah gasped. She squeezed Mary's hand with every bit of strength left in her weak body. "Promise." The urgency in her pleas was heart breaking.

"Oh darling girl. I will protect her with my life. You don't need to explain, Sarah. I heard you and Hannah talking. I am filled with shame for what that man did to you. I am so very sorry that I let you down. I should have protected you and I failed. I'm so very sorry." Mary sobbed as she confessed her sins to her dying child.

A tear trickled from the corner of Mary's eye and made its slow journey down her cheek. She felt the smallest of touches reaching out to her fingers as Sarah shared her last message. Was that forgiveness or just acknowledgement of Mary's sins against her family?

Mary did not notice the moment her daughter passed from this world. She wasn't conscious of her own body, only of the hand she was holding. She was listening carefully to each gasp of breath from her daughter, marking time.

Sarah was drawing breath, with long gaps in between, each intake arduous and harsh. All of a sudden the sound of breathing ended. Silence filled the room.

Mary knew her daughter was now at peace.

An almost animal like wail emitted from her chest as she collapsed across Sarah's body trying to bring her back. Her heart was breaking with the pain. The loss of a child was every mother's nightmare.

She had nursed Sarah in the early days of wedded bliss with John. She had picked her up as she made her first steps in the yard. She had comforted her as she cried for her Papa when he was taken too soon. Now her beautiful daughter would be with her poor father.

"How can I bear this pain," cried Mary as she sobbed into her apron leaving wet globules of grief.

Mary had gone through the pain of childbirth seven times. However the ache of watching her daughter die was like a knife to her gut. Wrenching through her torso, ripping her apart.

Her cries roused Hannah who was working in the kitchen below. She came running into the room to see the harsh truth. There lay Sarah's body with her mother collapsed over her.

Hannah was frozen as if petrified. She took in the scene, shocked to the core with trauma. She had been too young to understand when her father had died. This was her first real experience of death and in the last few days she had witnessed both her niece and beloved sister taken from her. As the reality hit her, she wept.

As Hannah cried, she gently took her mother by the shoulders and pulled her up from the bed and into her arms. Both women clung to each other and shared their heart-breaking grief.

CHAPTER THIRTY FOUR – 17TH APRIL 1861

It was later when Jack and Tom returned from the farm.

The younger children had been taken to Rachel's house on the village square. Mary didn't want the young ones to witness the aftermath of their sister's death. The younger siblings were confused and unsure what was happening. Rachel was a good friend to Sarah and, whilst she too was devastated and shocked by the news, she quickly took on responsibility for the younger Whiting children.

Hannah had helped her mother to lay out Sarah's body. They had washed her cold skin and dressed her in her Sunday best dress. It was an act of pure love as the two women worked together to cherish those last few moments before chaos would ensue. Mary had gently pulled the comb through her long hair and plaited it. Early spring flowers from the garden were twined into a form of crown resting on her still brow.

Like a whirlwind, Jack threw the kitchen door open in his usual aggressive way. His face was red and sweating from a day of labour. His clothes smelt damp with the cold. As he scanned the room he saw no evidence of the evening meal.

"Where's my bloody food woman," he shouted at Mary who was sat at the kitchen table, her hands wringing out a dirty cloth. Jack kicked his dirty boots off and threw himself down onto the rocking chair by the range. He slowly filled his pipe, striking a match on the range. He pulled deeply on the tobacco oblivious to what was to come.

Tom had entered the kitchen behind his stepfather. Being more intuitive and aware of death stalking the house, his gaze moved from his mother to his younger sister. "Mother are you alright," he asked with concern. Tom walked over to his mother reaching out for her hands.

"She's dead." Mary whispered. Silence enveloped the room as both men absorbed the news.

Tom was struggling to keep his composure. Small sobs were escaping from his throat as he looked to his Mother for direction. He was on the cusp of manhood but this was his first experience of loss as an adult. He had been so young when his father had passed. He was at a loss to understand whether it was acceptable to show his pain. He adored his big sister and had been heartbroken when he realised how sick she was. Mary saw the struggle and pulled her son into her arms, allowing him to hide his tears. That act brought forth his distress. She allowed him time to let his feelings out within the protection of her arms. Once the sobs had diminished, she held him away from her chest and kissed him gently on the cheek.

"She's in the bar. We laid her out in there for now so you can go and say farewell Tom" Mary explained.

Tom started to back out of the room holding Hannah's hand. Both children realised that emotions were at breaking point and just didn't want to be on the receiving hand of Jack's reaction.

"You stupid woman" shouted Jack. "Why have you left her there? How am I to open the bar tonight if she's lying out there in all her glory?"

His face was almost apoplectic with rage. It had not even entered his head that the bar would be closed. He was so wrapped up in his own selfishness.

Mary drew on a courage and strength never seen by her children since she had married Jack. She remained calm but determined to deal with her husband. Whilst she was not surprised by his complete lack of empathy or understanding of the family loss, she realised that now was the time for her to take control of this mess called her marriage. She had gone along with Jack for years, subjecting herself to humiliation and oppression. She had allowed him to treat her and John's children harshly and had allowed him to foist baby after baby on her poor tired body.

Well enough was enough.

"You will not be opening the bar tonight out of respect for my daughter. She will be buried tomorrow and tonight we will sit by her coffin and stay with her until the sun rises. You will show your respect for my daughter. My daughter who you wronged." Her look of disgust and anger should have made Jack more cautious; unfortunately for him he did not have the emotional intuition to pick up on her foul mood.

"Shut your mouth woman," he spat out the words with spittle running down his cheek.

"No I will not shut my mouth," cried Mary.

Jack made to move towards her as if to grab at her throat. Tom pushed himself between his parents raising his hands in conciliation. All too often Tom had witnessed his father lay his hands on his mother. Now was not the time for another beating.

"I know about your dirty secret. I made a promise to my dying daughter that I will protect Hannah from you. You will not do to Hannah what you did to my Sarah." Mary glared at Jack willing him to explode. She no longer cared if he hit her. The pain could not be more intense than the pain of losing Sarah.

"Mother," gasped Tom. "What are you saying? What did Father do to Sarah?"

Mary could see the pain and confusion cross Tom's face. He liked to think he was a man but he was still only 13 years of age. He did the work of a man but had the brain and understanding of a child when it came to relationships. She knew that he accepted Jack as his father whereas his sisters struggled with that concept. He was scared of Jack but held a measure of respect for his authority. Mary knew she was about to destroy that respect for good. There would be no more secrets in this family.

"He raped your sister and got her in the family way. It was his daughter that she gave birth to. Thank the Lord that the child did not survive. The poor babe would have carried the stain of incest all its life."

Mary clutched at her son's hands and drew them to her heart. She hated to destroy her son's world but the truth was spoken now and could not be put back in the box. "I am so sorry to have to tell you this, Tom. Your stepfather is an evil man. I have learnt a tough lesson about what happens when you don't protect your children from monsters." Gently she stroked Tom's cheek trying to offer some comfort.

"Sometimes those monsters are living right under your nose and you don't see them until it's too late."

Jack slumped back into the chair.

He physically seemed to deflate as he absorbed the anger of his wife's words. His head fell into his hands as the kitchen fell silent. All of a sudden he had lost his place as the principle bully in the household. How could he control the minds of his children if they knew the evil growing inside his brain?

Hannah reached out to take her Mother's hand. She was shocked that Mary knew the truth. Had Sarah shared the secret on her deathbed? "Mother, did Sarah speak to you today? Did she tell you what happened?"

"No your sister had so little strength left in her," replied Mary. "I heard you talking the night baby Jack was born. I found out the terrible news at the same time you heard it. I suppose I have been waiting to confront your stepfather since then. I was being a coward as usual."

"No mother, you are not a coward." Hannah reached out to Mary seeking comfort. Her little world had been turned upside down in the last few days. She was getting an unwanted lesson in adulthood.

"Oh Hannah, when your sister got so ill, I knew I had to do something to stop this happening to you too. I let your sister down. I will not let you down." Mary pulled Hannah into a comforting embrace.

Tom turned green as the colour started to drain from his face. He threw open the kitchen door and could be heard retching up his guts into the yard.

Silence filled the room.

Mary stood there in the middle of the dreadful nightmare and contemplated her next steps. She stared at her husband as reality hit. She hated this man for what he had done to her family.

Their marriage was over.

She would not share her bed with this man again. She would keep his house and bring up their children but any relationship with him was over. She knew that she shared the blame for her daughter's death. She had ignored the warning signs. No more. With courage Mary realised it was her time to dictate the future. No longer would she do what her husband demanded.

"I will never forgive you, you bastard. You killed my daughter with your evil ways. You may be my husband and I will have to live with the shame of that. But from now until the day you die you will do what I say. I will no longer be your puppet. I am in charge from now on and I will keep my children safe."

Mary grabbed hold of his shirt collar as both Hannah and Tom looked on with shock. "You will move out of this house and live in the farm from now on. I will run the bar with the help of Tom and Hannah. No longer will you drink yourself into a stupor on my profits. And most importantly you will never be alone with any of my children. Ever! Is that clear, you miserable little bastard."

All the fight had gone out of Jack Whiting. He knew he was beaten.

"And if you ever try to worm your way back in, then you will face me," shouted Tom. "I may just look like a lad to you but I will have vengeance if you touch my mother or brothers or sisters. You will find yourself dead in your sleep with a knife in your black heart." Tom was trying hard not to touch the man he had called father these last few years. If he hit him then he didn't think he could stop. The rage scared him. There was no way he would lower himself to the level of Jack because of his disgust and anger.

The shift in dominance was palpable.

Jack Whiting was no longer in charge. He would spend the rest of his miserable life on his own. His family would recover eventually. His children would grow up without him but under the protection of his name. From now on Mary Whiting would control how the family lived. She would pour her love into her remaining children in an attempt to compensate for her mistakes. And every day the small grave under the old oak tree would stand as a reminder of her guilt. She would be racked with the guilt of her grandchild's death until her poor mind was lost.

CHAPTER THIRTY FIVE

The party was in full swing.

Liz and Giles were excited to host their first New Year's Eve party inviting many of their new friends and some new acquaintances from the village. They had decided it would be a great way to cement their place in the new community. Not surprisingly a vast number of residents had accepted the invitation and the house was heaving with bodies as the New Year approached.

Liz moved gracefully from one room to the next handing out canapes and refilling glasses. As she entered the lounge she took stock, observing the milling crowd circulating around the room. Giles was in deep conversation with Ray Small whose farmland surrounded their house. Ray was dangerously waving his arms around as he held court. His portly stature struggled to remain in one place within what was probably his best suit. Liz smiled to herself as she recognised how out of place Ray seemed in their front room. All previous interactions with him had taken place when he was sat high up on his John Deere. Ray was never happier than when driving his beloved tractor with muck on his work clothes and under his nails. Jenny Small had forced him into the bath earlier as she was desperate to visit Crown House and was not having her husband ruin their image. Jenny didn't get out much so the idea of attending the first village party for many a year was the pinnacle of her year. She had been to the hairdressers this afternoon and splashed out on a new hair dye, a bright purple tint to match her best twin set.

Liz wandered over to talk to Ian and Margaret Greening. Ian was the church warden and his wife Margaret managed the village hall. They had lived in the village all their married life so were stalwarts of the community.

Margaret opened the conversation as she grabbed Liz's hand and pulled her in for a brief embrace. "Thank you so much, Liz, for the invite tonight. I have wanted a glimpse inside this house for ever. I hope you don't mind but I have had a sneaky look around. Nothing intrusive of course but just wanted to see what you had done with the place."

Liz smiled although she felt somewhat uncomfortable with Margaret's idea of a look around. "Of course that's fine," she lied. "To be fair we haven't really done very much to the house. Just a few superficial changes to make it our home. Our predecessors did all the hard work and we are reaping the benefits. Now will you excuse me, I really must circulate." Liz smiled sweetly as she retreated out of the room before Ian could enter the conversation. Ian was extremely deaf and was renowned for bellowing rather than talking.

Liz wandered through to the kitchen to pick up fresh supplies. Joyce was deep in conversation with Sheila and waved at Liz as she made her way across to greet her new friends. The three ladies had developed a strong bond during their regular coffee mornings.

"Lovely party," Sheila squeezed Liz's arm reassuringly. "I don't know how you make hosting look so easy, especially in your condition" she winked.

"That's the key thing. Making it look easy. It's all a big front. In truth I'm like the proverbial swan; smooth and gliding on the surface and underneath it all absolute chaos," laughed Liz.

Liz reflected on the afternoon just past. Giles had been tasked with running the hoover around which had been an epic fail. The last time Giles had been in charge of their Dyson he had managed to break it but needs must. Harry was on dusting duty leaving Liz and Joanne in the kitchen. Liz had tried to keep things simple but as usual her imagination had run away with her. A vast selection of canapes and small bites had been pulled together ahead of their guests arriving. There had only just been time for Liz to grab a quick shower and dress before the doorbell announced the first arrivals.

Liz left her friends to gossip and headed back through the house. She spotted a few hardy souls on the patio puffing on cigarettes. In the games room she could see Harry and Jo with their friends enjoying a table tennis competition. She stood and watched for a short while, basking in joy. Both of her children seemed to have settled in well with their new friendship groups and seemed none the worse for their parents' news about the new arrival.

Finally Liz made her way back to the lounge looking for Giles. The chimes of Big Ben could be heard on the radio as the year came to a close. Liz and Giles fell into each other's arms as the bell struck. They kissed.

"Happy New Year, darling."

The room burst into a crescendo of noise as neighbours shared New Year wishes and a rendition of Auld Lang Syne broke out.

Liz smiled as she looked out across the beaming faces. Tonight had been a huge success. The New Year was welcomed in surrounded by new friends. A fresh start for the family with a new addition due in the early summer.

"Perfect", Liz whispered to herself as she contemplated the year to come.

CHAPTER THIRTY SIX – NEW YEAR 1862

The kitchen clock struck midnight.

The house was deathly quiet.

Mary was sat in the rocking chair nursing baby Jack. The only noise breaking the silence was his snuffling breath as he dragged on her breast. Mary gently rocked back and forwards as her youngest child fed. He was a hungry child, demanding both food and attention. His demands exhausted Mary, who craved a good night's sleep.

As she sat alone welcoming the New Year in, Mary reflected on the changes since her darling Sarah had died.

The power balance within their marriage had shifted in Mary's favour. Whilst Jack continued to bully the household with his anger and bluster, it was without substance. He had not slept in the marriage bed since that fateful night and would make the lonely walk across the fields to the farmhouse nightly. As far as the villagers were concerned the relationship between Mary and Jack was unchanged. Outward appearances were maintained to protect the reputation of her children. Mary had treated him with contempt over the last months. She could not forgive him and just the sight of his abhorrent face was enough to turn her stomach. She had no desire to share a bed with him. She found it hard enough to hold a conversation with him.

Hannah had left home to enter service at Squire Cole's house outside the village. Mary had initially been concerned to let her go, knowing the bulk of household chores would rest on her weary bones. Allowing Hannah to go was her penance for not protecting Sarah. She would do all in her power to ensure her second daughter would grow up without the risk of attracting her stepfather's lecherous eye. Hannah was enjoying her life in service. She returned home each Sunday to visit with the family and regale them with tales from below stairs.

Tom was growing fast into a man. He had taken on more responsibility both in the farm management and running the inn. He treated Jack with indifference and would not allow his stepfather to bully him. Coming out from under Jack's yoke was benefiting the young man. He managed the sale of farm produce at the local market with youthful authority and was building a reputation for fairness and quality, unlike Jack. Local tradesmen had noticed the changes at Wood Farm but didn't fully understand the reasoning behind it.

The younger children Anne, Arthur and Emma had been too young to understand the power shift within the Whiting household. If they noticed the absence of their father as they broke their fast they did not mention it. The atmosphere within the household was calmer and more pleasant so did not demand questioning. The younger ones missed their older sisters but had the childhood ability to forget and move on with their lives.

That was something which Mary could not do.

Her life had improved. She no longer had to put up with the drunken fumbling of her husband. She was now her own master, making decisions around the inn and the household. She had discovered the true state of the family's finances and was able to enjoy a few luxuries to improve the children's nourishment.

Despite that her life felt empty.

She mourned Sarah with an all-consuming grief. She missed working together. The monthly wash day was a chore that bore no pleasure. Despite her moaning in the past, she had valued the time that she and Sarah would toil together. She missed her daughter's smile when she would enter a room. She had the ability to light up the room. Well at least she had, before that monster had put the light out of her smile.

How had she missed the changes in her beloved first born?

She changed so rapidly from a happy excited girl to a surly young woman. As a mother she should have noticed the change was something more that the pangs of growing up. She should have questioned Sarah sooner, before things had spiralled out of control. Perhaps she could have stopped it before it started. Perhaps she could have saved her daughter.

Lurking in the darkness of the kitchen sat her conscience. Mary Whiting was a murderer. She had ended the life of her first grandchild rather than bear the shame of its existence. She struggled daily with hatred for what she had done. Deep within she did not regret her actions but she was scared for the day of reckoning. At the end of her life she would pay the price for her evil act.

That thought stayed with her throughout the day and then screamed in her ears at night. It would be that voice in her ears that would take her mind. Gratefully she would welcome oblivion when it arrived.

CHAPTER THIRTY SEVEN

Giles woke with a start.

It was still dark. He could see the early tendrils of dawn light trying to break through the winter morning. Giles quickly realised the reason for the disturbance to his sleep. Sounds of a strong gale blowing outside dominated the morning air. The squally wind blasted against the bedroom window, peppering it with rain. The noise was frightening as the house was buffeted by gusts from the first January tempest of the year.

The weather forecast had mentioned a strong winter storm arriving overnight but this felt much more serious than anticipated. The noise of the squally gusts outside concerned Giles. The house was surrounding by large trees which would be vulnerable to wind damage. The gusts alone sounded strong enough to cause damage. On top of that, the rain was pelting down on already wet ground. It had rained almost every day since Christmas. It had been a rude awakening for Giles to see how massive the weather was in the countryside. It was surprising to see the weather fronts rushing across the fields before they smacked full force into the house.

Giles slowly eased himself from the bed, trying not to wake Liz. He pulled on his boxers and jeans and searched the floor for the jumper he had dropped there the previous night. As he fumbled in the semi-dark he heard Liz stir.

"Are you awake?" he whispered. Giles gently placed his hand on her shoulder as he spoke.

Liz rolled onto her side facing him. She groaned as she tried to delay the act of waking. "Morning," she slurred her words as sleep started to rescind from her mind. "What time is it? What's that awful noise?" As she became more aware she took in the blasting wind crashing against their floor to ceiling windows. The rain and wind splattered with force against the glass, with the noise and strength of a power shower.

Giles switched on the bedside light to continue his search for his jumper and pulled it over his messy hair. "It's that storm they mentioned on the news last night. It sounds like it's a lot worse than predicted. Sounds like a bloody hurricane out there. I think I better have a check out the back as I just don't like the sound of those trees. They are creaking big time. The last thing we need is storm damage especially near the swimming pool."

Liz had sat up in bed and pulled the duvet up to her chin as the cold air hit her. The central heating hadn't kicked in yet which told her it was very early.

Today was a working from home day and the couple had hoped for a bit of a lie in. The storm had other ideas.

"Give me a sec and I will get up and make some tea." Liz was building up the courage to stick her feet out from under the duvet.

"Take your time, darling. I'm going to take a walk up the garden to check out the trees. A nice hot drink will be lovely when I get back." Giles pulled the curtains back and gazed out into the gloomy morning. The field across from their house was empty at this time of year but in the distance he could see the violent movements being made by the trees on the horizon. That sight did not give him any reassurance of what he might find in their garden.

He made his way down the stairs trying his hardest not to wake Joanne and Harry. There was no point in the whole household being up this early. Grabbing his thick gardening coat and wellies, he let himself out of the back door. The wind hit him like a door slamming in his face. He was almost pushed back into the house with the strength of its power. The wind carried icy cold rain which slapped into his face. Giles seriously considered retreating back to the house and waiting it out.

Just at that moment of indecision, he heard a huge cracking sound. The sound echoed around the garden as the violent cracking noise escalated with a series of groans and creaks. Giles pushed his way forward making slow progress. His powerful torch wandered across the lawn picking out shapes in the early morning gloom. As he forced his way up the garden, the wind drove him back. It was one step forward and two back. The wind had made up its mind that Giles wasn't going anywhere fast. He was buffeted on all sides. Smaller branches were flying around the lawn as he made his way towards the orchard and swimming pool building.

As Giles made his way towards the bushes dividing the lawn from the orchard, a further boom of noise hit his senses. This time he instinctively knew that noise was not good news. The ground seemed to shake under his feet. The initial crack of wood was followed by a crescendo of noise as something huge hit the ground. Giles knew without witnessing it that a tree had fallen. He quickened his pace, worried to see the damage he faced ahead.

The sight which met his eyes was heartrending.

The beautiful ancient oak, which stood tall and proud at the edge of the apple orchard, had collapsed. Its huge roots had burst through the surface of the ground with their outer spindly knots shaking in the wind. The oak had fallen backwards taking a number of apple trees with it but missing the pool building. The "Armageddon" like scene spoke of destruction and waste.

The oak had stood over this land for over five hundred years and its loss would create a huge void in the landscape which could not be quickly addressed. It had stood strong and proud over the garden, bearing witness to many generations. It was devastating to see its sorry demise.

Giles carefully picked his way through the detritus. His main aim was to ensure that no further damage could be caused whilst the storm continued to rage. He would have to get someone round to help him clear the remains of the oak and some five apple trees but that could wait. His primary concern was the security of the rest of the trees and the swimming pool building which, whilst it was further away from the orchard, was taking a battering too. He quickly established that other than a fair amount of debris on the roof of the building, the pool area was secure and likely to suffer only superficial damage.

Giles approached the oak with the reverence due to such an ancient symbol of nature. A huge crater had opened up as the tree fell. Giles stood at the edge considering how he would need to fill that hole up before work on cutting up the beautiful tree could start. As he stood there in the pouring rain and gusty wind his torch picked out something unusual in the ground.

It took him some minutes to realise what he was seeing. A skull. Very small but defiantly an intact skull. It looked human; not animal. Giles figured it was unlikely to be the remains of a favourite family pet from previous house owners. His gut wrenched as he considered the implications of what he had found. He stood frozen, staring at the tiny skull unable to break his silent vigil.

"Oh my god," Giles suddenly spoke out loud as the enormity of the find hit him.

Splashing through the mud, he hurried back to the house in panic. He threw open the boot room door, pulling off his wellies and jacket. Shock hit him with a wave of emotion. He suddenly felt the need to vomit and only just made it to the toilet where he wretched the contents of his stomach up.

"Giles, what's up?" Liz was standing by the door as he raised his head from the toilet bowl. The concern was written all over her face. Giles was never ill. He had the stomach of an ox. It was certainly out of character behaviour.

It took him some time to form the words. His body was shaking as he cupped his hands to splash water over his grey face. "Fuck Liz. A skull. A fucking skull."

Liz took his hands and pulled him towards her. She was shocked to feel the shaking which had overtaken him. "Giles, you are not making sense. Come on. Slowly now. Tell me what happened." She guided him into the kitchen and placed a cup of hot steaming tea in his hands. Patiently she waited for him to take a few sips and allow him to gather his thoughts.

"The oak has gone. It fell. It's a mess up there. We've lost a number of trees. Where the tree fell there's a big hole and that's where I saw it. A skull sticking out of the mud. It's human, I'm sure. But what the fuck is a human skull doing in our garden." Giles put his head in his hands as he calmed himself down.

For the next few minutes both Giles and Liz sat in silence mulling over their own thoughts. Liz was the first to break the silence.

"Oh god, what in the hell do we do now," asked Liz. "Do you want me to go and have a look? Could you have imagined it?" A big part of her wanted her husband to say an emphatic no. The look on his face confirmed to her that this was not a scene she was keen to look at.

Giles stared at her as if she had lost her mind. "Liz, seriously? You don't just imagine seeing a skull. I can assure you it was definitely there sticking out of the mud. I couldn't tell if there was a body with it but it definitely was a fucking skull, believe me." Giles very rarely raised his voice to his wife. Sometimes she did state the obvious or the ludicrous and this morning it was the later.

"Sorry babe. I don't know why I said that. I guess its shock too. Of course you wouldn't be making it up. I just can't believe it." Liz wriggled into Giles's arms. She knew he couldn't stay angry at her for long.

"I think we should ring the police," Giles suggested. "Or Christine? I don't have a clue what the protocol is for this sort of thing." Giles squeezed Liz to his chest, unconsciously noting the small bump between them. He drew comfort from her as his body started to calm.

"It's still early so not sure we should wake Christine. Shall I find the number for the local police station? I guess it's not an emergency," smiled Liz trying to break the mood.

As she scrolled through the internet on her phone trying to find the number, she was knocked sideways by a sudden realisation. "Giles, could it be Sarah's baby? You remember we were trying to figure out why there was no burial site or information about the birth." Her brain was frantically trying to catch up with the speed of information she was processing. "And in those letters I got from Dave, it talked about Mary Whiting being obsessed with the oak tree. Oh my god. Could it be?"

Giles looked at Liz as she whirled around the kitchen in a state of confusion. "Stop Liz! This is not helping right now. Just stop jumping to conclusions and let's just deal with the facts in front of us. We have uncovered what appears to be a human skull in our garden and we need to report that. The police will have to investigate and once they have established the facts then fine, you can speculate at that stage but for now we don't know how old that skull is."

Giles could see Liz collapsing emotionally in front of him and he realised perhaps he had been a bit harsh in dismissing her reasoning. "Look we can tell the police about Sarah once they have ruled out anything more sinister. So keep your powder dry, my love. Let's make that phone call, shall we?"

Giles took control of the situation. The initial shock had passed and he was now back to his organised approach to any problem they faced. He was best when he was in control of the situation and could take practical steps forward. Giles made the call to the local police station. It took a good hour of being passed around various departments before he finally got to speak to someone in authority. The early hour obviously didn't help. Before Jo and Harry had surfaced from their beds their parents had managed to get a grip on their nerves and prepare themselves mentally for the hours ahead.

CHAPTER THIRTY EIGHT

Detective Paul Mallinder accepted a mug of tea as he perched on the sofa. He looked longingly at the chocolate digestives, knowing that his waistline would not allow him to indulge. He surveyed the room and its occupants.

The house talked money, with the sumptuous leather sofas and top-quality television and sound system. Both husband and wife were well turned out despite the drama of the morning's activity. Mr Stamford wore beige chinos and an Yves San Lauren fitted jumper. His wife wore a flattering wrap around dress in burnt orange. There was evidence of her condition as the small baby bump pushed its way proudly forward. They were an attractive couple who seemed confident despite the police presence. His normal experience with the general public instilled a level of nervousness. He had a way of making people feel guilty even if they had nothing to be guilty about. To be fair it was an atmosphere that Paul liked to encourage. Keep the public nervous and slightly in awe of him. It was a power trip and had been his modus operandi throughout his career. And it worked; normally.

"Right then. I just wanted to update you both on what we are doing." Paul flipped open his notebook to use as a reference. He nodded to his colleague Jessie who was sipping her tea politely.

It was now mid-morning and the police had arrived some three hours ago. It had been difficult for Giles to persuade the kids that they still had to go to school. Jo and Harry had been fascinated and at the same time, horrified with the news. Both Giles and Liz were relieved that it was a school day so that they could pack the kids off and deal with the mystery without the children getting over excited by the scandal of a body in the back garden. No doubt word would fly around the school anyway.

"Ok, I have our forensic team working in a controlled area by the fallen tree. That's why we have the tent over the area as the guys need to work in as clean an environment as we can make it to ensure we don't contaminate the evidence. They are working to remove the body from the soil and our aim will be to do that before nightfall. I have to tell you the area will be out of bounds for a couple of days. Once we have removed the body we need to conduct a thorough search of the area for any other evidence. As I understand it you have only lived here for under a year. Is that correct?"

Giles answered for them both to confirm the detective's question.

"Right. Well then I think we can eliminate you both from our enquiries," Paul grinned somewhat inappropriately. "I'm not revealing anything too sensitive if I let you know that the body has been underground for some time."

Up until now Giles and Liz hadn't been aware that their find was a full body and not just a skull. After discovering the grizzly find both of them had been reluctant to explore the site further. They were also hugely aware that this was potentially a crime scene.

"So what happens in terms of identifying the body," asked Giles. "You see these things on TV but it just seems surreal that this is all taking place in our back garden." Giles ran his fingers through his hair as he addressed the policeman. It was an unconscious habit he employed when thinking.

Paul seemed to ponder on the question before replying. This was an unusual case and the first of its kind for the detective. "That's something I am less sure on if I'm honest Mr Stamford. The initial view from our forensic expert is that this body is not recent. Basically you can tell from the decomposition of the body. Not to beat around the bush but there is no sign of skin and hair which could draw you to the conclusion that this body is very old."

As Paul continued to run through the possible scenarios they were interrupted by the sound of the doorbell. Liz excused herself as she went to answer it.

"Hi Liz, hope you don't mind me dropping in unannounced." Christine Abbott was in through the door before invited. "I heard a rumour and thought I could help." Christine was in the lounge before Liz could answer and was introducing herself to the two police officers. Liz and Giles smiled at each other witnessing Christine working her magic on Paul Mallinder. She really was a class act when it came to bringing officials back down to earth with a bang.

As everyone settled back down with a fresh cup of tea, Liz decided that now was the time to bring up the mystery of Sarah. She glanced across at Christine for moral support.

"Detective, I think it's probably worth me telling you about some investigations we have been doing into previous residents of the house. Christine has been assisting me in my activity as she has a real interest in the history of the village." Christine was nodding intently as Liz spoke.

"Without going into all the ins and outs of the story, we have found evidence that a young girl living in the house in the 1860s gave birth to a child but there are no physical records of that birth and subsequent death. We have letters and a journal which has helped us piece the story together but the missing piece seems to have been buried in the garden. It just seems too much of a coincidence that the body found today is not linked with the mystery of the missing baby. And judging by the size of the skull my husband saw in the earth, this is not an adult body."

"Mrs Stamford, I can see there is a certain logic to that reasoning but as you say there is no physical records that will confirm your assumption." Paul Mallinder was a pompous individual and he didn't take kindly to someone telling him how to do his job.

Giles could feel his wife's hackles rising at this irritating policeman. His whole attitude since he arrived had been one of passive resentment. Whether it was the fact that they were new to the area and that he saw them as London townies taking over the countryside or whether it was just his general demeanour.

"Detective, I can certainly understand your reticence in this case," Christine started. She smiled sweetly at Paul as she carefully expressed her view. "However I must inform you that we do still have a resident in the village that may have a blood connection with the body. I am sure you have the ability to run a DNA test which could rule out our theory and if it doesn't we will be able to give some closure to the mystery."

Dave Whiting would be shocked when he found out about the latest events, thought Liz.

"I am sure that if I was to speak to the individual concerned they would be more than happy to support your enquiries," continued Christine. "So why don't you go ahead and link in with your forensic team and then come and have a chat with me and I will see what we can do. You will find me at the rectory or in the church most days."

Christine rose to her feet at that point almost challenging Paul not to rise too. "Thank you for your time today, Detective, Officer. I'm sure you have plenty of work to be getting on with so please don't let us interrupt you any longer."

Both officials were swiftly but politely dismissed.

As she closed the front door Christine dissolved into laughter. "I just love my job some days," she giggled. "There is something about a dog collar which makes the most officious individuals behave like naughty school kids. Well at least that got rid of them for now. Anyway guys, how are you feeling? Who found the body? Tell me all?" Christine fired questions at her friends without waiting for an answer.

Liz motioned Christine through to the kitchen as she sensed that Giles was keen to get back to work. His day had been turned on its head by events that morning and whilst his PA had managed to juggle his diary around, he had a mountain of emails to catch up with.

Liz brought Christine up to speed about how Giles had found the baby under the roots of the great oak. For once Christine was silent as she listened intently to the story. It seemed inevitable that the baby would turn out to be Sarah's missing child.

"I am convinced that the reason I have felt Sarah's presence around the house is because of her baby," explained Liz. "She must have known that the baby hadn't been buried in the churchyard and she just couldn't rest until the baby was found. From those letters which Dave shared with me, it's clear that Sarah's mother never quite got over the death of the baby and perhaps she felt guilty that she didn't give it the proper burial it deserved."

"I think she probably was racked with guilt over the circumstances of the baby's conception. Not an easy thing to have to live with," agreed Christine. "Feeling like she needed to bury the child in the orchard may have been a direct result of the shame of the whole situation. It would be hard enough to deal with the death of your daughter in a small tight community like

Little Yaxley but to admit she died in childbed with no husband would cause huge reputational damage to one of the leading families in the area."

"I can just imagine," agreed Liz.

"Owning the inn and the biggest farm in the area would have made the Whiting family one of the most important families outside of the local squire. Can you imagine the fall out if it ever got out that the father of the baby was her own stepfather? In those days I am sure incest would have been classed as a criminal offence."

"I don't know how she could have protected that monster from paying for his sins." Liz struggled with the thought that any mother could forgive a man accused of violating their precious daughter. Unfortunately, her views were heavily influenced by her own loss. Despite the passage of time, Liz could not forgive Rebecca's killer.

Christine understood Liz's passion on the subject and her approach was definitely non-judgemental. She knew that Liz saw the situation as very much black or white. All too often the nastiest situations carried a tint of grey.

"It's hard to understand the motivations of Mary Whiting when you layer modern culture over the situation. In those days it was almost impossible for a woman to be independent of a man, especially as a landowner. The shame of her husband would be heaped on her head even if she was totally innocent of knowledge. So try not to judge her by our standards." Christine reached out to Liz. "I guess her whole being would be concentrating on protecting her other children and their reputation. She had six further children who need husbands and wives along with future employment. I'm sure she would have lived with the guilt of what happened until her dying day but realistically she couldn't have done anything more about it."

"I guess you are right, Christine. It doesn't make it any easier to contemplate. For me the priority now is how we bring peace to the past. Do you think Dave would agree to do a DNA test?" Liz hoped that Christine would take the lead in asking Dave. Whilst they had got to know each other over recent weeks, it was going to be a difficult conversation. Dave was going to be hit with the full story of his family's past which up to now, he had little knowledge.

"Well, with your blessing, I was going to suggest that I talk to Dave. It will need some careful handling. Let's just hope he hasn't got any criminal skeletons in his closet." Christine smiled to herself as she imagined Dave Whiting as Norfolk's answer to the Mafia. She hoped that he would be receptive to helping out. If the body was Sarah's baby there must be some form of DNA match to the ancestor of Sarah's younger brother Arthur.

"I'd really appreciate that, Christine. I don't feel comfortable asking such a big favour myself. If he agrees then I think you will be able to get Detective Mallinder to compare DNA and establish an identity. If we are right and its Sarah's baby, can we bury her? As vicar could you agree to open up Sarah's grave and place the baby alongside her?"

As Liz stared intently at Christine willing her to agree to her idea, she smelt the overwhelming scent of flowers. The smell grew in strength as it filled the kitchen. "Do you smell that Christine?" Liz grasped hold of Christine's fingers.

"Flowers, wow that's a beautiful scent. Which flowers are they?" Christine scanned the room looking for the source.

"That's Sarah. She's here with us now. I guess that's her way of telling me she wants the baby back with her."

Liz saw the shock on Christine's face as she struggled with the concept of just witnessing the supernatural.

"Honestly she has found a way to communicate with me. I can't really explain it but she comes through when she wants me to feel something or know something important. I then interpret her wishes. I'm over the moon that you have sensed it now. Giles and my Mum have been lucky enough to sense her so I know I'm not going doolally."

"Well blow me down with a feather!" Christine genuflected into the space around her. "Bless you child. Let's hope we have found your poor baby and we will bring her back to you. Then you can rest in peace."

As she spoke the scent dispersed. The kitchen appeared to glow with warmth despite the previous chill in the air.

CHAPTER THIRTY NINE

"Hi Giles, Christine here. Are you and Liz free this morning? That dreadful detective has been in touch and he has an update for us. He thought it would be worth getting us all together at my place. Kill two birds with one stone was the expression he used. Anyway, Dave and Sheila are on their way round as we speak." Christine had been the conduit between both Stamford and Whiting families and the police over the last week.

"No problem, Christine. Let me grab Liz and we will be over to yours shortly," replied Giles as he ended the conversation.

The phone call had arrived at last and it was with a level of trepidation that Giles and Liz took a swift stroll to the vicarage. It would be good to get some answers. Maybe they would get closure at last.

It had been over a week since the storm and the discovery of the body. Life had been somewhat of a whirlwind for the village of Little Yaxley since then. In the Stamford household, Liz and Giles had faced the disruption of the police crawling all over the garden. The children had played their part, supplying the police team with hot tea and biscuits. Their intentions had been twofold. Helping their parents deal with the excitement had been one factor but the main reason had been to observe the crime scene at first hand. It was great fodder for the gossip machine both around the village and, wider, at school. Both Jo and Harry had been very mature in dealing with the discovery. They had a good outline of the story which Liz had been unravelling so there really wasn't any apprehension about the discovery of a body. They seemed more interested in the process the police would have to follow to try and identify the baby.

Across the village the rumours had been cranked up as villagers observed the forensic tent pitched in the Stamford's garden. At the weekend the family had visited the Greyhound for Sunday lunch. Derek had tried his hardest to pump Giles for inside knowledge with little success. Giles had been reluctant to share any real information out of respect for the Whiting family. It would be up to Dave to tell the village if he wanted to and of course, if it was proved that it was Sarah Cozen's baby.

Giles and Liz hadn't spoken to Dave and Sheila since the discovery. Christine had been to see the Whitings to explain the find. She had reported back that Dave was shocked by the discovery but also intrigued about the story of Sarah and the potential that this poor baby had been part of his great great grandfather's family. He hadn't hesitated to provide the relevant samples to Detective Mallinder and was keen to understand the possible outcome.

Christine had been at the centre of activity over the last week. She had been the go between for the police and the village and everyone involved was impressed by how confidently she had orchestrated events to minimise disruption on the community and to try to avoid unnecessary speculation. If she was honest with herself, Christine would admit that she loved being in charge and was thriving with the importance of her position. Ever mindful of her pastoral role within the community she had led prayers for the soul of the poor baby at Evensong the previous Sunday.

She had also organised a quiet vigil for those who wanted to recognise the death of a child from their community. That vigil had taken place Tuesday evening and had been well attended by the villagers. In fact it had a bigger turnout than the Christmas Day services. Christine knew that a large number of villagers had attended to see if they could find out more about the grim discovery. Dave and Sheila had kept a low profile. At this stage no-one in the village knew about the possible familial relationship of the baby to one of the villagers.

Dave and Sheila Whiting were sat at the huge kitchen table at the vicarage when the Stamfords arrived. Christine was bustling around the range preparing the tea.

"Come in, come in," cried Christine as she carefully lifted the cast iron farmhouse kettle with a tea towel. "PC Edwards said they would be here around 11.30am so hopefully they won't be long now."

Conversation circled around the subject of the test results as the couples were joined by John Abbott, Christine's husband. John was a quiet mouse of a man who was obviously used to playing second fiddle to his assertive wife. He was often seen at functions hovering somewhere at the back of a room just keeping an eye on things rather than actively involved. Liz had warmed to John the moment they had met. He seemed so at odds to Christine in temperament. The more she had got to know him the more she understood why their relationship worked so well. He was the yin to Christine's yang. Their differences in character and behaviours complemented them as a couple, making them a strong and calming force within the community. John immediately set to work ensuring their visitors were fed and watered and settled in comfortably for what lay ahead.

Bang on 11.30am the doorbell sounded as Detective Mallinder and his sidekick PC Jessie Edwards arrived. It took them some minutes to get settled at the huge wooden kitchen table, accepting tea and acknowledging each of those who had made it to Christine's home to find out the news.

Paul Mallinder pulled out his trusty notebook and the file of information gathered during the course of the investigation. He cleared his throat as he prepared to hold court, enjoying his captive audience, which was waiting with bated breath to hear what the experts had discovered. He launched into his dialogue, glancing at each of the neighbours as she spoke.

"Ok. Let me talk you through the process first so that I can give you a bit of context to our findings. As you know the infant's body was fully decomposed so there was no evidence of hair or skin samples to extract DNA from. Our forensic pathologist conducted a specialist autopsy which examines length of time body was in situ. Their initial finding is that the body has been in the ground for at least one hundred and fifty to two hundred years. It is almost impossible to determine a cause of death due to the lack of visible evidence which could help us. If you think about the process we follow for a more recent death then the pathologist can see physical marks or do analysis of blood material to help determine a cause of death." He paused as he surveyed his audience.

"Our pathologist has extracted DNA from the bone sample. This bone fragment DNA sampling is not as accurate as blood or saliva as the DNA is seen as somewhat degraded. However it does give us a good enough reading to make comparisons with another DNA sample. We compared the sample with the saliva swab we took from Mr Whiting here. It is the opinion of our experts that there are enough indicators present in both samples to establish a link between Mr Whiting and the infant. Having reviewed the documents which Mrs Stamford shared with us, we can build a picture of historic events which support our assumptions. So in summary I think we can say that there is enough evidence to establish that it is likely that the baby is that of Sarah Cozen."

Paul Mallinder paused for maximum effect as he looked at the expressions of his audience. Dave Whiting looked stunned as he took in the importance of the detective's words. Christine and Liz took each other's hands and a tear rolled gently down Liz's cheeks. There was a profound silence as none of those present seemed to want to start the conversation up again.

Christine was the first to speak. "Thank you Detective. In a way I think that is a relief to all of us. It did seem to be too much of a coincidence for it to be anyone else. What happens next in terms of the infant's body?"

Paul Mallinder nodded slowly at Christine as he formed his response. "PC Edwards has been looking into the protocols with the Home Office as this isn't standard procedure as you can imagine," responded Paul. "Jessie would you like to run through what you managed to establish?"

Liz and Giles were surprised to hear PC Edwards speak. During their previous visits to the house Jessie Edwards had sat quietly in the background playing second fiddle to her boss. Given her moment in the spotlight, she addressed her audience in a deep Norfolk accent.

"Well there are certain procedures that we have had to follow as a definite identification cannot be completed. As the body pre-dates anyone alive now, then there is no formal requirement for next of kin to be contacted to ascertain their wishes. However with the knowledge we have available that Mr Whiting here is related to the baby we are quite comfortable to leave the matter with him. Mr Whiting may decide what he would like to happen to the body and of course the forensic team will release the body to you or to an undertaker of your choosing. Also we respect your wishes if this is not something that you would want to take responsibility for. The state can arrange for disposal of the body if that is your preference."

All eyes naturally turned to Dave who looked to be deep in thought. Dave had known deep down that it would be his decision, should a positive link be made. He had already thought long and hard on the decision. Strangely he felt quite divorced from any feelings about the child as it was hard to think of it as a relative. He could see the impact the finding had on the Liz Stamford who was more engaged with the poor mite that his own family. Dave cleared his throat and rested his hands on the vast kitchen table.

"Gosh, despite Liz and Christine sharing Sarah's story with me some weeks ago, it all seems so much of a shock. It's hard to imagine that one of my ancestors was literally buried in your back garden." As he spoke he directed his words to Liz and Giles initially. "I do feel a huge sense of responsibility to my family ancestors to deal with this poor baby's body with respect and dignity. I don't wish the state to deal with it as some faceless corpse to be disposed of as it sees fit. The baby should be laid to rest in the churchyard in Little Yaxley with its mother. Is that possible Christine?"

Christine stood up and walked over to where Dave was sitting. She rested her hands on his shoulders and squeezed in recognition of the decision he had made. It was a decision which all those present would support.

"Dave, leave that with me. I can get the necessary permissions from the Archbishop to arrange for Sarah's grave to be opened. Once we have all the necessary paperwork in place then can I suggest a small graveside service to lay the baby to rest? Would that work for you? I guess we will need an undertaker involved to sort out a small coffin or casket for the body but we can work through that together."

Christine already had a local business in mind who would deal with the unusual circumstances with sensitivity and with an eye to cost.

Giles jumped in at that point. "Dave, Christine, I really hope you won't be offended but we would really like to help. I know we aren't related but we have formed a close bond with Sarah's story. Liz especially. She has worked so hard to unravel the mystery. Please don't be offended but we would like to contribute financially to the cost of burying Sarah's baby. We would also like to be involved in the service if you wouldn't mind."

Giles hadn't considered the reaction he might get before expressing his views. It just seemed the right thing for him to do. He had seen his wife come back to life since she started to research the mystery of Crown House and its ghostly going ons. The drive to solve Sarah's story and the improvements seen in his wife were intrinsically linked.

Rebecca would never be totally gone from their life but as a family they were starting to learn how to live without her.

Dave continued with a huge smile on his face. "Giles, Liz. Sarah's baby could not have been reunited with her mother without your tenacity and care for her story. We would be delighted to share her burial service with your family along with ours. I am certainly not offended by your offer of help on the costs and I'm sure between us we can make it a special service for this poor child who didn't have a chance at life."

The new friends joined hands across the huge table, united in their desire to do the right thing for the poor child. It had not witnessed any kindness in its short life. These new friends would bring that kindness in death.

Detective Mallinder took the opportunity to extract him and Jessie Edwards from the conversation. It was time to leave. He was comfortable that the mystery had been put to bed and that the community could take forward closure for the poor mite. Despite his outwardly appearance of arrogance and bluster, Paul Mallinder had been deeply affected by the case. His wife had suffered two miscarriages in the last few years and was pregnant again with their third attempt at starting a family. He returned home every day expecting the worst. So far the baby had fought its way through to six months of pregnancy and both he and his wife were hoping that this time they would get the chance to hold their baby in their arms.

When he had stood at the side of that dirty hole in the Stamford's garden he had been overcome with emotion. Seeing those little bones blanched with time in the ground, had hit him hard.

The neighbours had the strength and passion to lay the baby to rest and reunite the past. It was now the time for him to step away and let them deal with next steps. He loved it when a case came together to such a satisfactory conclusion. It was the best part of the job. And, as he thought to himself, will definitely reduce the amount of paperwork he would have to produce.

CHAPTER FORTY

It was a bitterly cold morning.

The overnight frost was slowly receding from the grass, bringing a deep green colour back into each blade. The winter sun was peeping through the clouds bringing a modicum of warmth to those stood around Sarah's grave. A gentle breeze whipped around their legs as those attending huddled together for warmth.

Christine Abbott walked demurely across the churchyard cradling the precious bundle. The families had agreed to bury the baby in an eco-friendly woven basket which would degrade faster within the grave, joining the baby's bones with her mother's. The baby had been wrapped in the woollen blanket which Liz had found in the secret room. She instinctively knew that the blanket had been made with love by Sarah. It seemed right that her child should wear the garment for its journey.

As Christine approached the graveside, she smiled at those who had come to wish the baby farewell. Dave and Sheila were joined by Dave's distant cousin Josie and her husband Roy. Josie was a direct decedent from Hannah Whiting. She had been keen to attend and pay her respects to her great great grandmother's niece. She too had been shocked to hear the story from the past. She had been intrigued to read Hannah's letters to Arthur. For the Whiting family the story had revived their interest in their family story. Josie was keen to learn more about Hannah and had already made good progress in tracing back her family tree to learn more.

Hannah had married a vicar called John Greening in 1870 and moved to Eye in Suffolk. There she had raised her family of four children and eight grandchildren before her death in 1920 at the grand old age of 70. She must have seen some huge changes in the world during this time including the experience of living through the WW1 where one of her grandchildren died at the Somme. Hannah had cared for her mother when the fever to her brain had hit hard. Mary Whiting spent her last few years living with John and Hannah.

Dave had started to trace his family tree back to Arthur who had lived out his days at Wood Farm. He had made a thriving business of the farm and with a large family around him had lived into his seventies. Dave was descended from a younger son which accounted for the lack of connection held to the farm.

A review of the licensing records for the Crown and Hare revealed that Sarah's brother, Tom, took over the running of the inn in 1873 when his mother became incapacitated. He had reverted to using his father's name Cozen by this stage and was married to Jane. The inn remained in the Cozen family until WW2 when it was sold off and converted into a private residence.

Both Anne and Emma had married away from the village after their mother's death. To date investigations on their families were sketchy.

Jack, who had been born just before his sister's death in 1861 had gone into the army. This appeared to be common practise for a younger son. He had tragically died at the age of 19 at the Battle of Majuba Hill in the South African Boer Wars. His parents had both pre-deceased him but his early death must had been a tragic blow to his brothers and sisters.

Back at the graveside, Liz and Giles were joined by Joanne and Harry. The children had been given permission from their headmaster to start school slightly late this morning so they could join their parents. This decision had been the catalyst to the very early start around the graveside to respect the decision of the school and to try and minimise the time they lost.

Christine's husband John completed the small group of residents huddled around the grave, all trying to find a place to stand without showing any disrespect to the other graves surrounding Sarah's. This was not an easy task as the mounds of grass, still slightly frosty, seemed to suck the congregation's feet into the earth, anchoring them in place.

Christine started the short service with a reading from the gospel of John. "I am the resurrection and the life says the Lord. Those who believe in me, even though they die, yet shall they live, and everyone who lives and believes in me shall never die."

The congregation joined Christine in the Lord's Prayer. Hands were held across the group as they bowed their heads in reflection. The silence was palpable as each individual took time to consider their private thoughts.

Christine gently lowered the basket into the small section of the grave which had been opened to receive the precious bundle. She opened her arms in prayer as she spoke the words of committal. "We entrust our sister to God's merciful keeping, and as we now commit her body to the ground: earth to earth, ashes to ashes, dust to dust: in sure and certain hope of the resurrection to eternal life through our Lord Jesus Christ who died, was buried and rose again for us. To him be glory for ever. Amen."

All of a sudden Liz felt compelled to raise her eyes from the graveside. She looked across the graveyard towards the church. Standing by the wall, which surrounded the church grounds, she could see the shape of a young woman. Her outline was blurred but Liz had no doubt who she was. Liz smiled at Sarah and placed her hand on her heart as she made the connection between both worlds. She would swear to Giles afterwards that Sarah smiled back and made a similar gesture. Gradually the image dissolved into the early morning mist.

As her fellow mourners took their turn to sprinkle earth gently onto the basket, Liz recognised the strong smell of flowers surround the group. The scent was totally out of place with the cold icy February morning. Those standing around the grave would sense the changing atmosphere even if they did not realise at that point the significance of that they were witnessing.

As Christine returned the remainder of the soil to cover the basket and replaced the sod of grass to complete the burial, the scent gradually died in strength.

Liz pressed her lips to her gloved fingers and placed them on the tombstone. "Rest in peace now Sarah," she whispered.

EPILOGUE

Sunshine flooded into the bedroom chasing the early morning shadows away.

Fluffy clouds raced across the skyline, welcoming the new day. One of the joys of their bedroom was the floor to ceiling windows that gave them such a welcoming sight as the day began. Being able to see nature at its finest was the perfect way to start the day.

The sun caressed Liz's cheeks as she woke slowly from a fitful sleep.

Beside her Giles glanced down at his wife and smiled. He had woken some time earlier to make a cup of tea but was reluctant to wake Liz. She had been up a couple of times in the night and he knew she was exhausted from her toils.

Liz stretched out, emitting a sigh as she reached her arms above her head. She ached everywhere but it was a beautiful sacrifice, she thought to herself. Her breasts felt tender and were telling her that it was nearly time. Slowly and with care she eased her aching body up the bed, plumping the pillows behind her for additional support.

From beside the bed a faint cry could be heard. The baby snuffled as it woke from its sleep and decided it was time to feed. All too quickly the faint cries escalated into a hungry wail.

Giles quickly jumped from the bed to pick up the baby and cuddle to his chest as his wife readied herself. Liz pulled up her vest top opening the unflattering nursing bra to release her breast. Within moments the baby had engaged and was pulling hard on Liz's nipple.

As they watched their new daughter feed, Giles and Liz were overwhelmed with love. Giles sat with Liz cuddled into his chest whilst their baby snuggled between their bodies, protected within a circle of safety.

The baby had entered the world yesterday morning in the comfort of their bedroom. The midwife had initially not been keen for Liz to have a home birth at her advanced age but nothing was going to stop Liz from enjoying the satisfaction of giving birth with her family surrounding her. She had given birth to all her children at home and wasn't going to give in, just because she was a bit older.

The birth had been textbook in nature, with no complications. Giles had been with her throughout. Jill Wynn had been there to help her daughter and to welcome her new granddaughter into the world. Jo and Harry had been on hand and were able to meet their new sister within a few minutes of her birth. They were both overcome with joy at the sight of the bloody wrinkly body; the new addition to the family. Both had cried tears of happiness when they first held their tiny sister. It had been so precious for Giles and Liz to share this beautiful moment with Jo and Harry.

Despite it being early the sounds of Jo and Harry moving around broke the silence of feeding time. A gentle knock on the door signalled their presence.

"Morning Mumma," whispered Jo as she stuck her head around the door. "Can we come in?"

Liz pulled her vest top down to cover her modesty as her children entered the room and settled down on the bed with them. The baby continued to feed, its sweaty hair sticking to Liz's skin. The morning sunshine was warming the room which, added to skin on skin comfort, kept the small child settled.

"Oh Mum, she is the most beautiful baby in the world. I know we are slightly biased but she looks like an angel doesn't she?" Jo had fallen for her little sister immediately.

The baby was gorgeous. Her features were so well formed and she had the most stunning blue eyes which Jill had remarked gave the impression that the child had been here before. She had a full head of auburn hair and the sweetest chubby cheeks. She was the most angelic of all Liz's babies. All babies are precious but this new arrival was truly a blessing to this family.

Liz knew the time was right to share her thoughts.

"I think I have decided on a name for our new bundle of joy. I hope you like it." Liz gazed at her husband and two grown up children as she prepared to speak. "I think we should call her Hope. It makes me think of positive thoughts for the future."

"Hope, I like it," said Giles.

"Hope will never replace Rebecca but her arrival will give us the strength to go forward without Rebecca. Rebecca will always be in our hearts and Hope will be in our arms." Liz looked at each of her family in turn as if to confirm her words and the importance of them to her.

A mother's loss was devastating.

To have lost Rebecca in the prime of her life was an unbelievable pain which Liz had felt she could never recover from. This beautiful gift was the final piece of the jigsaw. Bringing love and healing to her mother.

The whole family could move on to a new chapter in their lives.

Sarah would rest in peace.

Rebecca would live on in their hearts. The Stamford family was once again complete.

Liz knew without any doubt in her heart that her next suggestion was the absolute right thing to do.

"Darlings, if you all don't mind I would like to give her a middle name. Sarah. Hope Sarah Stamford. It feels the right thing to do. Sarah's story brought us together in love. Sarah will always have a special place in our hearts and, of course, in this family."

"Hope Sarah," chorused Giles, Jo and Harry.

The sun shone its healing light on the family as they surrounded the new baby with love.

The End

ABOUT THE AUTHOR

Caroline Rebisz lives in Norfolk with her husband. She has two daughters.
Having worked in financial services throughout her career Caroline retired
to the countryside and fulfilled her passion for writing.
A Mother's Loss is her debut novel.

Printed in Great Britain
by Amazon